FROM THE ASHES OF MADNESS

Jᴀᴍᴇs K. Dᴀᴡsᴏɴ

Speir Publishing

**Published by
Speir Publishing
2200 Carlisle Avenue
Oklahoma City, OK 73120
www.speirpublishing.net**

Copyright © 2009 by James K. Dawson

ISBN10: 0-9801725-8-6
ISBN13: 978-0-9801725-8-4

Library of Congress Control Number: 2009923575

Manufactured in the United States
10 9 8 7 6 5 4 3 2

Cover Design: Paul Michael Speir & James K. Dawson
Book Design & Production: Paul Michael Speir
Author Photo by Carol Dawson

www.jameskdawson.com

When he opened his eyes a pool of thick, dark blood had soaked the ground beneath his right thigh. The cigar-shaped stick he'd stuck between his teeth lay in two pieces, one on each side of his head. He spit out the middle section which he'd crushed between his teeth. Then trembling with exhaustion, he leaned forward and carefully removed his leg from the fork in the now horizontal stick, which had come loose from the pile and fallen to the side. When he felt strong enough to move again, he ripped the sleeves from his shirt and pulled them both over his leg. He bound them tightly with the makeshift splints and tree bark twine. He gathered is remaining strength, got up slowly, fighting off yet another wave of nausea, and....

This story is dedicated to my children.

Rebecca Benton: my greatest appreciation for your thorough and insightful editing.

For those who believed I could do it, many thanks.

"Crede quod habes et habes"

Augustine

CHAPTER ONE

3:55 P.M., APRIL 8TH, 2008

I s this how I die?" Greg whispered to himself. The gripping pain in his left arm would not give in, and a mounting fear began to claw at his throat. He silently cussed himself. His buddy, Mitch, unaware that death was so near, snored lightly as he rested in the passenger seat of the Comanche. Greg didn't understand how his friend could sleep as they flew over the pristine wilderness of Idaho's high country. Unknown to him, Mitch had slept little the night before, fitfully at best, a nightmarish dream waking him in the early morning hours, when he'd found himself on the floor in a cold sweat. Mitch had complained of a migraine and had gone to sleep within a few minutes of take-off. At that very moment Mitch shuddered as the same nightmare haunted him once again.

Greg was tempted to rouse him, but his friend settled down; escaping the horrid dream; retreating into a peaceful slumber.

Cold sweat dripped off Greg's chin as the warning signs of an imminent cardiac arrest multiplied. He refused to turn back, ignoring his condition, believing the discomfort would go away as it had so many times in the past, but he knew the odds were against him. He fought it as he stared down into the forest below, watching their shadow as it trailed the south fork of the Salmon River. He was a stubborn man, and a fool.

The watercourse shimmered in the warm afternoon sunlight, threading its way north, dipping and diving, twisting and turning through the remote and rugged mountains.

Thunderclouds rumbled and boiled in the distance as a bolt of pain shot up his left arm and into his jaw. He jerked with the pain, then braced himself and continued to fly. When his pain had started they had already flown too far to turn back. Should I wake Mitch and let him take us into Missoula?

To the northeast he could faintly make out Chamberlain Creek. His plan was to follow its serpentine course to where it joined the main fork. Then he would turn north again and follow the compass into Montana. Up ahead the storm grew worse; lightning flashed, thunder boomed.

Mitch slept soundly despite the noise; while Greg studied the dark and ominous clouds ahead. They boiled and grew as he watched a dense wall of rain advance across a snow-shrouded peak. Both men jumped in their seats as lightning suddenly ripped the sky. Mitch adjusted his position and slept on. Greg cursed the storm and weighed the options. He chose to fly west, behind the storm. He banked in that direction. His pain intensified. A few minutes later, he banked right as he passed the storm, glancing at Mitch as he started the turn.

In that moment Greg finally realized he could cheat death no more. He laughed out loud, and with great difficulty, said, "Wake up, buddy, I'm...." He choked and sobbed; suddenly realizing he was as good as dead. He gasped and said, "This is going to be hard on the women," and then he grinned defiantly as pain struck him a solid blow and he felt himself sinking into darkness. Greg tried valiantly to reach over and shake Mitch awake, but to his dismay he found that he was too late. He couldn't move. Stuttering and spitting, turning blue, choking on his words, he managed a barely audible, "Hope you make it," before his chest was crushed in the vice of a massive heart attack. He struggled defiantly for a few seconds more, and then he stiffened, his eyes rolled back in his head, and he died. His head fell on his chest and his heavy, limp body slumped slowly against the yoke, pushing it forward.

While Mitch slept soundly, his seatbelt lose at the sides of his seat, the Comanche plummeted toward The River of No Return.

CHAPTER TWO

Will the rain ever stop? It's been fallin' all night and it'll rain all day. We've so much to do. Springtime is near and we'd best be cuttin' next winter's supply of firewood."

The old man relaxed in his living room on a large, winged-back couch, smoking his wooden pipe. His dog sitting quietly beside him, they both stared into the flames of the early morning fire.

Thomas J. Braden rose early every morning and stirred the night's fire back to life, adding more wood to take the chill from the big log cabin. Even in the summer, the mornings in the mountains could be cold. Most mornings after breakfast, and always after supper, Tom would sit before the fire with an open book. Sometimes he read aloud so Barney could hear. He often spoke his mind to the dog, having no one else to talk to. The Golden Retriever, seldom far from his side,

11

had wandered out of the woods two years ago and had adopted Tom and his late wife, Natalie.

"Barney, watchin' the fire reminds me of something. The fireplace needs cleanin'. Maybe tomorrow, if the rain lets up, we can spread the ashes in the yard along the walk. When the snow's gone we can plant more roses," he said. "Roses are said to flourish in ashy soil."

It didn't take much to excite him these days, nor to sadden him. "Nat' used to do that. Maybe we'll plant some more at her place by the river. She'd like that. You know how she loved her roses." He paused a long moment and then said, "I should've planted more for her when she was still with us."

The old man's bottom lip quivered and he became silent. A tear sparkled in the firelight as it crawled down his left cheek. Barney drew closer, his soft brown eyes glowing and his thick fur shimmering in the light of the flames.

Tom had lost his wife early in the previous spring. She was his first and only wife, his lifelong companion, and their relationship had seldom known bitterness. She died in her sleep early one morning as he held her in his arms. She just took a deep breath, let it out slowly, and was gone. Her death was sudden, without warning. He had tried to save her but his efforts were useless. She was gone. Emotionally, Tom had not been the same.

He had called his son and then waited.

Jeremy showed up a day later to find his father still in bed, holding Natalie's body to his chest, crying, and rocking back and forth in his misery. Barney whined at the foot of the bed, shivering, for warmth, in more ways than one, had retreated from the cabin.

After the funeral, beginning to doubt his father's sanity, Jeremy tried to force his father to sell the expansive property, and then settle into a "retirement" home in Boise. Jeremy and his wife lived in Salt Lake City, Utah, many miles distant from there.

Tom would have none of it.

"I may be an old man, but I'm still fit and strong. And I'm not crazy!" he had shouted.

It took a lot of argument, but Jeremy finally gave in. They let him stay at home in his mountains, but only after promising to keep in touch. His son told him that he would visit often. At first, he did, but that did not last, and now it had been months since his last visit or phone call.

"He has become so damned greedy. All he wants is the money from the sale of *my* land, as if he didn't have enough already. With Jeremy appearances were always most important. And I can't understand it; we were very careful to give him an authoritative atmosphere. We were fair and loving with him but there were rules. He should have become confident and secure and pro-social. I don't know how and why he became so self-absorbed. It's almost as if...." Tom paused a few moments, looking off into space.

Then said, "Barney," the dog looked up at Tom, "he doesn't have a lick o' sense. That's the way it seems to me sometimes, but he's a sharp kid, just the same. Something just isn't right, but I can't put my finger on it. He drives up showing off his fanciness, but yet it seems he's always hungry for more, as if we hadn't provided enough for him in his youth. He thinks he's going to get my land, but he better think again. I have a thousand acres of virgin forest, and I'll be damned if I'll give it to him when I die. And he's all set for my death. I saw it in his eyes when he was here last. He thinks I'm just an old coot; fit to die and rot.

"Jeremy is my flesh and blood, but I didn't raise him

like that. It's that damned city, or the result of living in it. The city has ruined him. I guess maybe I tried to hold on too tight to him; he was our only child. In opposition of my wishes, he didn't stay up here where he belonged. 'I just have to get away for awhile, Dad,' he'd said. Said he wanted to see the world. We hoped he'd get his education and then come back home, or at least stay in Idaho. Barney, my son never returned.

"I know why he wants this land. I overheard him talking to Sally when they were here for the funeral. He wants to sell it to a developer, take the money and run. Says he's going to move to Europe. Greed has plumb ruined him, Barney. Yet I sense something more is at the root of his problems.

"I can't give him the land. I won't do it. My father insisted it stay in the family. In spite of how he's treated me of late, I love my son. But if I give him the land, Jeremy will not keep it. I just don't know what to do."

The old man held his last friend close, and they watched the fire die down. It was warm and soothing in the cool morning, the embers glowing, and sap-filled wood expanding, crackling, and popping.

"We've much to do, dog. Soon we'll have a visitor. Mother always knew when company was coming. She'd get up in the middle of the night and make sure the guestroom was ready. She'd turn the porch light on. She'd do things like that. My mother had a way about her; she knew things.

"I have that feeling now. I don't know who it is, but someone will be here in a couple of days."

CHAPTER THREE

MUCH EARLIER THE SAME DAY,
BEFORE DAWN...

The night lingered dark and crisp over Boise, as a cool breeze drifted down from the mountains, carrying with it a freshness hinting of spring. The city slept quietly, peaceful, its tranquility broken only occasionally by the bark of a dog alerted by nocturnal prowlers. As morning approached, the stars winked out and dew covered the sleeping city with a crystalline blanket. On the eastern horizon grayness crept forth. Marching boldly away from Europe's yesterday, on it came, the sun's prophet, spreading the news to the western lands, heralding the rising of the morning sun.

Columns of smoke spiraled from chimneys in the older homes as early risers stirred smoldering coals to flame and added more wood to take the chill off hardwood floors and cold feet. Lights that had jumped out of windows in the early hours disappeared as the sun's rays leaped over the treetops. The wind whispered across the waking city, prancing lightly through the trees on frosty toes. Morning dew was heavy. Roofs sparkled brightly while the trees shimmered and danced with the breeze, their needles and new leaves shooting arrows of dazzling light in every direction.

In a modern, two-story home on the southwest side of town, in an upstairs bedroom, after a fitful night of tossing and turning, Mitchell Cooper lay sleeping soundly. The covers were thrown back on his wife's side of the bed. An early riser, Donna was up and brushing her teeth. In the bedroom at the end of the hall their son also lay in deep sleep, but for another reason: he'd studied far into the night.

Donna finished brushing, gargled, and stepped into the shower, hollering over her shoulder, "Mitch, it's time to get up."

Her husband's chest rose and fell as he breathed, his eyeballs darting back and forth beneath his eyelids, unhearing and unheeding her words.

"Mitch! Wake up!" she shouted over the water raining down on her tall, brown, and shapely body. This time Mitch did hear her, but her voice was hoarse and ugly, echoing in his ears.

"Leave me alone," he grumbled.

"GET UP!" the voice roared in his ears. Mitch snapped awake and sat up, angrily throwing the covers aside. The color drained from his face as a rubber-like arm reached through the closed window beside his bed. The arm pulsated and stretched as it pushed the molecules of glass aside.

Mitch stared, unbelieving, blinking his eyes, trying to clear his sleep-fogged vision. His disbelief soon vanished as the arm punched through the glass, exploding the window, sending glass shards across the room. The muscled and sinewy arm grabbed him roughly around the throat, plucked him easily from the bed, and yanked him out the window.

Mitch started to yell, but without any sense of time or circumstance, he found himself naked, walking aimlessly down a fog-shrouded mountain slope. He heard a sound and turned abruptly to find a dark horse standing behind him, head down, staring into his eyes. The stallion was so black it virtually blended with the night, except for the faint glint of its shiny coat in the moonlight.

The horse kneeled and touched its nose to the ground. Mitch was puzzled at first, but when the horse, with near imperceptibility, motioned with its head and a slight glance with its eyes for Mitch to mount, he understood, grabbed a hold of its mane, and swung astride.

With a thunderous squeal of rage, the horse bolted and ran, charging down the mountain as fast and mean as the West Texas wind. Mitch held tight with his knees, fearing for his life as the horse jumped creeks and ravines. The stallion raced blindly, crashing through the undergrowth, winding around trees so fast Mitch nearly fell, but the horse would always jump back under him, saving him from certain injury. Mitch's heart raced in his chest. He screamed into the night for understanding, but the night ignored his pleas and closed tighter around them. The dark horse ran until its sides were foamy with sweat and its breath became ragged. It wheezed, struggling for wind, but ran as if pushed by madness. The forest darkened as the trees tightened their grip, the thick branches blocking the moon and stars until the path ahead disappeared. The night thickened into black cotton.

Mitch pressed close to the horse, holding onto its

mane with both hands, pressing with his knees, strain-
ing to see, fighting to hold on, scraped and bleeding.

A cold wind hit his face. He smelled water and heard
a roaring torrent ahead. Then with the crack of a sonic
boom, they burst from the forest and Mitch felt the terror of their flight abate. His relief vanished as quickly
as it came when the horse leaped and pitched headfirst
into a dark chasm, where they fell helplessly into a
fathomless void.

A woman called his name as they fell.

Mitch flailed with his arms, separating from the stallion, reaching for anything, finding no holds, screaming
and hearing his screams bounce and echo, wasted on
the cold wet walls of the abyss. Mitch heard a bone-
shattering crunch as the horse slammed into an out-
cropping below him, and he was met with a spray of
blood as the stud careened back and forth against the
narrowing walls.

Mitch's stomach rose into his throat and his heart
raced inside his chest as the walls suddenly closed in
on him, slowing his fall, trapping him in a cocoon-like
grasp. He fought desperately against his bonds, but in
vain, for his limbs had become lifeless and heavy. A
chainsaw buzzed somewhere below as the woman's
strangely calm voice called to him from above. Without
warning, the saw ripped through the darkness, plung-
ing into his gut as he hit bottom in a burst of light and
searing pain. He awakened to the sound of his own
screaming to find his legs tangled in his blankets on
the floor beside the bed. The alarm clock buzzed insis-
tently on the nightstand that his head had narrowly
missed.

"Oh shit!" Donna said under her breath as she ran
to her husband's side.

"Mitchell, are you alright?" she said, looking for signs of injury.

"Yeah," he groaned. "I just had a nightmare, literally, only it was a stallion. It must have kicked me out of bed," he said, trying ineffectively to laugh it off, to push aside the terror that gripped him so severely.

With just a towel around her waist, Donna knelt by his side. She took him in her arms and held him there on the floor, loving him without question. He clung to her, unashamedly, trembling, afraid. A cold sweat beaded his ashen face.

"I-I've never dreamed anything so terrible," he said as the nightmare began to fade away. "I was pitched off a horse, or we both fell, I'm not sure now, but the ground was suddenly gone, and we fell for what seemed like a long time. I think we fell down a crevasse, or a mineshaft. I couldn't move; I was wrapped in . . . my blankets," he said, grinning with embarrassment.

"Yeppers, you just fell off the bed," Donna said as she reached up and turned the alarm off. Mitch tried again to laugh, but could not find any levity in the situation. Donna helped him up and onto the bed, where they sat and talked quietly, trying to make sense of the dream. She held a Ph.D. in psychology, and though she didn't presently work in the field, she used her education daily. She knew what he needed, what they both needed. She told him it might be the full moon, then kissed him lightly on the lips, and returned to the bathroom. A minute later she came back.

"Lie back and relax. I'll get the coffee going."

Mitch closed his eyes and pondered the vision of his wife's backside. He usually would not tolerate laziness in himself, but this was the first day of his vacation. His thoughts turned to the trip at hand. Moments later, as he smelled the aroma of fresh brewed coffee, he smiled to himself, thinking how good it would smell over a campfire in the mountains. He started to rise out of bed.

"No you don't, old man," Donna said, running into the bedroom; her energy seemed limitless. She threw off her robe and climbed in beside him. Her brown skin contrasted sharply against his tanned, athletic physique.

"Who're you callin' an old man?" he asked.

"You're getting old and you know it." Donna ran her fingers through his collar-length black hair.

"Ya think?" Mitch replied. "Well, I'll just show you what an old man can still do." He kissed her passionately and then said, "It's a little late in the morning for this. Steven might be up."

"Don't worry about it," she said.

CHAPTER FOUR

Steven, your father wants you to join him for breakfast," Donna spoke through her son's bathroom door. On the other side, Steven winced and shut off his hair dryer, sighing, shaking his head impatiently.

"Gimme a break, the Boss Man always wants me to join him for breakfast; it's getting old." As soon as he said it, he regretted it, and though the door was between them, he took a half step away, knowing what was coming.

"Steven R-a-n-d-a-l-l COOPER, don't you *DARE* use that tone of voice with me."

"Wait! I'm sorry!" Steven said.

"I didn't mean it, it's just that...."

The maturing young man struggled with his feelings. It was natural for him to be upset. He loved the mountains as much as his father did, and even more, he loved the time spent with his dad. Even though he knew he needed to stay and study, he'd been hoping his father would relent and let him go along. Soon enough he'd go away to college and they'd have even less time to spend together.

"Mom, does dad have any idea how bad I want to go?"

"Listen, Dear. I know you're upset. Yes, your father and I know how disappointed you must be. He'd love to take you with him, but you know you cannot afford to miss one day of school; you're too close to reaching your goal. The plans you've made for the life you designed hinge on your acceptance to Sul Ross University. You know where your grades have to be. You've said it more than I have."

Steven didn't comment right away; his heart was at odds with his mind. It was his desire to study Equine Science at Sul Ross University in Alpine, Texas. He wanted to get a solid education in animal husbandry and then go on to Veterinary school. All the classes he had taken thus far had been geared to that end. Sul Ross, situated high in the mountains of southwest Texas, was called the "Cowboy College." It was THE place to go for anyone interested in a career with horses.

"Steven? Did you hear me?" His mother waited, listening, knowing what he must be feeling.

"Yes, Ma'am. I'll be down in a few minutes."

"OK," Donna said. "Be respectful to your father at the table. Eggs in five."

"Yes, Ma'am." Then he said, "Mom?"

"Yes, Hon'?"

"I'm sorry."

"I know, Darling. Don't worry about it."

Steven returned to the mirror and his hair, thinking to himself how nice he had it. So many kids his age were on a much different road these days. He reminded himself to thank his parents for caring so much.

"What was that all about?" Mitch asked over his newspaper as his wife came down the stairs.

"None of your business. How's your coffee?" she asked, fighting a rising irritability.

"It's fine. Time for the shot, isn't it," he said with a knowing grin. Donna frowned over her shoulder.

"Does it show that much?"

"It's beginning to," Mitch admitted, smiling sympathetically. Donna returned his smile and remembered their lovemaking as she gazed out the kitchen window and became lost in thought. Mitch sipped his coffee and tried to read the news.

Donna had grown up in San Antonio, the daughter of a wealthy American father and Sicilian Spanish mother. She'd traveled with her family extensively, and they had given her a first-rate education. She'd earned her doctorate in psychology from the University of Texas. Her handsome husband, who looked so much like a young Sam Elliott, was younger looking than his thirty-eight years. He was tall and ruggedly good-looking. Gray had just begun to edge into his black hair, but a reflection of rambunctious youth still twinkled in his fetching blue eyes.

Mitch was ranch-raised in South Texas; he had been a genuine working cowboy. Western at heart, Mitch loved the rough life and never minded hard work. Professional rodeo competition had been part of that life, but he traded a chance at becoming a modern rodeo celebrity for the more rewarding life of a full-time husband and father.

He struggled for a few years to make ends meet, working as a carpenter, while his wife built her practice. Then, while she supported the family, he returned to school and became an electrical engineer. Mitchell

Anthony Cooper was now the wealthy owner of Cooper Electronics Manufacturing and Distribution Company, in Boise, Idaho. Hard work was his secret to success, but he also liked to play. This afternoon, Donna would see him off to Missoula, Montana, where Mitch would meet his guide and then be flown by bush pilot back into Idaho's Selway-Bitteroot Wilderness Area.

Donna always worried when her husband took these extended trips, but Mitch had it together, and his friend Greg was an exceptional pilot with over 20 years in the air, including two tours of duty in Vietnam. Greg had been teaching Mitch how to fly, and it was reassuring for Donna to know that her husband could take over in a pinch. She always worried, but this time Mitch's girl felt different, uneasy. She felt that something wasn't right.

"Mornin', Dad," Steven said, jogging downstairs with a full backpack slung over his shoulder.

"Good morning, Son! Sleep well?"

"OK, I guess. Until about six. Something woke me. I thought I heard someone yelling." He sat down across from his father

"It was your dad," Donna said from the kitchen. "He had a nightmare."

"Hm? Maybe you should stay home, Dad. It could be a bad omen."

"I'm not superstitious; don't believe in that stuff," Mitch said, turning a page.

Donna put breakfast on the table and sat down beside her husband. At that moment, Mitch saw something in her eyes that set him back a notch. Was it fear? He had to admit that he'd felt something nagging at him, too. It was a fleeting, almost intangible feeling darting in and out of his subconscious.

He ignored it and put the paper aside. Donna said

the blessing and then they ate.

"Good feed, Mom," Steven said after inhaling his breakfast. "Excuse me, but I have to run. See ya, Dad. Good luck, and be careful. Oh, are you going to be back in time for my birthday?"

"Thanks, Son, I'll be careful. I should be back before you turn twelve."

"Seventeen! Dad, I'm seventeen!" Steven exclaimed.

His mother gave him a stern look.

"Seventeen? You can't be," Mitch retorted. "I'm only twenty-three!"

"No, you're thirty-eight and still counting," Donna interrupted. But you sure as hell act like twenty-three half the damn time."

"What the blazes set your hind end on fire?" Mitch asked.

"I'm outta here," Steven said, and was gone out the door so fast he didn't hear it shut behind him. The hot rush of emotions vanished with their son, and left Donna and Mitch wondering why they were snapping at each other. It rarely happened between any of them. Perhaps they felt the impending emptiness that would be with all of them when Steven departed for college.

"We could adopt another child," Donna said, sensing one of his thoughts, as she so often did. Donna had been mechanically raped and beaten by a boyfriend two months into her freshman year at college. She had nearly bled to death from the internal damage; she would never be able to carry and deliver a child. Her doctor, against her instincts, had later talked her into a complete hysterectomy. Thus, Steven wasn't their natural child. He was *chosen*, as he was fond of telling his friends. Donna and Mitch had talked on occasion of adopting another child, but they also knew that they had probably waited too long."

"Are you really ready for all that again?"

"At times I think I am" she replied, "but then I think about our age and I wonder if it's too late."

"It's not too late, and it's not inconvenient financially," he said. This surprised Donna, and her heart danced.

"Are you serious?"

"It would up our chances of having grandchildren. But let's talk about it when I get back."

"You're right," she said, and with a new spring in her step she said, "I'd best get busy in the kitchen," and you'd best get to the office. I know you want to check on things one last time. You are never satisfied until you do."

"I know. Kiss me where I like it, and I'll be on my way."

"Come and get it," Donna said.

"If I have to come and get it, then I don't want it."

"Meet ya halfway?"

Mitch gave her his crooked cowboy grin and playfully accepted. As he held her in his arms, looking down into her eyes, he saw immeasurable love, and again, something else he couldn't quite fathom.

He kissed her.

"Let's go back to bed," Donna said. He followed her swinging backside up the stairs as the haunted look retreated from her eyes.

CHAPTER FIVE

I n the driveway Donna leaned on the broom she'd just shooed Mitch out of the house with and watched him drive away to the office. She smiled, knowing he would soon be back.

"What're you so happy about?" a deep but feminine voice hollered from next door. Her best friend and neighbor, Sherrie Spencer, always nosy, pretended to check the mail, which would not arrive for another hour yet. "If my husband was leaving for two weeks I wouldn't be jumping for joy."

"Looks are deceiving, girl." Donna said with a heavy sigh as she noticed a robin in the grass by the sidewalk in front of her house. It searched for earthworms and insects below the pine needles scattered on the dormant grass beneath the two tall pines shading her front yard.

"You need to talk," Sherrie said as she turned back into the house. "I'll be right over."

Donna watched the robin, thinking it was a forerunner of spring. It cocked its head from side to side as it hopped across the grass, listening patiently for the telltale signs of movement below the needles. It found a tasty worm and tried to pluck it from beneath the dry grass. The worm clung tightly to its purchase in the earth and, for a moment, Donna watched a tug of war ensue between the robin and the worm. Then the worm broke and the bird tumbled backward with half of it wiggling in its beak. Donna wanted to laugh but merely smiled and started to turn back to the house.

"Spring is finally here," Sherrie said, abruptly materializing beside her. Donna jumped as if shot.

"Sorry, I didn't mean to scare you."

"Don't worry about it. It's not your fault; my nerves are about gone."

"Hormones?"

"Yep!" Donna said with pursed lips. "Let's go inside."

The morning sunlight reflected off the heavy walnut door as Donna closed it behind them. Mitch had spent most of a summer three years ago, tucked away in his back yard shop, bent over the door with a chisel and a mallet. His pastime and passion was woodworking. He was fond of saying that a laborer works with his hands, but a craftsman works with his hands and his mind. Mitch worked with his hands, his mind, and his heart. That made him an artist. He milled his own lumber, constructed the door, and then carved the figure of an elk at the edge of a clearing with a crescent moon overhead. Mitch had been offered several thousand dollars for his work of art, but he would never part with it. He treasured it nearly as much as he did his wife.

Inside, Donna and Sherrie were finishing a brunch of doughnuts and coffee.

"If my husband knew I was pigging out he'd throw a

fit," Sherrie said with her mouth full. Grace was not her strong point. "I'm supposed to be on a diet." Donna wondered about that; Sherrie had never been overweight.

"I hate diets, I hate exercise, and I detest chocolate-covered doughnuts," Donna said as she reached for another one.

Sherrie sensed that Donna needed to talk but did not press it. Her best friend would confide in her when the time was right. In the interim, she would be supportive.

"Here, let me get these," she said as she reached for the dishes and rose from the table.

"Whatever," Donna said. "Let's just rinse them and put them in the dishwasher. I'll do them later with the supper dishes."

"Harold's bowling tonight," Sherrie commented as she carried the plates and doughnut box to the sink. "Come over and we'll play cards or watch a video."

"Might just do that," Donna said, handing a rinsed glass to her ditzy friend. Donna rinsed another and handed it to her. "Steven's going out with his girlfriend."

"She's adorable," Sherrie said. "They'd make a terrific couple."

"She's smart as a whip. She's never had a grade below a B+, and few of those," Donna said.

"I'm jealous," her friend said. "I didn't have a grade above a B+, and few of those; I was too busy chasing boys. It was great fun, too, at least while it lasted."

"What happened?"

"I caught one!"

"Oh you!" Donna squealed, throwing a plastic cup at her. "I thought you were serious." Donna dried her hands and threw the towel to Sherrie. "Let's go into the living room. I want to show you something."

Donna opened a large cedar chest and removed a quilt she had been secretly working on. She spread it over the oak coffee table, which Mitch had also built, then turned the air conditioner off and opened the front windows to let in the fresh spring air.

"It's a surprise for Mitch. It tells the story of our life together. Donna's creativity with needle and thread was inspiring, yet the pattern was simple: it consisted of a single square-foot block in the center, surrounded in a spiral by blocks half that size. The smaller blocks built around the larger as their life story unfolded. Each colorful section of appliqué told a separate chapter of their life. It was a picture album in cloth.

Enchanted, Sherrie listened as Donna explained her art.

Donna and Mitch were artistically talented, but Steven had yet to show an interest or aptitude for art; however he sure could play the guitar and his academic prowess bested them both.

Sherrie asked Donna about a block close to the center that displayed a pine tree.

"That one depicts our honeymoon in Colorado."

"Is this your campfire?" Sherrie asked, pointing at another block across the quilt.

"No, and it's odd, but that one was not in my plans. I'm not sure why I included it. I was drawing some patterns last month, and it just came to mind. It's Mitch beside a campfire with a big yellow dog. It doesn't fit the theme of the quilt, but...somehow it just seems to work."

Suddenly they heard Mitch's jeep pulling into the drive, and Donna jumped to her feet.

"He's back already! Hurry, open the chest, I can't let him see it." Donna hastily folded the quilt and stuffed it in the chest, closing the lid just as Mitch walked in the front door. Donna ran to him and gave him a quick hug and kiss.

"You're home sooner than I expected. What's up?"

"Alex, that's my vice president," he said for Sherrie's sake, "ran me off. He said I was wasting valuable vacation time and to get my butt out of there." He shrugged. "So here I am. Hi, Sherrie! What're you and my lady up to? You look like you've just been caught at something."

"You're imagining things, Darlin.'"

"Oh crap!" Sherrie said. I have a cake in the oven. I gotta go. See ya."

"Bye, Sherrie," Donna said, winking at her. Sherrie winked back and slipped out the door, closing it softly behind her.

"What was all that about? She doesn't bake!"

"Don't worry about it. So, they ran you off? Figured they would," Donna said as she guided him out of the living room. "Finish packing. I'll be upstairs."

"So that's how it is? First Alex acts like *my* boss, now you?" Mitch said, shaking his head and looking with a grin at the cedar chest. He'd go on letting her believe she had a secret.

"Until you get back, you'd better believe it!" she said, poking him in the chest. "And don't *you* forget it!"

"You little wench. I'd best bend you over my knee," he said, pretending to go after her as she ran squealing up the stairs in mock fear. Laughing, Mitch opened the door to the garage and plucked his checklist off the tool bench.

CHAPTER SIX

Good morning. This is meteorologist Charlie Burns, bringing you today's weather. It looks like we're going to have another fine spring day. The high should be in the upper sixties; tonight's low, about 40 chilly degrees. In the upper elevations, look for temperatures ranging from thirty-six for the low, to fifty-five for the high.

Temperatures should rise steadily all week and through the weekend. Look for highs in the mountains to reach into the upper sixties, while in Boise we could see seventy by Saturday.

At the weather station we now have fair skies and forty-nine degrees. Look for fair skies all week in the valley with a small chance for thunderstorms in the mountains...."

"That's all I need to know," Mitch said and turned off the television.

"Hon'," he hollered up the stairs. "You about ready?"

"Be down in a sec'."

"I'll meet you out front."

Mitch walked through the house, room by room, on his way to the garage and out to the driveway, making sure he hadn't forgotten anything. Donna met him at the car.

"I feel as though I've forgotten something," Mitch said as he opened the door for her. As he climbed into his side of his red Jeep Cherokee, his wife said, "You did," and handed him the hunting knife that his father had given him on his sixteenth birthday. It had been his grandfather's.

"Thanks, Babe. I don't know how I could forget this. It's been on every wilderness trip I've made since dad gave it to me. Maybe I *am* getting old."

"Nah, you just have a lot on your mind. I made you guys some sandwiches for the trip." She put a paper sack in the back amongst his gear.

"Turn on the heater, please?" she said.

"Nope, can't do that."

"Stop teasing. It's cold in here!"

"The switch is out. It hasn't worked in two weeks."

"You've been driving without a heater for two weeks? Until two days ago we still had snow on the ground!"

"It wasn't that bad," Mitch said as he turned west off their street. "You know the cold doesn't bother me that much. Dad used to call me the "Eskimo Vaquero." What kind of sandwiches?"

"Plain old ham and cheese."

"That's fine. Greg and I'll eat them later. Why don't you and I just eat here? We have a little time," he said as they pulled into Donna's Mexican Restaurant and Cantina, which, by the way, they half owned, which served some of her own family recipes. Unbeknownst to Donna, Mitch had called ahead and placed an order with one of the girls, gambling on what Donna would like to eat. He wanted to keep to the flight plan, *and* spend a little more time with his wife.

Arm in arm they walked across the crowded lot. Donna held tightly to her husband as they went inside and selected a secluded booth. After only a moment a young Mexican girl named Helena brought their menus and water, and then some chips and salsa. Mitch and Donna quietly studied the menus for a couple of minutes, and then Helena returned and took their order, although it was already being prepared. Mitch grinned. He was thankful that his gamble paid off.

The pretty Mexican waitress winked at Mitch.

"Beats Ham and Cheese," he told Donna.

"I suppose I can handle it," she said, rubbing her knee against his as she dipped a chip. "But this salsa is hotter than blazes. George must have stubbed his toe on the cayenne." Donna sniffed and blinked her eyes. Mitch was quiet, suddenly subdued.

"What's wrong?"

"Just thinking. Are you going to be alright? You're not going to just mope around for two weeks, are you?"

"No, I'll keep busy. I've still got some shopping to do for Steven's birthday, some reading to catch up on, sewing, gardening, and stuff like that."

"Here's your beer, Sir, and your Margarita, Ma'am," the waitress said, suddenly appearing at their table. "Would you like some more salsa?"

"No thanks, 'Lena, this is plenty," Mitch said, glancing at Donna to be sure. She nodded and took a soothing sip of her drink. Mitch knocked the top off his beer, and out of the corner of his eye he watched the young waitress walk away, thinking Donna wouldn't notice.

"Does," Donna cleared her throat, "Little, Miss 'Lena, have a nice tush?"

"What?" Mitch said.

34

"Getting a bit familiar with the help, aren't you? I'm not blind, you know." Of course she was *teasing* him. She knew he'd never stray and she tolerated his flirty nature...within limits.

"I was looking at her hair. She has beautiful hair."

"Don't give me that bull. Her hair didn't go down that far."

"OK, so I peeked. Does that mean the honeymoon is over?"

"No," Donna said, smiling over her drink, "as long as you look at mine, too."

"Every chance I get and you know it."

"Here you are," Helena said. "Careful, guys, these plates are *very* hot."

"Geez! That was fast," Donna said.

"Can I get you anything else?" the waitress asked, winking at Mitch again.

"Thanks," he said, "we're fine."

"Very good, Mr. and Missus Cooper. It's always good to see you. If you need anything else, please, do not hesitate to ask."

"Thanks, 'Lena," Donna said and smiled at her. "She is a doll," she added, "and speaks better English than you. Oh, and don't think I don't know you ordered ahead. But it's a nice surprise anyway."

"Si, Señorita," Mitch said, already lifting a steaming forkful of chicken enchilada to his mouth. "Ahora, cierre su boca y coma." She didn't have to be told twice. They were both hungry and the food was delicious.

Within twenty minutes they were on the way to the airport.

Greg was pulling the plane out of its hangar when Mitch and Donna drove up. Mitch quickly jumped out and gave his friend a hand. It only took a few minutes to load the gear, and then they were ready to take off.

Greg fiddled with an imaginary problem inside the cockpit while Mitch and Donna said their farewells.

"He's ready to go, hon'," Mitch said.

"Hold me for a minute?"

Mitch took her in his arms and buried his face in her hair. She fell into his arms where she still fit like they had been molded to each other.

Greg smiled and wished he had been so lucky.

"I love you," Donna whispered.

"I love you, girl. Take care of yourself, and don't worry; I'll be fine. It's a routine excursion. What could go wrong?"

A dozen terrifying scenarios sped through her mind, but she knew he was right; he could handle himself. She had no reason to worry.

"You'd best go," she said. "Greg's finished fixin' whatever didn't need fixin'."

Mitch laughed and said, "Yeah, but you don't want to let me go."

"Kiss me," Donna whispered.

She got what she asked for, and more, maybe too much. She tore herself away, looked into his eyes, and knew the feelings were mutual. But still, something was wrong, and suddenly she was scared and wanted to cry. *Damn hormones,* she thought. She held back her tears, but the lump in her throat remained. She quickly kissed him again and then ran to the jeep. Mitch watched as she sped off. Donna would get over the tears and eventually swallow the lump in her throat, but a knot of fear grew inside her, and, try as she might she could not shake it.

She left the airstrip, drove a mile, and then pulled to the side of the road as her tears came in a flood. It was not just her hormones; she was really frightened. The knot of fear, heavy inside her, said that something was dreadfully wrong. As her husband disappeared over the mountains, a cold panic gripped her. She gunned the Jeep's engine and raced away hoping to outrun her fear.

CHAPTER SEVEN

Hold on tight," Greg said. "That wing on your side was loose last time I took her up. We may have a rough flight. I suppose it'll hold together until we get to Missoula."

"Not funny, Bud! In fact, that's just the kind of humor I can do without."

"All kidding aside, this could be a rough flight, bro'. We've some bad weather between here and Missoula. I would've told you on the ground, but your old lady didn't need to hear it. I know she's worried enough as it is."

"You're right about that," Mitch said. "She's been a bundle of frayed nerves lately. She's hiding it, but not as well as she thinks." Mitch got a puzzled look on his face, and then said, "I watched the weather this morning. Burns said there was only a chance of a thunderstorm. He didn't call for anything serious."

"That was this morning. I called the National Weather Bureau a few minutes ago. The storm that stalled in

Washington is on the move again. It's coming across the panhandle right now. If it doesn't move south, we'll be fine. We should be able to skip quickly behind it as it passes through. We're gonna be OK. I just thought you should know what's ahead." Mitch shrugged it off and said he was going to take a nap, complaining about a restless night and the beginnings of a migraine.

"OK by me," Greg said. "Hold on now, we have a stiff crosswind; as we leave the runway she'll slip sideways."

"I trust you," Mitch said, as he tightened his seatbelt. Greg noticed and grinned around an unlit, Black & Mild, plastic-tipped cigar.

"You rookies are all the same," he said; though he would have insisted Mitch secure his belt anyway.

"You were a rookie once," Mitch said as they roared down the runway. "Weren't you ever just a *tiny* bit concerned for your safety?"

"Nah, never," Greg said as they lifted off at a tangent to the runway. "Oh, I got a little nervous once when I lost power twenty miles off the coast of Nam.

"It was August of '64. We were countering an attack against Navy destroyers in the Gulf of Tonkin. Our mission was to bomb their bases along the northern coast. We had just refueled and were getting into bombing formation when my engines quit. I restarted and kicked it in the ass only five hundred feet above water."

"Man that was close," Mitch said.

"You forget, friend, whether it's under power or not, an aircraft will usually remain stable at the minimum speed at which it was designed to fly. I was going pretty damned fast when I lost power. I just stayed with it until I could figure out the problem and restart the engines, and, of course, I could have ejected at the last minute. But man, what a crunch that gives your spine.

"It's like this Comanche, if we flew straight up, like

this," Greg pulled back on the yoke, and as they began to climb, he cut power. Seconds later, Mitch's stomach rose into his throat as the plane stalled and fell. It felt like the bottom had fallen out of his seat and for a moment he was weightless and then the G-force caught him and threw him back in his seat as the plane raced Earthward.

"As you can see, all we have to do is put the nose down until our airspeed increases enough to recreate the conditions necessary for lift, and then we pull the nose up and we are flying again." Greg eased back on the wheel and within a few seconds, they were climbing back to altitude, straight on course. "It's more complicated than that, but you get the drift. You'll learn all that and more in ground school."

He paused a moment to check the gauges and adjust the fuel mixture.

"Damn you! I hate it when you pull that crap on me," Mitch said.

"Get used to it! You'll have to do it on your own soon, or you won't pass the exam."

"Well, you could have warned me."

"Your engine may not warn you before it quits."

"I suppose."

"To be honest with you, when my jet lost power, it pissed me off more than it scared me. If I had lost that jet it would have tarnished my near perfect flight record, not to mention my pride. No, I had to stay with it. It wasn't in me to bail out, but my weenie of a co-pilot was ready to jump. I guess what I'm saying is that it's no shame to admit fear once in a while.

"Fear is what got us through that hell. Mix a little controlled anger with that fear, and *man*, watch out! That's what makes heroes. A hero is nothing more than a person who is scared near to death but keeps his wits. He's angry enough to overcome the fear and clear-headed enough to handle the situation. Well, that's how I see it.

"Relax, we'll level off in about five minutes, and hopefully it'll be smooth sailing into Montana."

Greg was five years Mitch's senior, but looked fifteen years older. The Vietnam War, three greedy wives, and a love affair with Jim Beam had taken their toll. At five feet, ten inches, he weighed well over two hundred pounds. He was not in the best shape—far from it—but he was as stubborn as he was brave. He ignored the pain in his chest and insisted he was fit for the hunt.

Mr. Cooper had his doubts about that.

Unlike Mitch, who ran 5 miles most every day and worked out every other day in his company gym, Greg seldom exercised. He often overate and overslept. Greg reminded Mitch of a lethargic, tree-dwelling sloth. They were total opposites, but they were best friends. Greg was simply a—no cares, no worries—kind of guy who never let hard times get the best of him.

Until now, that is.

"It's sure good to be in the air again," he said a few minutes later as he leveled out. He unbuckled his seat belt. "You can take yours off. It'll be two hours before we need them again." He glanced at some menacing clouds in the distance, "unless we run into bad weather."

"OK," Mitch said. He yawned, unbuckled his belt, and then took a deck of playing cards out of his shirt pocket and began cutting them with one hand as he watched the wilderness pass beneath them.

"That's pretty fancy work," Greg said, as he leaned forward to adjust his fuel mixture.

"Watch this." Mitch shuffled the deck in mid-air without the aid of a table.

"Where'd you learn to handle cards like that, and how come you never showed me?"

"I taught myself years ago when I was rodeoin'. It helped to pass the long hours on the road."

Suddenly Greg groaned and nearly doubled over.

"What the fu...."

Greg groaned again and leaned back in his seat.

"I'm OK. Whew, bad gas pain. Hurts like hell." He drew a deep breath and leaned back as if to take the pressure off his lower abdomen.

"Level with me," Mitch leveled at him. "Are you alright? What the hell is going on?" *Bad gas my ass,* he thought. "You don't look so good. We better turn back and get you to a doctor."

"Nonsense! I just saw him last week. Really, I'm fine," he lied as he subconsciously acknowledged they'd just passed the halfway point in the flight.

"It ain't worth it!" Mitch threw the cards up on the dash. "If it's your heart we've got to turn back."

"It's not my heart. You can forget that. I may not be in the best shape, but my heart is fine."

"Then what the hell was that all about?"

"OK. I'll admit I'm not in great shape like you. But my Doc' said my heart wasn't that bad."

"Are you sure?"

"Yeah, I'm sure," Greg said, breathing easier.

"Well, let me take over for awhile."

"Alright, you go ahead," Greg said, wiping sweat off his brow. He wondered if he was going to make it. Mitch wasn't the only one who was anxious. It was the first time he'd ever lied to his friend. His doctor had threatened to have his pilot's license revoked if he didn't lose some weight.

Mitch continued to fly under Greg's instruction, but in the back of his mind, he wondered if it was worth it.

His instincts warned him to turn around and head back to Boise, but he had never known Greg to lie to him. He recalled his nightmare, and his wife's negative feelings, feelings she'd tried to hide. Against his better judgment, thinking they were probably near the halfway point anyway, he kept the plane headed north by northeast, deeper into the wilderness.

It wasn't long until his eyelids became heavy, and his headache became more pronounced. He turned it back over to Greg and took two aspirin.

"I've got to get some sleep," Mitch said, taking his billfold from his hip pocket. "Don't let me forget this; it's wearing a hole in my ass."

"I don't see how you can sleep. Man, look what we're flying over." Greg waved his hand over the mountains. "There's places down there no man has seen." They had this conversation every time they flew somewhere together.

"Like I said, I didn't get a lot of sleep last night, and we won't get much tonight." Mitch closed his eyes as he squirmed for a better seat.

"Have it your way," Greg replied with a sigh. "Hey, did I tell you about the time I shot...."

"Stow it, Doughboy," Mitch said, "or I'll tell your wife about your girlfriend."

"I don't have a girlfriend."

"I'll make her think you do."

"You'd do that, wouldn't you?"

"You're damned right I would."

"Figures," Greg said. "I furnish the plane and the fuel and...."

"And I paid for everything else. So quitcherbellyakin and let me sleep."

"You sound like my mother," Greg said.

It was Tuesday, 3:50 P.M. when they flew over the

43

Salmon Mountains. They were just over an hour out of Boise, a few minutes south of where they would be hunting tomorrow. Greg was tempted to wake Mitch when they flew over their hunting grounds, but Mitch was just ornery enough to stir up trouble with his wife —or make him think he had. In a little more than an hour, weather permitting, they would land in Montana, where they would meet their guide, eat, and then retire to his ranch for a short six-hour rest. Just before dawn, they would have breakfast and then be flown by bush pilot into a spike camp in the heart of the beautiful, but rugged and potentially dangerous, Selway-Bitteroot Wilderness Area.

♠ ♠ ♠

Donna watched until the airplane could no longer be seen, cursed Greg for stunt flying, dried her face, and drove home, stopping briefly to pick up a few groceries. She arrived home at 3:00, and by 3:50 she had the groceries put away, sorted the mail, and had been working on the quilt for thirty minutes, trying not to think about Mitch.

Try as she might, she couldn't concentrate and kept poking herself with the needle. Finally, she put the quilt aside and reached for one of the magazines that rested on the coffee table. Before she could pick it up, the phone rang. She jumped up to answer it, but the ringing stopped as soon as she got to her feet. Then she heard a thumping sound that seemed to come from everywhere. She became dizzy as the sound grew louder, booming like thunder in her ears. Then the floor fell from beneath her and her stomach rose into her throat. She screamed as she felt herself falling. As she fell, she understood that the thumping noise was her own heart racing in her chest.

"My God, what is happening," she screamed. Then she came to her senses to find that she was still standing by the couch. In horror, she realized that she had not been the one to fall.

"No!" She screamed. "Mitch? MITCH?" Then her world began to spin; the knot in her stomach exploded; darkness overcame her, and she collapsed in heap.

♠ ♠ ♠

Mitch woke knowing something was wrong. He sat up blinking the sleep out of his eyes and saw Greg slumped over the controls. He quickly looked out the windows. They were in a steep dive, the earth rushing up at them with blinding speed. He began to shake as panic welled up inside him.

"Greg? Quit playing games. You're scarin' the hell out of me."

Greg didn't move.

Nearly blind with panic, Mitch punched him in the shoulder. When Greg didn't respond, Mitch lifted his friend's head. It took only a glance to see that his friend was no longer among the living. Mitch lurched for the yoke and tried to pull it back, but Greg's body was so heavy he couldn't move it. He looked out the front windows at the mountains rushing toward him and knew he was also going to die unless he did something, and did it quick. He grabbed the yoke again, closed his eyes, screamed his wife's name, and heaved with all his might, shoving his feet hard against the rudder controls.

"Come u-u-u-up, you son-of-a-bitch!" Mitch felt a little give in the yoke and opened his eyes. Greg's body began to fall back and he felt the yoke begin to come to him and the nose begin to slowly rise toward the horizon. Donna, sweet Donna, be strong for me now, honey. Help me out here, girl. C'mon, girl, I know you can hear me. We're not out of the woods yet. As the nose rose higher toward the horizon, Greg's body fell back in its seat and Mitch gained full control. The plane began to climb, but not soon enough. He folded his arms over his head as the nose of the plane took the top off a tree.

Just up ahead a river gorge waited to swallow the wreckage as Mitch screamed more in anger at his fate than in fear. The Comanche ripped through the forest, shearing off the left wing, then the right wing and the tail. The shorn off parts splashed into the roaring torrent and disappeared quickly from sight. The remaining fuselage spun sideways through the trees, down into the canyon, tumbling and rolling, breaking apart, tossing Mitch into the far side. The misshapen fuselage with Greg's body trapped inside hit water and went under. It came right back up, bobbed in the current for a few moments and then slowly sank as it was carried swiftly downstream. A single, jagged end of a wing tip, the only piece of the wreckage the river had yet to take, dangled precariously at the top edge of the cliff above. It lay there waiting for a gust of wind to send it crashing down into the gorge, where it would join its sister parts, erasing any visible trace of the crash. Mitch's body, along with the fractured airplane and the body of his friend, had completely vanished from sight.

The forest's relative silence was shattered by the destruction. The wilderness, in its innocence, was suddenly, forcefully thrust into terror. A mule deer bounded away into the woods, shedding an antler, snorting its fear, awakened from its afternoon bed.

As the plane fell, its engine screaming, a female black bear sat up in its den as its cubs ran to its side.

Birds stopped singing. A badger dove into a hole under a rock. A half-mile south, a moose brought its head out from under the waters of a shallow lake, its muzzle dripping and vegetation hanging from the corners of its mouth. It stood knee-deep in the cold water, nostrils flaring, listening.

The plane struck the earth like a bomb, piercing the air with sounds of tearing metal and shattering glass. The moose turned and plunged through the reeds and mud. Leaving the lake, it retreated from the happening and disappeared into the darkness of the deep woods where it waited in fear to forget.

CHAPTER EIGHT

Donna blinked her eyes open. Her muscles twitched and she tingled all over as she stared at the fuzz under the couch and fought to regain her senses. Groggily, she pushed herself to her knees, then sat back and leaned against the coffee table. What the heck just happened? Are my hormones that out of whack? She leaned her head back and stared at the oak beams in the ceiling. She started to feel dizzy and leaned forward, rested her elbows on her knees, and held her head in her trembling hands.

Then it all came back.

"God, no!" she said. Shaking fiercely, she began to sob, her heart breaking. Then she heard her son's pickup coming up the driveway. She jumped to her feet and ran upstairs to her bathroom. She choked back her sobs and splashed her face with cold water. What am I going to tell him? You know what to do. Hide it until you are sure.

"God, I'm white as a sheet," she said as she saw herself in the mirror. She slapped herself a few times to bring the color back, pulled herself together, dried her face and hands, and then went to her son.

He was on his way to the kitchen to get his afternoon Coke from the frig'.

"Dad make it off OK?" he asked before he tipped back the soda and guzzled half of it.

"Uh huh, I'm waiting for his call." She stepped off the landing and turned toward the kitchen.

"How was school?" Donna asked as she greeted Steven with a hug.

"It was alright, I guess. We had a little excitement this morning. Jeff Bowers broke his leg running hurdles. You should have seen the blood," he said as he sat down at the table. "The bone was sticking out...."

"Spare me the details, please. Are you hungry?"

"Yeah, I could eat." He took a long look at his mother.

"What's wrong? You don't look so good."

"I just miss your father."

Steven didn't buy it.

"I guess I can cook," she said too quickly. "Soup and sandwiches sound OK?"

"Sounds good," Steven said, watching her closely as she walked too briskly into the kitchen.

"How was school?"

"You already asked me that a minute ago." Steven tipped the can back and finished off his soda, giving his mother an appraising glance. "I'll be upstairs studying, if you want to talk about it."

"All right," she replied, barely able to hold back the tears while he walked up stairs. When she heard him enter his room she let herself go and ran into the garage where she cried convulsively. A few minutes later, finally pulling herself completely together, she had the soup coming to a boil and she was just about finished with the sandwiches. Spreading mayonnaise, she wondered if her hormonal imbalance could have caused her to feint. She searched her feelings, finished the sandwiches, and concluded that Mitch was in trouble.

Donna called Steven for supper. Three minutes later, he sat down with her at the table. Holding hands, they said a prayer of thanks, as was their custom. Steven did not squeeze and release her hand as usual; instead he held his mother's hand firmly and looked into her frightened eyes.

"What's wrong?"

"Nothing."

"Mom, I'm not a child anymore. Please don't tell me a white lie and dismiss me with a nod of your head. What's wrong?"

The sudden ringing of the telephone made them jump in their seats. Donna rushed to answer it.

"Hello? Oh, hi, Sherrie. No, of course not. I'm sorry. I thought it was Mitch. Expecting him to call any time now. Thanks. I'll call you later. Bye."

She returned to the table and stared at her untouched meal. No longer hungry, she put it all away and cleaned the kitchen in silence. Steven cleaned up after himself and returned to his room without a word.

He felt her fear.

Unable to concentrate on his homework, he descended the stairs and walked quietly into the utility room. He came out with a garbage bag and then went through the house emptying all the trashcans. Donna sat in the living room staring at nothing. Steven took the garbage outside to the street and deposited it into the can by the curb. On his return, he found his mother talking on the phone.

"Yes, he left a little after two. Uh huh, I watched them fly off. He was supposed to be there by four-thirty. It's nearly five."

Steven shut the garage door and stood breathless, listening. He broke out in a cold sweat as he heard terror surge in his mother's voice.

"Alright, I'll wait. Thank you, Sam." Steven ran to her side as she hung up the phone. Donna turned and buried her face in his shirt.

"They probably detoured around the storm," he said.

"What storm?"

"Mom," he said, pushing her back so he could see her face, "it's been raining up there for two days." He followed her into the living room, where she stared out a window toward the mountains. Didn't he tell you?"

"No, he didn't tell me. Oh God, I knew something was going to happen. I knew it, a-a-and I-I-I didn't try to stop him." Donna collapsed on the couch. "I should have stopped him" she said and wept face down on the cushions.

Like a zombie, Steven walked slowly to the phone and called his girlfriend. With a strained, fear-edged voice, he said, "Molly, I have to cancel our date. Dad's missing."

♠ ♠ ♠

A restless hour later, they received another call from Missoula. It was the Montana Civil Air Patrol. They had been made aware of Mitch's plight, and were calling in pilots, making ready to begin searching for the plane. Donna listened, outwardly calm, crying inside, as the officer told her of things she needed to do, and about what *they* were going to do. When she hung up, she turned to her son, who had been listening at her side.

"Let's go sit down," she said, heading toward the couch, barely able to stand, much less walk. Steven sat down beside her.

"That was the Civil Air Patrol. Your father and Greg are listed as missing. They are making ready to search for them." Donna took a deep breath, searched her son's face, and then continued. "Your father is alive." Steven screwed up his face, puzzled.

"Listen to me very carefully," she said as she took his hands in hers, holding them tightly. "I've known for two hours that your father was not going to call. I sensed it when they went down. I also know that he did not die in the crash. I don't know about Greg." Steven drew back, afraid, concerned for his mother.

"I'm scaring you. I'm sorry." She hugged him like an injured child and whispered in his ear, "You may think I've gone off the deep end, but I know in my heart that what I feel is true. You have to trust me."

"Mom, don't do this," he said, choking on his fear.

"Steven, you are not following me. Now please, listen! Your father and I have a special and unique relationship. We knew from day one that our marriage would be as perfect as God could make it." She paused a moment to take a deep breath and hold back the tears so she could finish.

"When was the last time you saw or heard us fight?"

"I-I've never seen you fight."

"That's because we know each other. I mean, we don't have to talk about some things, uh, we feel them, and I'm not making any sense, am I?"

"No, Mom, and you're scaring me." Donna pulled him to her and hugged him to her breasts, knowing he was too proud to cry in front of her, but being there for him just the same. However, she cried silently, only her tears showing her loss of control. After a few moments she pulled away and continued.

"Son, your father and I wanted to let you in on our secret, but we weren't sure you would understand, or even believe." She grabbed a tissue from a box on the coffee table and blew her nose, and then she continued. "Your father and I don't always have to speak to be heard. We cannot explain it. We just look at each other and know what we are thinking. Call it telepathy of some kind, but we can sense each other's thoughts and feelings. Your father and I are very close, Steven. So, when I tell you that your father has crashed and survived, it's because I know it deep inside. If your father were dead, a part of me would have died. Both parts are alive, and I know your father is alive. He may be lost, and probably seriously injured, but he is very much alive."

"I've seen how you guys are, I knew there was something special, and Molly has noticed it, too. I believe you. But what if he's really bad off? What if he's dying? It's cold up there and he doesn't have any food."

"He does have food if he can get to it. Greg carries two survival kits in the plane. It's alright to be scared. I am scared for your father, too, but we can handle it. We have to. We must lean on our faith and your father's strong spirit."

Donna took her son's hands in hers again and they prayed together.

As they finished, the doorbell rang and Donna answered it.

It was Molly; Steven ran to her. The three of them embraced in the doorway, beginning what would prove to be a long and difficult test.

CHAPTER NINE

As the Earth turned on its axis, the sun sank over the mountains, setting the western skies on fire. The brightening stars rose into the thickening blackness of night, tiny bursts of light marching over the horizon like soldiers carrying torches to war. Slowly the moon emerged, bright and glowing in its fullness, like a general on the battlefield standing tall and proud over his army.

Throughout the long, cold night, led by their commander, this battalion of lights stood guard over Mitch encased in his icy prison. In the morning the stars and moon would sleep while the day's sun took charge, driving away the cold and showering the Earth with its life-giving warmth, melting away the winter's frozen tears.

Many a lesser man would have died, but Mitch was too strong of heart to die without a struggle. Through endless harsh hours, at the bottom of a twenty-foot-deep snowdrift, his inner strength kept his broken body alive. During the night, Mitch pulled himself into a fetal position, but not to die. The heat from his body sealed the inside of his cocoon, turning it into a life-saving shelter with fresh air circulating from above. The snow staunched his bleeding wounds, and, at the same time, insulated him from the frosty nights as he lay precariously floating between life and death. The snow both saved him and at the same time could kill him. Heat from his body was constantly melting the snow around him, and he was sinking ever lower in the snowdrift and closer and closer to the rising river.

The river waited hungrily for three days and nights while the cycle repeated, until noon of the third day, when the sun's heat, gaining on the moon's cold, caused the river to rise. The sun blazed forth, showering the land with thawing heat. The temperatures soared, snow melted, and as the river rose, Mitch slipped ever closer to the river's edge. In tortured sleep, he dreamed tortured dreams.

CHAPTER TEN

Neither Donna nor Steven slept much that first night, in spite of the fact that Donna knew Mitch was alive. Sherrie stayed with her until late in the evening. Molly stayed the night with Steven, sleeping beside him on the couch.

By Friday morning, the search teams had covered the entire route between Boise and Missoula, at a width of two hundred miles. They covered every inch. Nothing was found.

Donna kept herself busy managing the house and Mitch's businesses, yet the quilt occupied most of her time. She spent hours at the couch, with the quilt in her lap, talking soft encouragement to her husband as she sewed.

As she worked on the quilt Friday morning, Steven stared out a school window, up at the mountains. Both of them were weary from lack of sleep and the endless hours of waiting.

But Donna, unlike her son, had the secret assurance that her husband was alive. Steven had his doubts about that and began to wonder if his mother was not hiding her fears behind a dangerous fantasy.

She was nearly finished with the quilt. It was all there, the story of their life so far, but it lacked three blocks to be complete. Now she must wait and let time stitch the rest of the story. Yes, the quilt would have to wait, but she could not.

Restless and frustrated, she picked up the phone. She called the Air Patrol and asked to join the search. They refused her request, saying she would be better off waiting at home. They suggested she call family, if she hadn't already, but of course, she had. Mitch's father and his new bride were away on a cruise, and had conveniently told no one where they were going, or who they were sailing with. Donna couldn't find Mitch's mother. When her husband had ditched her for a younger woman she'd disappeared. *Her* parents had died in a car collision five years ago in Spain. Both of her brothers were fighting in Iraq, they'd been notified, but the Corps' take on that was that if it wasn't immediate family, no go. So it was just herself, and her son, and their friends.

After the Air Patrol called the first time, she had called Greg's wife, Barbara. They had never been friends, but Donna made every effort to console her, inviting her to stay with them. Barbara had refused, saying she would be fine and to leave her alone. Donna called back several times, but all she got was a cold shoulder.

Sherrie was a Godsend, insisting on helping with everything. The pastor and several members of the church had been by; the kitchen was overflowing with prepared foods. Everyone she knew turned out in her time of need. She was comforted, but it was not enough; she had to *do* something.

If it were she out there instead of Mitch, he would not rest until she was found. Donna took Steven from school, hired a pilot experienced in search and rescue, and joined in the search against much protest from friends and associates.

First, they studied charts and maps of the mountains under the flight path. Then for three days, hour after fruitless hour, they searched, resting only to refuel, eat when their stomachs would let them, and sleep a few hours a night. For all the effort, they saw only miles of wilderness, except for one thing passed off as insignificant.

About noon on Sunday as they flew along the Salmon River, they spotted a tree at the edge of a canyon that had been shattered by something. They flew low, cruising at near stall speed. They saw nothing more, except an old man and a dog sitting idle beside the river. They wrote the damaged tree off to lightning and searched on.

At the end of the day they had to give up because their pilot had other business. So they reluctantly returned to Boise, exhausted and discouraged.

In her heart, Donna knew Mitch was still alive, but she had expected he would be found by now. At home on Sunday evening, she sat on the couch, held the quilt to her breast, and cried herself to sleep as she had every night since his disappearance. She was drawn to the quilt, and in the days to come she would seldom be without it.

CHAPTER ELEVEN

Early Friday morning the river found Mitch feeling the cold on a conscious level, with his feet dangling in the water, its icy tongue licking at him hungrily. He dreamed of a red-eyed beast that dragged him into its lair. Drifting through that vague nowhere between sleep and waking, he was oblivious that just moments before, the last of the snowdrift that had saved his life, had slid into the water, nearly taking him with it.

Slowly he awoke, groaning with pain and stiffness, blinking his eyes at the sunlight. As his vision cleared, he saw the river. Wild-eyed and frightened, he shrank back, cringing against the wall of the cliff, his mind gone, gasping at a sharp pain in his right side.

What was Mitch Cooper three days ago was now an empty shell. He was broken, bruised and battered, with no memory of his past, no knowledge of his where-abouts, or of how he had arrived alone in the remote wilderness.

His voice reverberated off the canyon walls as he threw back his head and vented his anguish. He saw a cliff towering a hundred feet above him. He gaped, un-believing, until merciful unconsciousness took him once again.

A sheer cliff rose behind him. Boulders, uprooted trees, and several tons of tangled driftwood littered its base. Mitch was trapped on a narrow, slanted ledge on the side of the cliff. Before him flowed the mighty Salmon River. It was full and rising steadily in the spring thaw.

Mitch awoke again later that afternoon and man-aged to sit up. His head throbbed ominously and he groaned as he moved, feeling what must be a few bro-ken ribs. He coughed and tasted blood. For a few min-utes he sat unmoving, his back against the cliff, trying to figure things out. As he leaned against the sun-warmed rock, surveying his surroundings, he became aware of a raging thirst. He stood up to a pain that sent shock waves through him, and he fell hard to his knees, vomiting in the sand between his hands, trem-bling with agony: the jagged end of a bone was poking out of his right leg, just above the ankle.

Dry heaves washed through him like the waves that crashed against the ledge. It was then that Mitch real-ized how utterly alone he was. He cowered in the sand, closing his eyes against the horror mounting inside him, and nearly passed out again from the intensity of the pain and anguish.

Vaguely aware of his surroundings, Mitch's mind reeled as he tried to remember who he was. Fear and pain washed through him, until he thought he might throw himself into the river and just get it over with. Then slowly, strength deep within him began to emerge, and he felt a calm filtering through his panic. He started to relax, breathing as deeply as his broken ribs would allow. In a moment, his mind cleared, and he began to talk to himself.

"Ain't gonna die," he groaned. "Can't die. Won't."

He forced himself to ignore the pain, and, for the moment, to push fear aside and take no counsel of it. Slowly, easing himself up inches at a time, Mitch once again tried to stand. For several minutes he fought nausea, but finally it receded. Thirst drove him forward, and he hobbled drunkenly to the river's edge, dragging his right leg behind him. The river seemed to reach out as he got close, its waves tossing spray into the crisp mountain air, bathing the canyon in mist. He stopped a few feet back from the edge. The water was too swift, deep, and dark with silt. Caution forced him back away from the river's edge.

The ledge was twenty feet wide at its widest and over a hundred yards long. It slanted down toward the river at about a twenty-degree angle. He searched for a safer place to drink. About forty yards upstream to his left as he faced the wide river, he saw the mirror-like surface of a small spring-fed pool nestled in a cul-de-sac of rocks. Mitch made his way slowly between the many obstacles, falling several times. Dragging his leg behind him, he gasped for breath, having to stop and rest often, sometimes crawling. A trail of blood followed him closely.

It took him an hour, but he finally made it, dropping heavily to his knees and easing himself down to drink, but hesitating as he saw his image reflected back at him. He stared at the bloody and unshaven face of a stranger. The man looking back at him had a full mustache that drooped at the ends and met with three day's growth of beard. The face was rugged and handsome beneath the blood, cuts and bruises, and dark stubble. He gazed at himself until thirst pushed him forward. At first he just took a mouthful to wash the sand and blood from his mouth, and then he drank slowly, a swallow at a time, careful not to take too much at once. In his concentration, he was unaware of the mountain lion tracks in the dirt between his hands.

His thirst quenched, he crawled to a boulder and leaned against it, wincing at the pain in his side. A tickle in his throat caused him to cough and he spit up blood. He wiped his face with his sleeve and stared across the canyon, exhausted. As he looked around, he felt uneasy. He sensed a threat, but could not see or hear what caused his alarm. As he leaned against the boulder, he checked his pockets and was relieved to find a large and well-made knife, along with a cigarette lighter. But he found no billfold or any kind of identification. He probed his sore head and found a gash over his right ear. He doubled over and vomited when he found cracked, exposed bone.

He woke moments later to find himself lying on his face in the sand. Steeling himself, angry at his situation, he crawled back to the pool. He drank again. Then he peeled off his shirt.

He almost dipped it in the water so he could cleanse his wounds. He thought again. He looked around. This was his only fresh supply of water: the river was too muddy to drink.

Reluctantly, he crawled to the river's edge. He thrust his shirt into the near freezing water. The swiftness of the current almost wrenched it from his grasp, but he held on and pulled the now heavy cotton shirt from the river. He cleansed his bleeding wounds and rinsed the shirt before wrapping it around his shoulders and crawling back to the pool to drink again. Then he spread his shirt out on a flat rock to dry in the sun.

He noticed his reflection again and leaned over the pool to appraise his image. He was stout of arm and broad in the chest. The body shimmering beneath the surface was used to hard work or frequent exercise, and appeared to be quite strong. He smiled in spite of his predicament; he was beginning to like this stranger, though this unfamiliar person was getting cold. He glanced at the sky and knew he had best find shelter soon, build a fire, and find something to eat. He turned from the pool just in time to see a grizzly bear lumber out of the forest on the other side of the river. Mitch was instantly on his feet, staring at the bear, wincing at the pain shooting up his leg. He stared, frozen in place as the bear approached the frigid water.

As Mitch watched, the bear reared up on its hind legs, forepaws held out in front, its long, black, deadly claws shining in the waning light. The huge bear stood motionless, testing the wind. Involuntarily wincing at the pain in his leg, Mitch retreated. Saliva dripped from the grizzly's massive jaws. It blinked, sniffed the wind, then dropped to all fours and charged into the river.

Mitch jumped back, gasping in pain and falling, grabbing at his left side, his injured leg folding underneath him. But the bear only splashed a few feet into the river before it stopped and roared a challenge across the water. Shocked by the bear's sudden rush Mitch sat trembling, suddenly dizzy, encased in agony, as the enraged animal voiced its anger. He somehow knew the bear's eyesight was poor, that it could not possibly see him. But if the wind were right, it could smell him a half mile away.

With little strength left, he watched, gasping for

breath, as the grizzly drank. After several minutes, the bear left the swift water and began feeding on grubs and insects it found beneath rocks and the scattered logs along the shore. Then, as if by signal, the bear turned from the river and disappeared into the forest. Mitch noticed several white spots of hair on the bear's rump as it retreated.

"That bear's been hit with buckshot!" Mitch heard himself say. Then a premonition sent a shiver up his spine. They would meet again.

Mitch looked up at the sky and told himself to get busy. He made his way to his shirt and managed to put it back on, but it caused him to shiver; the shirt was not yet dry, and the air was getting colder all the time.

As the sun began to set and paint the sky orange and pink, he searched the ledge for some sort of shelter. In searching, he noticed that he was literally standing on the side of the cliff, and that when the water receded this ledge was inaccessible. Just as he thought his luck had completely run out, he found a small fissure in the base of the rock face. The triangle-shaped cleft was about six feet wide, twenty feet tall, and sloped back into the wall farther than he could see. It was close to the driftwood and hemmed in by several tall rocks.

He found a good stick to use as a crutch as he collected firewood. Some of the driftwood was worn smooth from the action of water and sand working against it. Some of it seemed to have been at rest for ages, some for only a short while. Mitch had enough fuel to last months, if necessary.

Abruptly a thought that had been nagging at him from his subconscious came bursting forth. He looked toward the river and knew his fight was just beginning and that the worst was yet to come. The river was on the rise and he would soon be engulfed by its mounting volume. He turned too quickly to continue his task of gathering wood for his fire and felt the bones in his right leg grate against each other. Agonizing pain shot up his leg and he felt himself falling. The lights went out once more.

The moon was high and glowing bright when he awoke to find himself lying face down in the sand. He pushed himself to his knees, crawled to the pool, and drank as though it was his last drink. He knew it was much too late now, but tomorrow he had to find something to eat. He looked at the river; the lip of the ledge was now two inches underwater.

He turned wearily from the pool and dragged himself inside the shelter. He gathered a few small dry sticks, then took out his knife and shaved off some bark to use as tinder. He covered the shreds with a pyramid of small, medium, and then larger sticks. Shielding the stack from the cool breeze, he clicked his lighter and lit the fire. It didn't take long before fire took hold of the dry wood. It crackled in the flames and the sound calmed his soul. As the fire burned, Mitch added progressively larger chunks of wood, until he had a healthy blaze going.

Sick and weary but warming, Mitch rested on his uninjured side and watched shadows dance on the walls of his small cave. The fire quickly heated the small enclosure, and he began to feel somewhat better. He picked through the firewood, found several fairly straight sticks, and cut them to length to fit his leg below the knee. He stripped some bark, made some twine, and prepared a makeshift splint for his leg. Realizing he had to set the bone, he searched for and found what he needed: Lodged in the driftwood, standing vertically was a branch with a fork. If I can lodge my ankle there,

and if I can muster the strength—and remain conscious—I might be able to set the bones. Mitch crawled
the ten feet, turned around to where he could place his
foot in the fork, but found he had nothing to hold on to
for leverage. Yet there were two boulders on each side
of him. If I could find.... There, off to the left.... He saw
what he needed: a fencepost, rotten at one end, but
sufficient. On his way to it, he searched for and found a
small stick the size of large cigar. He placed it in his
shirt pocket. Then he crawled to the fencepost and
pulled it free from the pile. Nearly exhausted, he
dragged it back and placed it behind the boulders.

He rested, counting ten minutes in his mind.

Then he put the cigar-shaped stick in between his
jaws, leaned back, wrapped each arm around and under the post, and by stretching his body to the limit he
managed to wedge his ankle securely in the notch.
Without giving it any further thought, he sucked in a
deep breath and pulled with everything he had. The
pain was excruciating but he somehow distanced himself from it, and then with a grating of bone against
bone and a crack and a pop everything went black.

When he opened his eyes a pool of thick, dark blood
had soaked the ground beneath his right thigh. The
cigar-shaped stick he'd stuck between his teeth lay in
two pieces, one on each side of his head. He spit out
the middle section which he'd crushed between his
teeth. Then trembling with exhaustion, he leaned forward and carefully removed his leg from the fork in the
now horizontal stick, which had come loose from the
pile and fallen to the side. Blood had dried on his leg,
so he must have been out for some time. When he felt
strong enough to move again, he ripped the sleeves
from his shirt and pulled them both over his leg. He
bound them tightly with the makeshift splints and tree

bark twine. He gathered his remaining strength, got up slowly, fighting off yet another wave of nausea, and forced himself toward the mass of tangled debris to gather more firewood.

The fire and the moon provided ample light. Like a drunkard, he stumbled about looking for sticks large enough to last a while, yet not too heavy to carry back to his fire. He found an armful and carried it back to his shelter with the threatening roar of the river following and the alarming feeling that he was being watched.

Mitch was nearly done in and didn't know how much more he could take, but he returned for more wood, aiding his movement with a stout branch he'd fashioned as a crutch. As he approached the towering mass of driftwood, he heard a noise from within it. Goosebumps crawled on his skin as the feeling of being watched intensified. He sensed movement again and heard a low, snarling growl directly in front of him. He warily removed the crutch from under his right arm, and leaning on his left leg, lifted the stout branch over his head, his pain and sickness forgotten. He readied himself as a mountain lion crouched low to the ground, growling deep in its chest, the black tip of its tail twitching, ready to spring.

♠ ♠ ♠

A half mile upstream and across the river, the spotted grizzly lumbered along the rocky shoreline. Every twenty yards or so, she stopped and sniffed the breeze and stared across the swift watercourse, sometimes taking a few tentative steps into the icy flow but always retreating to continue upstream.

Weary from old age and the day's wanderings, the

bear finally abandoned her desire to cross the river and headed into the forest. Fifty yards from the river she found a rocky escarpment and began searching out a place to rest. She traveled three hundred yards alongside the wall, crossed a small feeder creek, and disappeared into a cave behind a copse of trees. She crawled inside and curled up on the sandy floor. The cave was one of her many dens; her odor permeated the walls. She sniffed the air briefly then sighed contentedly—knowing she was home—and then she closed her piglike eyes, and slept.

Eight years earlier, further back in the depths of the cave, she had given birth to her last set of cubs. Now twenty-two years old, at the end of a sixty-mile journey from exile, she was barren, tired, and just pure mean. Tomorrow she would cross the river and find the source of the blood odor. She would find the man, kill him, and eat him. Then she'd find the place where the hogs were, where she had killed so much and enjoyed the killing. She was hungry for blood and her appetite was insatiable.

♠ ♠ ♠

Back at the cliff, Mitch readied himself, adrenaline rushing through his veins. Then with a snarl of fury, the big cat jumped at him, and knocked him sprawling before he could even manage to swing the club. Then it disappeared silently into the shadows, leaving Mitch shaken.

On his hands and knees, holding his side, he laughed at the absurdity of what he had just attempted. Then he wheezed and coughed up more blood. He began to tremble with weakness as the unused adrenaline wore off. Sapped of energy, dizzy, his mind reeling, he knew his chances were slim. Too sore to move, too tired to think, he slumped to the ground where he was, and he lay staring at the grains of sand and bits of wood, and an ace of spades.

In early dawn, without remembering the trip, he awakened to find himself staring at the glowing coals of his fire.

"Must be spring of the year, whatever year it is," he mumbled. "Smells like it." The sky was graying in the East, and soon the sun would loom over the treetops and bathe the canyon with serene warmth. A sliver of anxiety shot through him as he stirred the fire to life and remembered his dilemma. He scooted closer to the flames. He wrapped his arms around his knees and then waited for daylight.

Suddenly he felt wetness beneath him. He turned and saw that his ledge was half covered with water. The outcrop sloped from the face of the cliff to the river, losing about two feet in the descent. One foot was gone, and he was quickly losing ground.

He groaned and stood up, his body wracked with pain. The river had taken his crutch, so he leaned against the cliff, trying to find strength. Remembering the events of last night, he began looking for cougar tracks. He found them immediately. They were everywhere. Why didn't I notice them before? He found a well-used trail against the base of the cliff. He started to follow the trail but was interrupted by a hissing noise behind him. He turned quickly, grabbing his side, and saw his fire put out by a wave of water. Terror engulfed him, propelled him, and he stumbled along the wall like a lunatic. He followed the cat's trail along the base of the cliff, until the tracks mysteriously vanished.

Mitch stood gasping for breath, unable to comprehend what he saw before him. He dropped to his knees and studied the tracks, noticing how several of them seemed to be rough at the edges as though the cat had turned and leaped toward the cliff.

Blood oozed from the cut on his head. He wiped it out of his eyes and leaned against the rock face, steadying himself, studying the cat's trail, and searching for how it had fled the ledge. He looked all around him and saw no escape. The shelf tapered back into the cliff at both ends, leaving a sheer face. He saw nothing but smooth rock above and rushing water below. He studied the face of the cliff and to his amazement found bits of fur clinging to a crack in the otherwise smooth rock. He hobbled back a few steps, water lapping at his boots, and tilted his head back to gaze at the high wall of rock. He examined the crack intently as a wave wet his jeans just below the calves; the ledge was now almost covered in water.

The crack was six to ten inches wide and at least sixty feet in length, running up the cliff at a 45° angle to his right, the lower side jutting out from the upper about twelve inches, maybe less, more in some places.

Mitch knew he had to climb it, not knowing where it led, knowing only that he could not wait. The river had him in its grasp and soon he would be swept away by it to be drowned or crushed to death on the rapids he could hear downstream. As he reached for the crack, a portion of the pile of driftwood was torn away.

He lay down in the water, drank his fill, then turned to the cliff as the sun's rays leaped across the treetops to illuminate the canyon and reveal a second ledge just above where the crack in the wall played out.

Mitch's hopes soared and he began to climb, pulling outward and down with his hands, as if trying to pry the cliff apart, at the same time pushing himself up with his one good leg. Desperately, he ascended, oblivious to the pain, his mind reaching ahead, planning his every move. The sun beat down on his back. Time crawled. Sweat poured off of him, stinging his eyes, burning the cuts on his face, making his hands slippery. His muscles screamed. Blood oozed from the wound in his head. He'd had to use it for leverage. The blood ran down his cheek, and he could taste it at the corner of his mouth.

After ten minutes of painful ascent, he held tight with raw hands and risked a glance down to find he had only climbed forty feet. The river had risen a foot, engulfing the ledge, coming after him like the monster in his dreams. He looked up, away from the river and was dismayed to see the top still sixty feet above him. A hundred yards to his right, upstream, he could see a pine tree leaning over the edge, as if watching him.

Mitch wasted no more time or energy sightseeing; he resumed his climb, but only scaled another five feet before the crack closed up tight. The next ledge was just three feet overhead but still out of reach. He searched for a handhold, but the rock was smooth. His one good leg trembled, his muscles ached, and his breath came in ragged, bloody gasps. He closed his eyes against the pain, squeezed the sweat and blood from them, and searched his brain for an idea. Panic began to creep up on him and then a voice in his head spoke to him. From memory it came, distant, yet familiar. "A hero is nothing more than a person who is scared near to death, but one who keeps his wits, angry enough to overcome the fear and clear-headed enough to handle the situation."

Mitch forced himself to calm down. As he slowed his breathing, relaxed his mind, let his anger at fate overcome his pain, an idea began to form. He knew he had to bridge the distance between himself and the ledge

above. He must find a handhold; he had to push higher. He needed both legs, but he needed something
more. He needed a lever, a rope, an anchor, something
to push against.

Crazy with pain, he nearly grinned when the idea
that had been forming came to fruition.

Holding tight to the crack with his left hand, Mitch
slowly let go with his right and removed his belt from
his pants. He put the D-shaped buckle between his
teeth. Quaking with the effort, Mitch shoved the end of
the leather belt through the buckle, and then tied a
knot in the end. Keeping the belt tight between his
teeth, he changed hands and shoved the knot deep into
the crack, gouging his knuckles.

Nearly give out, Mitch took a painful deep breath,
and then reached as high as he could with his left hand
and pressed it against the smooth face of the cliff. He
searched for anything to hold fast to, and found a small
indentation. Grasping it with his bare fingertips, bal-
ancing precariously, expecting to fall to his death, he
lifted his right boot and worked it into the loop formed
by the belt going through the buckle. He took another
deep breath and felt a tearing inside as he slowly trans-
ferred his weight to the loop. The leather stretched and
the knot shrank as it tightened; yet the belt held. Mitch
moaned as bone grated against bone in his leg. He
yelled out his pain and pushed harder as he slid himself up the face of the cliff, reaching high with his left
hand, feeling desperately for the ledge. Just as he
thought he could push no farther, his fingers curled
over the edge. But in the same instant, the belt slipped
free, and he was left clinging by ragged fingertips,
searching frantically with his feet for the crack, his fingers slipping fast.

His left foot found the crack. Mitch jammed his boot

into the opening. Reaching with his right hand, he found the ledge and with a hoarse, blood spitting roar, he heaved himself up onto the narrow, gravel covered shelf. He collapsed with his back to the wall.

His body yearned to die, but something deep in his soul fought to live. For several intense minutes, he struggled to regain his senses and overcome his terror and pain.

Overhead, in the forest, silence ruled; nature waited to see if Mitch had the courage to go on. He had escaped the river; he'd won the first battle, but his fight had only begun. Would he crawl away now only to die alone? Would the ants carry his flesh back to the earth? Would nature reclaim his dust? As if in answer, a hoarse whisper burst from Mitch's bloody lips.

"No!" he said as he pushed himself up. He pushed harder, trying to stand, but he fell hard, bruising his face. He groaned and tried again but could only get to his knees. He kneeled, head hanging, gazing down at raw and bleeding fingers with torn fingernails, fingers that danced before his eyes as madness overtook him.

"Can't let it get me. Gotta run faster. Move over, Ugly. Get the hell out of my way, you bastard. No, I don't want any of that. I hate that crap. Steven, you listen to your mother. Buck, you son of a bitch, buck! Is that the best you can do? I'll ride you and spur the hair off your ugly hide." With those words, Mitch fell on his face again, grunting as the wind was knocked from him.

"Get off me!" he tried to yell through clenched teeth as he struggled to get his knees beneath him again. "Gotta get home. She needs me." Then he fell silent, shaking his head to get rid of all the thoughts milling crazily about in his mind.

He saw the mountain lion's tracks in the dust beneath his hands and told himself to concentrate on following them one at a time. He began to crawl. First he crawled an inch, then another, then a foot, and one more. Never taking his eyes off the tracks, Mitch crawled slowly on his hands and knees up the trail. He did not think; he did not look over the edge; he just followed the tracks, one by one, up the narrow ledge to freedom.

Mitch crawled until he sensed a change in his surroundings and his mind began to clear. He smelled grass and pine needles and mountain dirt beneath the leaning pine tree. He curled up against the tree, where he slept and dreamed of an immense bear. He dreamed of a whirlpool in an endless sea, within inches of sucking him under. He dreamed of a cedar chest with a piece of cloth sticking out from under the lid, and a faceless, nameless woman who cried herself to sleep.

Throughout the day, Mitch hugged the tree, his tortured body more dead than alive. He lay unmoving as dark clouds rambled over the mountains, closing out the sun, chilling the forest with cold rain. Mitch hunched his shoulders and coughed. He shivered as the rain washed away the blood that bubbled from his blue lips.

Miles away, thunder boomed and lightning lashed at the forest like a pirate beating a prisoner with a cat-o-nine-tails. The wind raced through the trees, pushing limbs aside, shaking pearly raindrops from the needle-clad branches, and causing the last evidence of the crash to tumble into the river and vanish.

Lightning struck close by and lit up the forest like a flare on a battlefield. The bolt of electricity pierced the air and jolted Mitch awake. He closed his eyes tight against the storm, hoping the nightmare would end, praying that all this was just a bad dream. Lightning struck thirty feet away and shook the Earth violently. Mitch's eyes flared with an insane rage. He drew his feet underneath him and stood up. Madder than a bee-stung rattlesnake, he tucked his head and limped into the depths of the forest, searching for a better place to die.

A mile upstream, the grizzly woke and resumed her search for a place to cross the river. She was one of Idaho's last grizzlies. She had evaded man and his far-reaching rifle for twenty years. Now she hunted him. She found a shallow spot in the river and she waded in as though swift water were no more than wheat waving in a summer breeze. She was formidable, and it seemed she could not be stopped but as she neared the middle, she slipped. She tumbled downstream thirty yards be-fore she slammed up against a boulder. Undaunted, she snarled angrily, gathered her massive paws under her and continued across.

♠ ♠ ♠

Another bolt of lightning illuminated the forest and Mitch saw a tight group of trees. He stumbled and limped, making his way from tree to tree, cursing his fate. He made it to the stand of blue spruce and dropped to the ground. Near blind with pain, driven by pure instinct, he crawled inside where it was dry and curled into a fetal position. At the same moment, the sodden grizzly crawled from the river and collapsed from exhaustion.

CHAPTER TWELVE

"Barney, let's go for a ride; I need to cut some wood," Tom said as he took his breakfast dishes to the sink where he washed and rinsed them, then set them on a towel to dry. Barney barked eagerly, leaped into the air and ran to the front door where he swept the floor with his tail. Then he ran back to Tom, jumped in the air, spun around, and raced back to the door.

Tom laughed heartily.

"Why, I think I'll dance me a jig, too." He grabbed the broom from beside the refrigerator and danced a waltz around the kitchen. Barney watched curiously for a few seconds, and then barked loudly, scratching at the door.

"Alright, I'm coming. Be patient, my furry friend." Tom replaced the broom in the corner and then stood motionless as memories of his late wife flooded his mind. For a few precious moments, he stood dreaming of a time when he and Natalie danced in the kitchen. In his memory, her long dress billowed outward as he spun her around, both of them laughing, the laughter flowing around the room, mingling with the sunlight as it shone through the curtains over the kitchen sink.

Barney tugged at his pants leg.

"Alright, Barn'," Tom said, "I'm coming." He grabbed his Levis jacket from where it hung on the back of the nearest kitchen chair to the back door, and put it on. Then he plucked his worn hat and new leather gloves off a shelf by the door. He swept a lock of silver hair off his forehead, donned the old gray Stetson, and pulled the leather gloves over his hands. He smiled as he opened the door and drew a deep breath of crisp mountain morning.

The dog, in his youthful haste, nearly knocked Tom over as he bolted out the door.

"Barney! Get your butt back in here. Get inside; you know better than that!" Tom wasn't mad; he just couldn't abide rudeness in people or animals. He smiled through his long gray moustache, his eyes sparkling from under the brim of his hat as Barney ran back inside with his tail tucked.

"Now wait," Tom said, motioning to the dog with the flat of his left palm as a cop would hold up a lane of traffic. Then Tom went out the door first and let Barney follow only after the doorway was clear.

"Good, dog, Barney! You're a good ole boy." Barney ate it up and ran around the yard in excitement, having already forgotten the scolding, and Tom wore the grin of a more or less happy man, yet loneliness and grief shadowed him. He was an old man, with an old man's weathered face. Crows feet scratched at the corners of his eyes, and his cheeks were creased from an almost permanent smile. For in spite of recent hardship, he lived the life he loved. Today he was eager to get busy at living. Thomas Joshua Braden loved the outdoors, and he looked forward to gathering firewood and the exercise it afforded him.

Before breakfast, Tom had packed a lunch for himself and the dog. After the morning's work, they would sit at his favorite place on the Salmon River for lunch, and then while Barney roamed the woods nearby, Tom would smoke his pipe and reflect on life. At the river's edge, he'd relax in the relative quiet of the forest, watching the river slide by, listening to its tranquil voice, at peace in his mountain home.

Something ancient flowed with the blood in his veins, something that drew him to the river and its forest border. Perhaps in another time, he'd been a mountain man the likes of Jeremiah Johnson. Maybe he had crossed the wilds with Jim Bridger, fought beside Custer, or against him. All he knew was that he could never leave his mountains. This was the world he wanted to see, the world that he needed. He drew his life's breath from the trees, he listened to the stories told by the wind whispering through their branches, he drank from the springs, he fed on the berries in the underbrush, and he fished in the waters of the pond behind his cabin. He was kin to the mountains he called home, and he would have it no other way.

He checked in the back of his Chevy Silverado Suburban, made sure he had all his gear, and then opened the door and slapped the side of the silver-and-blue truck.

"C'mon', Dawg!" Tom hollered. Barney barked once from somewhere out back and then came racing around the cabin, jumped into the cab, and sat on his haunches, eagerly awaiting his master. He barked twice at Tom, as if to say, "Well, come on! We're burnin' daylight."

Tom grinned and climbed inside. He felt under the seat for his revolver. Reassured, he started the engine, let it warm up a few seconds, and then drove out of the yard. Gravel crunched under the all-terrain tires as he maneuvered down the winding, tree-lined, and shadowed drive. Within a hundred yards, his two-story log cabin disappeared into the forest.

Tom always carried a sidearm or rifle with him when he left the cabin, mindful that he could run into a bear at any time, and he had his suspicions the old she-bear "Patches," or "Spotted Bitch," as he called her, might be coming home.

"Haven't seen her in a couple of years. Really don't care to. Last time I saw her she chased me thirty feet up a tree. The old sow held me up there nearly six hours before she wandered far enough away for me to make a run for the truck. Yeah, Barn'," the dog looked over at him curiously, "she sure had me treed." Tom laughed as he recalled the incident, happy that he could laugh at himself, considering the danger he had been in.

"That was right before you came along. If you'd been with me, we'd have put an end to her meanness once and for all.

"Know why we call her Patches? It's because she's got six little white spots of hair on her rump; scars from an old buckshot wound." Tom paused in his story as he reached the end of the narrow drive and turned left onto the county road that paralleled the river. Behind him the road quickly came to a dead end, ahead the road curved with the watercourse as it meandered toward the Snake River and to town. Barney searched the road ahead as the old man talked. He barked whenever he saw a critter scurry across the road, which was often enough to get on Tom's nerves.

"Old Patches—Barney, get quiet—was gettin' after Ted Collins' hogs six springs ago. Ted, he come a-runnin' out with his shotgun and gave her a solid blast in the ass. He figured it would scare her off. What'd she do? She chased him back into his cabin and killed his hogs anyway. I asked him why he didn't just use his 7mm Magnum on her. Well, the old fool had forgotten where he'd put his ammunition. Ted wasn't too bright."

Tom slowed down for a pothole as he laughed at the memory of his old friend.

"Collins," Tom continued, "had to call Fish and Game, and they had to rescue him out of his own house." Tom was laughing so hard he nearly ran off the road.

"Two years ago, Fish and Game finally had enough of her shenanigans, so they drugged her and carried her sixty miles east of here, deeper into the wilderness, hoping she'd take up new residence away from people. But she's back," Tom said, suddenly serious. "She was seen headin' this way two weeks ago. I've got a bad feeling, Barney." Barney looked over at him with his head curiously and comically cocked to one side. "Yeah, I've a feeling she's somewhere close, out there," he said, pointing out his window toward the river. Barney thought Tom was pointing at a chipmunk and jumped in his lap trying to look out the window.

"Sit down!" Tom yelled, thrusting the heavy dog aside. "Damn, Dawg! You're going to make me run into a tree," he said as he turned off the county road and back onto his property. He followed a narrow trail that wound like a snake into the woods.

Tom owned nine square miles of virgin forest. The land spanned the gap between the road and the river for a length of six miles. It began a half-mile east of the cabin, and stretched five and a half miles west of it. A ten thousand foot-peak rose up behind him. Tom's land ran south of the road, along the base of the mountain. Eighty percent of his land was dense forest, most of it was Idaho White Pine, but there was plenty of Ponderosa Pine, Douglas fir, spruce, cedar, and hemlock. Bubbling streams wound through several lush meadows, and behind the cabin, within a stone's throw of the barn, was a six-acre pond, deep and full of bass, catfish, and perch.

Tom drove about a quarter of a mile and then pulled to a stop at the edge of a clearing. He stepped out and, for a few minutes, just stood smelling the fresh pine-scented air. He listened to the wind in the trees and the rushing of the river. The sights, sounds, and smells of the forest always thrilled him. His home had a singular beauty that never escaped him and that he never failed to appreciate.

He counted his blessings as he reached under the seat for his holstered, fully loaded Ruger, Super Blackhawk .44 Mag. It wasn't Ruger's most massive revolver, but it packed plenty of punch and fit his hands. He'd never seen anything on his property a .30 caliber couldn't handle, but he always like to be prepared for the worst.

He strapped it on.

"Can't be too careful," he said, looking around the woods as he walked to the back of the truck. He opened a long, gray toolbox and found a can of white spray paint. With the can in his left hand and the revolver loose in its holster, Tom walked into the forest and began marking trees to cut for firewood.

He did not select any young or healthy trees; he only cut those with disease, damage, or old age, endeavoring to preserve a healthy forest. He spent an hour choosing and marking trees, planning his attack and then returned to the truck for his chainsaw. He fueled it, checked the oil, and then carried it to the first tree. Tom studied the tall tree for a few moments, and then dropped it into an opening.

The whine of the saw reverberated throughout the woods, driving deer and other smaller animals from their feeding places and causing the birds to fly off to quieter surroundings. The noise reached far into the wilds, drowning out the river. The old Grizzly lumbering through the undergrowth, gorging on delicacies she found under rocks and logs, seemed at first to ignore the sound, but after a few moments she began to feed toward it, heading downriver. Curious at first, then irritated, she hurried her pace, suddenly remembering why she had crossed the night before.

Tom continued to topple trees for another hour, and then he prepared to fell his eighteenth and final tree for the day. He wouldn't cut them all up into firewood today, but he wanted to get as many down as he could so that he'd have plenty to work with in the next few months while the weather was nice. As he walked around the tall pine, planning its descent, he found her tracks.

"Can't be more than a few hours old," Tom said as he searched and found several more footprints, following her trail. "She's heading north along the river." He took off his hat and mopped his brow with a red bandana. "Crossing into her old haunting grounds."

Three miles downstream, at the west end of his property, the river widened considerably and became shallow enough to cross. Tom had seen bears do it in the past, and he thought with a little trepidation that there was nothing to keep her from turning around and coming back.

"Damn! I don't need this. Barney? Barney? Here,

dog." Tom yelled at the top of his lungs, fearing for his dog, whose nose and ears he needed.

Tom yelled again, but the dog was nowhere in sight. He set down the chainsaw and walked quickly back to the truck, stumbling and nearly falling twice in his haste. When he got to the truck he reached inside and blew the horn. At the same instant he felt something brush his leg. With a coarse yell Tom jumped back and to the side. Barney yelped in surprise.

"Kee-rist!" Tom said as he saw Barney.

"You scared the devil out of me." The surprise was too much for Tom; his legs buckled and gave out from under him as he slid down the side of the truck. Barney tried to console him, whimpering, wondering what he'd done wrong. Tom raised a shaky hand to Barney's head.

"I'm getting too old for this crap," he said. "Dawg, I thought you were her; I thought I was a goner." Tom rested a minute to slow his heart, then said, "Barney, she's out there, I just found her tracks. We've got to be careful. She's old and mean, and this time of year she has one thing on her mind, and that's eatin' whatever she can get her claws on. She almost got me once when I wasn't paying attention. I won't make that mistake again. Come on," he said as he got shakily to his feet. "Let's keep a sharp eye out." He retrieved the chainsaw and exchanged it for an axe. He checked the blade.

"This won't do." He rummaged through the glove box and found a flat, circular whetstone about three fourths of an inch thick, spat on it, and touched up the edge for about ten minutes, periodically checking the sharpness with his thumb. Finally satisfied, he leaned it against the side of the truck and palmed his revolver. He checked the loads and then replaced the gun in its holster, leaving it loose and easy to get to. He again

looked in the glove box and retrieved a box of car-
tridges. He placed an additional half-dozen rounds in
an inside pocket of his denim jacket.

"I better have easy access to more ammunition if she
shows up," Tom said as he wiped sweat off his brow
with his red bandana.

He could not recall when he had picked up the habit
of talking to himself and to the dog, but he couldn't
care less. He felt it kept him sane, as sane as an old
man could be under the circumstances. He called Barney to his side and took him to the tree where he found
the bear's tracks. Barney caught her scent immediately, and the hair rose up on his back. He growled and
followed the trail a few feet, then stopped and looked
back at Tom, alternately growling and whimpering.

"That's a good boy; you keep a watch out for me."

With the dog at his side, Tom put the axe to work.
He could have used the saw, but he preferred the axe
for the workout it afforded him. Starting at the base of
the tree and with the skill of a man born to the woods,
he hacked away at the branches. He threw the severed
limbs aside. He paced himself, trimmed a half a dozen
trees, and then stopped for lunch.

"C'mon, Barney," Tom said, heading for the truck,
"time to eat." Tom grabbed his lunch box, and with
Barney running happy circles around him, he strolled
down to the river. Tom watched his dog play, smiling at
his antics. As they drew nearer the river, the sounds of
its antics grew louder and Tom's smile became more
pronounced.

"Wow! It hasn't been this high in years," he said as
he sat down on a log that had long since been polished
smooth by the seat of his denim jeans. An odd rose
bush grew at one end of the log. Barney sat facing Tom,
his tail wagging impatiently, saliva dripping from his

jaws.

"This time of year she should be high, but she's nearly out of her banks. I bet she's wiped Sampson's ledge clean." He tore open a small, plastic container and handed Barney a piece of leftover steak from supper a few nights ago. Barney started to take it, but something caught his attention; he raised his ears and cocked his head to one side. He listened for a second, and then his hunger brought him back from his distraction. He took the steak Tom offered. He ate it quickly, and ran downstream a few feet, barking at something he could hear but couldn't see. Then Tom heard it—a low-pitched whining noise—coming from the east.

As they listened, the whine grew louder as it drew nearer, and then Tom knew it for what it was. Suddenly it was before them, an airplane, flying low, following the river. It cruised around the bend so slowly Tom was surprised it didn't stall. It was so close Tom could easily see a pilot and two passengers, all three intently gazing out the windows. The brown-and-white Cessna disappeared around the next bend, and soon the interruption was forgotten. Tom removed his tuna sandwich and hungrily tore off a bite. As he chewed, he remembered the bear, took his revolver out of his holster, and laid it on the log beside him. Barney ran back to him and looked up at Tom expectantly.

"Glutton," Tom said, and took another bite of his sandwich. He chewed thoughtfully, teasing the big Golden Retriever. Looking over the dog's head, Tom noticed that the river was heavier with silt and driftwood than usual for this time of year. He watched the river for a few minutes, and then noticed something floating with the current only a few feet from the bank. He stood up and stepped down to the river's edge for a better look. What he saw was a playing card, a three of diamonds.

"Damned city folk threw out their car trash upriver. Maybe it was tourists. Folks around here wouldn't do that. Some people just don't give a hoot about nature. They don't think. They just toss it out the window, wanting the river to take it out of sight and away from them. They don't take the time to consider the folks downriver."

He shook his head in disgust as he turned back to his log. As he turned, he saw a water-soaked billfold wedged in the grass at his feet. "Now what's this?" He picked it up. It was hand-stitched, western-styled. "Hm? Bet someone is looking for this."

His gaze went skyward, remembering the airplane, and he had the feeling he was holding more than a billfold. He sat down on the log and opened it, finding a thousand dollars cash and a few photos in a plastic binder. If there had been any credit cards inside, they had been washed out of it. Most of the photos were of a nice looking woman with jet-black hair and gray eyes. The rest were of a tall, young man, who didn't resemble the woman. He took the photos and money out of the billfold and spread them on the log to dry.

Looking again at the money, tom said, "Now who walks around with that kind of pocket money?"

Barney barked impatiently. Tom ignored him for a few seconds, and then he said, "What? You want mine, too? Well you better think again."

Barney danced around, spun on his tail, and then looked down at the lunch box, and back up at Tom, whining eagerly.

"Did I forget something?" Barney nuzzled the box, pushing it across the grass toward Tom. It was a game they played each time they came down to the river, which was at least once a week in good weather.

"Well, let's just take a look; maybe I did forget something." He opened the box slowly, watching the dog from under his hat brim. "Well, I suppose I did." Tom removed a bag of dog biscuits. Barney came unglued.

"Lay down and play dead, then you can have a couple." Barney hesitated a second and then laid down and rolled over on his back. Lying quietly with his long, golden hair bright against the green grass and his tongue hanging out of his mouth, he grinned up at Tom.

Tom had to laugh. As soon as he opened the bag, Barney sprang to his feet and sat on his haunches; his tongue quivering, he waited for his treat. Tom fed him two biscuits. Barney accepted them gracefully, one at a time, chewing each one slowly, savoring the taste. Then the game was over, and the dog leapt away and ran into the forest to chase critters.

"That's it, just eat and run," Tom said, suddenly lonely but happy, too. "I'll just sit here and watch the Salmon River swim by."

Tom sat alone, feeling good, watching the river and enjoying the thriving forest. A butterfly lit on his knee. A blue jay squawked somewhere overhead in the pines. A deer drank from the river on the opposite side. A ground squirrel watched Tom, bobbing its tail as it munched on a pine nut.

"I can still feel you here beside me, Nat'." He leaned over, picked a wildflower, and laid it gently on the grave beside the log. "I love you, honey. I always will." Suddenly he heard his dog barking. Its bark was different, like nothing he'd ever heard before. Tom looked in the direction the dog had gone, listening. Then, with at first a puzzled, then concerned look on his weathered face, and gun in hand, he went to see what was up. Abruptly Barney quit barking and goose bumps rose on his skin.

Tom ran fast and hard for fifty yards, then his age failed him and he had to slow to a walk.

"Where are you, dog," he yelled." In return the dog barked twice. He was just up ahead. Tom quickened his pace a little and hurried after him. A clearing soon came into view, and Barney was on the other side, sitting on his haunches, peering into a thicket of spruce trees.

"What is it, Barney?" Tom asked, breathing hard. The dog looked worried, but not afraid. He whimpered and looked over his shoulder at Tom. Then abruptly his ears sprang forward and he rose from his haunches and stepped forward, listening to a sound that came from inside the trees.

Tom heard a tortured moan. Kneeling beside the dog, he moved a branch out of the way and peered into the dark interior. He heard a pain-ridden cry of relief, and then two words spoken slowly and with difficulty.

"Thank, God!"

"Barney, move!"

Tom crawled inside, pushing the dog out of his way.

"Oh my God!" he said, "Oh Lord of Mercy."

Staring back at him from inside was the sick, gaunt, pain-wracked face of a man too close to death for comfort.

"Mister, please help me. I'm...dyin'."

"You are not going to die, Son," Tom said just as he noticed a red froth bubbling from Mitch's lips and wondered if he'd eat his words.

"What is your name, friend?"

"I don't know. Don't know how . . . long . . . I've been here. River . . . almost . . . had to climb, big cat, I followed, I-I, can't, re-re-remember...."

Mitch stopped, breathless, as Tom kneeled nearer to him to hear better, to examine him more closely.

"Take it easy, Son. You will be all right." Tom felt a sudden compassion for the man. "We'll take good care of you."

"Mister," Mitch whispered raggedly, "I never quit. I couldn't."

"I know, Son, I know," Tom said. Though he didn't understand what the man was trying to tell him, Tom felt it was important to him; he could see the determination to live in Mitch's eyes.

"You made it, Son. You went the distance for sure," Tom said, trying to keep that will to live alive. For a brief moment, Tom saw triumph in the man's eyes, then only pain—pain that Mitch could no longer refuse.

Tom was afraid this man was not going to make it, but he was not about to let him know any different.

"You say you have forgotten your name?" Mitch didn't answer. He just stared off into space.

"Son?"

Mitch raised a trembling and swollen hand to his forehead and gazed up at Tom with a look that chilled him to the core, and said, "It's empty. The bucket's empty."

The words fell out of Mitch's mouth and smacked on Tom's ears like hailstones on a truck roof, leaving Tom cold and frightened for Mitch, for suddenly Tom knew he was not only dying physically, but his past was already dead. The fear and loneliness that Mitch conveyed was such that Tom had to look away; it was more than he could take. He recalled an accident from years ago, and a brain-injured man who had never regained even the slightest vestiges of his prior self. The unfortunate man subsequently had been placed in a mental hospital, where he remained in a semi-vegetative state.

"I need to leave you here for a few minutes, Tom said." He was afraid to leave him, but knew he must.

"No," Mitch groaned. I don't want to die alone."

Patiently, knowing that Mitch was not in his right mind, or in it at all, Tom convinced him of the necessity, and, leaving Barney with him, Tom ran for the truck, praying for divine intervention and hoping the bear wouldn't show up suddenly. He hoped the god he prayed to was stronger than his instincts.

Tom reached the truck gasping for breath and barely able to open the door. After just a few moments to catch his breath, he climbed in and started the truck. He sped around the fallen trees and bounced up the mountain. Thick timber hindered travel that had been relatively easy on foot, and twice he had to back up and find another way. It was slow going, but he pressed on until he found his way completely blocked. He groaned as he realized he'd have to cut his way through and use up precious time. He parked and started to get out when suddenly the hair prickled up on the back of his neck, a sure sign to him that a bear was near.

Thomas Joshua Braden broke out in a cold sweat as a terrifying memory came back to haunt him, taking him unwillingly into the past....

♠ ♠ ♠

Several years earlier...

Tom was out enjoying the day, harvesting a few of his trees, meeting old friends, smelling old smells, and seeing old sights that still thrilled him.

The wind rambled lazily over the hillside, carrying the man's scent to the huge bear. She stood on her hind legs, pulling the wind through her nose, and blinked her beady eyes as she saw him. She huffed and dropped to all fours and then stalked through the forest. Once out of sight of the man, she began to circle around behind him.

Tom wiped his brow and took a long pull from his canteen, then wiped his face with his sleeve and gazed out across the meadow, breathing deeply of the fresh summer air. He corked the canteen and ran his fingers through his hair. A wasp buzzed past his head and he jumped and turned away, swatting at it with his hat. As he turned, he saw the grizzly rise up on all fours. She roared her intent as Tom fell back and rolled aside just in time to escape her murderous charge. He kept rolling and made it under the truck a split second before she'd have raked him into her grasp with her four-inch claws. Her hot breath was rank with the rancid odor of carrion. Tom gagged and scooted frantically to the other side as she thrust both platter sized paws underneath the truck and tried to turn it over.

Tom took his only chance and made a run for the trees. Fifty feet separated him and the safety of one tree he knew he could climb. The bear was right behind him, shaking the Earth. Suddenly the tree was before him and he jumped, caught a branch, and pulled himself up as her claws raked his right leg. He screamed as hot streaks of pain shot up his leg when the bear ripped his right boot off. Tom climbed frantically, reaching ever higher....

♣ ♣ ♣

In an instant, Tom's scream from the past manifested itself in the present and brought him quickly alert to the future.

"No! Not again! Not now!" Tom threw open the door and scrambled out of the truck. He jerked the chainsaw out of the back and ran into the brush and trees that blocked his path. Tom cut and ripped like a mad man.

He came to a healthy tree and cut it down without reservation. He cut another, and yet another, dropping trees out of the way of the vehicle like a tornado clears a path of destruction. After twenty minutes of frantic work, he could finally see his way through. He ran back to the truck, threw the saw in the back, climbed in front, and threw the gears into four-wheel drive.

Tree limbs smacked against the hood and windshield as Tom weaved through and over the brush and the fresh stumps, heedless of the damage he was inflicting on the vehicle. Moving too fast, too carelessly, he suddenly smashed into a tree. Pinecones thudded against the cab and hood, and the impact sent shock waves through the truck, slamming him into the door. Tom fell back in his seat, dripping blood from a cut on his head.

Single-mindedly he shook himself out of his daze, wiped his forehead with his sleeve, then more carefully maneuvered around the tree and raced up the mountainside.

Barney ran out to meet him as he reached the clearing and turned around to back up to the stand of spruce. When Tom got out of the truck the dog was looking toward the river, a low growl rumbling deep in his chest.

Tom pressed into the trees and found Mitch lying on his back, staring blankly up into the darkness. At first, Tom thought he was dead, but Mitch slowly turned his head and looked at him, managing a crooked grin.

"'Bout time you got back," he said. "My right leg is broken, but I can walk if you help me." Tom smiled in spite of his premonition of imminent danger, but he was serious when he said, "Son, listen carefully. Don't ask me to explain, but we have got to get you out of...."

Tom's voice was silenced by another wave of goosebumps.

"We've got to run. There's a rogue grizzly headed this way. Do you understand?" Mitch nodded, fear edging into his eyes.

"Let's go," Tom yelled, dragging Mitch out of the trees. Then they ran as one, stumbling, even falling once, but they managed to make it to the truck. Mitch held his left arm to his side, grimacing at the pain stabbing at him, as hot knives cut at his leg. Then Tom stopped suddenly and Mitch gasped as his leg twisted and he fell at Tom's feet.

Tom stared at Barney, who was staring at the bear standing forty feet away at the edge of the clearing. Towering nearly a dozen feet above the forest floor, the monstrous grizzly stood glaring, her lower jaw hanging, saliva dripping from massive teeth. With evil intent blazing in her eyes, she huffed, dropped to all fours, and charged.

"Get in the truck!" Tom shouted, picking Mitch up and shoving him with one hand as he grabbed for his revolver with the other.

"Not this time you ornery bitch!" Tom raised his revolver, aimed, and found Barney in his sights. The dog had thrown himself in front of the bear. Caught off guard, the grizzly halted her attack fifteen feet from Tom. Barney tore at her fiercely, unafraid. Now he was running back and forth in front of her, snarling his fury, confusing her.

Tom took a gamble and ran to help Mitch into the truck and to safety. Then he leaned across the hood. He aimed, but he couldn't fire; a golden blur kept filling his sights. Barney was fighting for all he was worth, and the bear wouldn't stand still. Hair flew, flesh was torn, and Tom heard a sickening thud as the bear slammed Barney into a tree.

The big bore revolver bucked in Tom's hands. The impact threw the bear over on her back, but she didn't stay down. As soon as she hit the ground she was back up and coming at him. Tom squeezed the trigger repeatedly as she relentlessly bore on. It seemed she couldn't be stopped, and Tom fell backward and rolled under the truck as she came over the hood at him.

The springs groaned as her bulk slammed onto the truck. She bounced back and instantly tried to jump around the front of the truck at him but toppled and fell against the hood before sliding in her own blood to the ground.

Tom was instantly on his feet. He quickly reloaded, dropping one round between his boots. He heard ragged breathing at the other side of the truck. He backed up as far as the forest would let him and then worked his way around the front, keeping plenty of distance between them. A tremendous paw twitched where it stuck out from behind the left front tire. Tom had backed up thirty feet, when she suddenly lurched to her feet, and with six heavy slugs inside her, she charged yet again.

Blue steel smoked in his hands as Tom stood over the bear that lay shuddering within inches of his boots. He couldn't remember firing, but a dime-sized hole smoked between her eyes, and her right ear was gone.

"Is it dead?"

Tom looked up, astonished by what he saw. Mitch was out of the truck and standing beside it with the axe raised over his head, ready to step in and fight the bear off Tom.

"If she ain't, she soon will be." Tom stuck the hot muzzle in the hole where her ear had been and delivered a final, brain pulverizing shot.

The silence in the woods was complete. The bear

twitched its last as Tom holstered the revolver and ran to Mitch who had slumped to the ground at the sound of the final shot; he could go no further; could do no more; he was done in.

"OK, let's get you back in the truck." Tom helped Mitch into the passenger's seat and then examined his injuries before he tended to Barney, whom he feared dead anyway.

"Grit your teeth, boy; I've got to check you out before I move you too far."

"Ribs broke," Mitch groaned, "head, leg."

It was all Mitch could do just to sit up, but he endured this final agony while Tom examined him and did his best to make him comfortable for the rough ride back.

"You're fortunate; your ribs are not completely broken, just cracked bad enough to perforate your lung." Tom appeared rock solid, but inside he was nearly insane with terror and grief for his dog. Nonetheless, he was able to keep things in perspective and take care of Mitch.

"I've got to check on Barney," he said after a few moments. You rest here." He turned away.

"Mister," Mitch grabbed Tom's arm, "thanks."

"Name's Tom, but don't thank me. Thank Barney." He looked over his shoulder at the crumpled body of his dog. I hope he's still alive." Tom ran to his dog and knelt beside the crushed body. His eyes filled with stinging tears. Barney was ripped from head to midbody down his left side. His left foreleg was badly broken and he wasn't breathing.

"You danged fool dog. Why'd you have to go and get yourself killed?" Tom cried shamelessly as Mitch watched from the cab of the truck.

"Damn you!" Tom screamed as he picked up Barney's inert body and held it to his chest. Why'd you have go and get yourself killed?" Tom hugged the dog and cried his heart out. He squeezed the dog's body tightly, afraid to let go of his last friend. But soon the professional side took over and he forced his thoughts back to what he could control. He wrapped his dead dog in a blanket he kept under the back seat, and laid the dog between himself and Mitch, and then he took it easy going back to the cabin so as not to cause Mitch too much pain.

Tom prided himself in his stoicism; nonetheless, overcome with grief and excitement of the moment, he started crying again. He could hardly see to drive from the tears in his eyes and relied mostly on instinct to get him home. They managed to make it without incident, and once there he immediately got Mitch comfortable in the spare room and went to work. Only after an hour of cleaning and stitching Mitch's worst wounds did he take time out to tend to his dog. To his great surprise and relief, Barney was breathing, albeit with difficulty. Tom said a silent prayer of thanks, cradled Barney in his arms, and took him inside to begin the healing.

Tom spent the rest of the afternoon taping Mitch's ribs and Barney's leg and side, and sewing them back both back together with over two hundred stitches. He had also had to re-set Mitch's broken leg. He administered antibiotics, fed them, and then they all rested.

In Dr. Thomas Joshua Braden's thirty years of family practice, which he hadn't practiced in twenty years, he'd never seen a man suffer as much as Mitch must have, and dare to live. However, it was an hour-long, thirty-seven-mile drive to the nearest hospital in Grangeville. He'd conveniently forgotten about calling for a Med-Evac chopper: he was lonely. So against his better judgment, he committed himself to their care.

Tom sat on the couch in front of the fireplace, smoked his pipe—his only vice—and pondered the day's events. Barney slept on a pallet of blankets before the hearth, and Mitch slept in a bedroom down the hall. Blissfully under the influence of morphine, Mitch drifted through a painless, dreamless sleep, more dead than alive, but still fighting. The meaty aroma of the stew Tom had re-heated for their supper wafted around the room and mixed with his pipe smoke. He wanted to eat, needed to, but he hadn't taken the time. Now that he had time, he didn't have the energy. He fell asleep, his pipe cold in his hand.

Chapter Thirteen

6:30 A.M.

ONE WEEK AFTER THE PLANE CRASH

Tom fried bacon, eggs, and potatoes, yawning, and sipping a cup of coffee. It was tough waking up on the heels of three restless nights. Mitch had slept straight through, unmoving, but Barney hadn't fared so well, awakening several times in the last two and a half days. Tom had knelt by his side and spooned water into his faithful pet's muzzle, giving back precious fluid. The dog was wrapped with bandages and tape from his head down past his rib cage. His left leg, broken twice, was cast in plaster.

Tom brewed a second cup of coffee. He usually only allowed himself one, but it had been a long night and he'd overslept by an hour. It was the first time in many years that he'd allowed himself to sleep past five. He hadn't slept at all the night before.

Barney was resting quietly. Neither a sound nor the

slightest movement had come from Mitch since Tom had put him to bed two nights ago with an IV feeding him saline solution and anti-biotic which, out of habit, he always kept in fresh supply. He'd been through quite an ordeal, neither of them knew to what extent, and Tom was hoping he'd sleep another day through and on into the night. On the other hand he was beginning to feel a bit of concern, because the stranger had not moved at all since he'd fallen asleep. Tom was starting to fear that maybe he'd made a mistake by not getting proper help.

Tom finished preparing his breakfast and sat down in the dining room to eat. He bowed his head, prayed a silent prayer of thanks, and then began to eat.

"Coffee sure smells good!"

Tom jumped in his seat and turned so quickly he nearly fell out of it, not believing what his ears told him. Between the living and dining rooms was a high, wide, timbered archway, and leaning against the wall on one side was Mitch, haggard but standing on his own, the IV pole at his side.

"For Christ's sake! You shouldn't be out of bed. By all rights you should be dead." he started to get angry, but then he smiled. "If this doesn't beat anything I've ever seen. Now there stands a man."

"Bacon doesn't smell bad either. Mind if I join you?"

"By all means, you're already up," Tom said as he rose to help him to the table. Mitch eased himself down into the chair, already exhausted.

"Heard you in here cookin'," Mitch said, resting his elbows on the table, cradling his throbbing head in his hands. "Then I smelled the coffee and opened my eyes. When I smelled the bacon that did it; I just couldn't stand it any longer."

"Next time holler at me, you stubborn fool," Tom

said as he stared at Mitch in awe. Then he turned and walked to the stove, shaking his head in disbelief. "I'll bring your meals to you."

"Sorry about your dog."

"Don't be," Tom said, "turns out he's as tough as you are. He's alive. I fixed you up and then went to bury him and the danged fool pup was breathing again. Well, barely. He's going to make it now. And I guess so are you are, too, although I was really starting to worry about you. You slept without moving for a long time. Barney's in the other room by the fireplace.

"He's lost a lot of blood and his leg is badly broken, but he'll pull through. Now what about you? How are you feeling?"

"I've felt better, I suppose."

"Here, drink this," Tom said, "it's hot and strong."

"It'll do," Mitch said, managing a lopsided grin. He sipped his coffee and watched Tom work in the kitchen, which was at the other end of the large room. The cabin had a lot of space.

Tom was only a few minutes at the stove before he brought a steaming plate of bacon, eggs, hash browns, and toast to Mitch.

"Judging by your condition, I doubt you've had a bite to eat in a week, except for what little stew I could spoon down your stubborn gullet the other night before you passed completely out for nearly three days; you might not be able to eat much."

He poured himself some coffee, topped off Mitch's cup, and then sat down across from him.

Mitch stared at his plate.

"What's the matter, Son?"

"I was just thinking." Mitch sipped his coffee, liking the taste.

Slowly Mitch began to eat, savoring each bite, letting

his shrunken stomach get used to having food again. Halfway through the meal he suddenly looked up at Tom.

"Thanks for fixin' me up, for the bath, the shave."

Embarrassed, Mitch looked down, took a bite, and chewed thoughtfully.

"You're welcome. And it was no trouble; I'm...used to it."

Mitch looked up at Tom curiously, then through the wide doorway into the living room at the dog. He looked down at the cast on his leg, and then felt the bandages on his own head and saw the stitches in his hands.

"Are you a doctor? This ain't no amateur patch job."

"My name is Tom Braden, M.D. I've been retired for a good while, but I still keep up with the technology...a little. I still read a few journals...now and then."

"Well, I haven't a clue as to who I am," Mitch said, offering his hand to Tom, "but I'm pleased to meet you."

Tom gripped Mitch's injured hand firmly but gently. "The pleasure is mine."

Mitch finished his breakfast, much to Tom's pleasure, and pushed his plate forward. He picked up his coffee cup and looked at Tom.

"I know you're curious, so I'll try to explain." He took a sip of his coffee, the IV tube following his arm, thinking a moment. "I woke up from oblivion, it seems like an eternity ago, but just a few days I guess, I don't know. I was lying by the river with my feet in the water. I was trapped in a canyon...downriver...on a narrow ledge...on the side of a cliff."

Tom raised his head and sat back a bit in his chair, goose bumps crawling on his skin.

"I was all busted up and I have no idea how I got there." Mitch put his cup down and stared into the clouds swirling on the surface of the dark brew. "The river was rising; I was trapped."

"My God, you escaped Sampson's ledge! No one has ever done that! You climbed up?"

"I didn't have any choice. I had to climb the cliff or drown in the river."

"No wonder you're such a mess. You are the first to climb out of there, and not the first to be trapped there."

"What I can't figure is how I got there in the first place. I can't remember anything before then. Mitch recalled the bear across the river. "But I wasn't alone.""

"What's that?" Tom had been thinking and missed what Mitch was saying.

"I wasn't alone; I saw a bear on the other side. Saw a cougar, too. It was on the ledge with me. I was gathering wood for my fire when I saw it. I was so hungry I was fool enough to think I could kill it with a stick. It jumped at me, knocked me down, and then disappeared. I must have passed out then, because the next thing I knew I was back by my fire. I stirred it back to life and added more wood. That's when the river caught up to me." Mitch started talking rapidly. "I went plumb crazy then, or maybe desperate, but I searched every inch of that cliff for a way out. That's when I saw the cat's trail. It was a good thing, too, because the river was over the shelf and rising fast." Mitch paused to catch his breath and sip his coffee.

"So what happened next?"

Mitch was tired; his mind wandered. He stared at Tom with a puzzled look on his face.

"What?"

"You said the water was rising," Tom pressed on, following a hunch.

"Yeah, Joe, that's when I found the tracks. I followed them along the base of the cliff until they vanished, like that cat. I couldn't understand it, but the trail simply disappeared. I almost gave up, almost quit, and then...Montana threw that long pass and.... But then, I saw hairs in the crack...Luke, we gotta fix that fence before we lose another cow." Mitch grew silent and stared off into space. "Gotta fix that goldurned fence."

"It must have been hell going up that cliff," Tom said.

Mitch took several sips from his cup and then said, "It might have been hell if I hadn't." He sipped more coffee and then looked Tom in the eye.

"I climbed the crack."

He stared into space a few minutes, then took a deep swallow of his cooling coffee and continued.

"I don't remember much after that, except that I found the second shelf. I remember crawling along it. Then things get fuzzy. I woke up by a tree that leans out over the side." Mitch put down his coffee, and looked at his hands.

"Joe, I forgot what I was saying."

"You said you had climbed out on top, by the leaning tree."

"Yeah, right, I remember now. It was dark, lightning was striking everywhere, and the rain was coming down in sheets. I got mad. I got hellacious mad then, and I jumped up and stumbled down the mountain until I found shelter. Next thing I know, Barney was licking my face."

"Son, you'd best get back to bed now. You need your rest."

"Yeah, I know," he paused, his cup halfway to his lips, his hand shaking. He set the cup down and shook his head angrily.

"Dammit all to hell! It ain't fair." He slammed his bandaged fists down on the table.

Tom winced.

"I've been robbed," Mitch said, slamming his fists down again. "It ain't fair."

"I know it isn't fair, Son," Tom said, "and I know how frightened you must be. Let's just try to stay calm, try to find some peace within you. It's not going to help you to worry about it now. We can figure out the why and what for later. The most important thing for you to do now is to get your health back. Let's go. Back to bed."

Tom helped Mitch to his feet.

"Do you mind if I just camp out on the couch?" Mitch said. "I'd like to be close to the dog."

"I suppose, for now," Tom said, combating Mitch's anger and frustration with a gentle self-control. He made Mitch comfortable on the couch, stoked up the fire, and then checked Barney. The big dog was sleeping, so Tom left him alone and returned to Mitch.

"Son, if it's any comfort, I'd like you to know that you are not alone, not anymore. You have friends here. Don't be afraid to let yourself go like you did a while ago. Don't keep it bottled up. God and I have big ears."

"Thanks," Mitch said. He forced a grin but didn't open his eyes.

"Son, before you drift off, I need to ask you something." Mitch nodded and yawned.

"Was it a big bear?"

"Big as the one that jumped us."

"Did she...it have a spotted rump?" Mitch was quickly falling asleep, but managed a nod.

"Damn her ornery hide." Tom knelt closer, "Don't worry if I'm gone when you wake up; I've got some business to attend to."

"I'll be fine," Mitch said, and then caught the first wink.

CHAPTER FOURTEEN

I t's good that you killed her, Tom; she's been a
pain these last few years, especially after Collins
wounded her. That buckshot just pissed her off,
and she's been mad ever since." The Idaho Game
Ranger stooped to examine the carcass. "This is odd,"
he said. "The ground is wet all around the carcass, and
dry everywhere else."

Tom laughed.

"It was ice. After I'd fixed him...after I'd fixed Barney
up I went to town and bought up all the ice I could
find. I covered it in ice. I wanted to save the meat, but
especially the hide."

"Makes sense," the ranger said.

"You know, Billy, if I hadn't left my sidearm in the
truck those years ago, she'd have been dead then, instead of me up a tree. And Barney wouldn't be laid up."

"How is he?" The ranger asked.

"He'll be alright, Billy, if infection doesn't set in." Tom thought about his other patient and reminded himself to get some stronger antibiotics before he returned home.

"Tom, don't think you've done wrong by killing her. She was old and worn out; I doubt if she'd have lived another year. She's better off, and so are we. Do you want the county to remove the rest of the carcass?"

"No, that won't be necessary."

"Well," Billy said, rubbing his jaw thoughtfully, "I should impound your weapons and your home, etc, for taking the law in your own hands, but I suppose we'll let it slide in light of the fact that it was self-defense." He grinned.

"You darned well better," Tom said. "Your father and I go back a ways. And I figure I did the state a favor. - How is your father? I haven't talked to him in a while."

"Dad's doing really well. He bought the old Treadwell mine and he's working it from time to time. He finds a little gold now and then, nothing much, but enough to keep him interested. He still fishes when the weather isn't too chilly. How're you doing Tom? I miss Natalie."

"I'm doing better, thanks. Yeah, I miss her, too. She was too good for me. Well, I best get busy if I'm going to salvage any meat."

"Be tough as old shoe leather," the ranger said.

"Not if you know how to prepare it. Most of it will go for dog food anyway. Barney's going to need a lot of fresh meat in the next few weeks."

"Sounds like a plan. I have to go, Tom. You be careful; she wasn't the only bear around."

" I'll be fine. Say hello to your dad for me."

"Sure. See you later."

Tom watched as the ranger drove away, then he went to work. From a sheath on his belt, he drew out a skinning knife. He shaved some hair off his left forearm to test the edge and then with a mild vengeance burning in his eyes, he turned toward the dead bear.

While Tom was butchering the carcass, Mitch slept a deep, uninterrupted sleep. Shortly after Tom had left the cabin that morning, Barney awoke and looked around as if trying to place himself. He saw Mitch sleeping on the couch and he pushed himself off the pallet with his good legs. He dragged himself painfully across the polished wooden floor. When he reached the couch, he lay down at Mitch's side.

The fire was dying down, but the day was warm and the cabin was cozy. Barney watched Mitch and whimpered. Mitch snored softly, resting easy, and soon Barney was also asleep.

About two in the afternoon, Tom returned to the cabin and climbed wearily out of the truck. In the back was some of the wood he'd cut yesterday. He left it where it lay and went inside, carrying a brown grocery sack.

The cabin was huge, two stories high, with a long veranda on the front. On the left end of the raised deck was his stack of seasoned and split wood, ready for the fireplace. On the other end was a long-unused porch swing. Budding rose bushes surrounded the veranda. Leading from the drive to the steps up the porch was a flagstone walk lined with shrubs and more roses. The cabin had been built in a natural clearing, and it appeared to have grown there.

His father had made a fortune in the early logging days, but in his later years he turned against the old ways and adopted the new. He began planting where he'd cut and eventually quit cutting and sold out.

In repentance, he'd bought a thousand acres of what remained and built the cabin on it. From that time until his death, he'd refused to cut a tree that he didn't need for firewood.

The cabin had an oversized living area with a huge fireplace at the front. Behind the living room, divided by a bathroom, were two bedrooms. These were separated from the living room by a long hallway. At the right end of the hallway was a staircase that led up to two more bedrooms, a full bath, and a study. The kitchen and dining room were at the opposite end of the hallway, joining the living room at a right angle. The kitchen was at the far end where it shared the back of the cabin with the garage and utility room.

Outside, the yard was natural, except for the shrubs and roses. The log cabin blended harmoniously with its surroundings.

Tom sat at the large dining room table in one of four high-backed wooden chairs, where he rested his head in his hands. The excitement and labors of the last seventy-two hours had taken their toll. He stared at the back of the couch and at the fireplace.

Something was different.

At first his tired mind couldn't detect it, but then it dawned on him that Barney was not where he'd left him. Tom found him lying on the floor next to Mitch. Barney opened his eyes and looked up as Tom knelt by the dog's side, groaning at the ache in his tired muscles.

"How's it going, pup?" he whispered, not wanting to wake Mitch. Barney whined and looked up at him.

"He'll be fine-thanks to you." He retrieved the dog's blankets and laid them by the couch. After he made the dog comfortable, he looked up and saw that Mitch was awake.

"How's it going, Mountain Climber?"

"I feel like it fell on me, the mountain, I mean. You

don't look so good yourself."

"Been cuttin' wood."

"From the looks of your clothes, that ain't all you've been cuttin'."

"I took most of the carcass to the butcher for processing into dog food, but I saved the choicest cuts. You partial to bear meat?"

"Don't know," Mitch said, after thinking a minute, "but hungry as I am, it don't matter what bones the meat was hung on."

Tom laughed and his weary old eyes twinkled under his hat brim.

"Set tight. I'll clean up and then fry us some big old bear steaks."

He brought Barney's water bowl close so the dog could drink at will.

"Thirsty?"

"Parched, but first I need to use the restroom."

"Of course, I bet you're sick of that bed pan." Tom helped Mitch to his feet. Mitch winced and groaned.

"Damn, my chest hurts. Feels like I got a thousand needles stuck in it."

"Show me where," Tom said.

"Right up here." Mitch touched the area beneath his left collarbone.

"Have you had much difficulty breathing?"

"I can't take a deep breath, and it hurts like the blazes when I move. As long as I sit still I'm fine, but the slightest movement shoots fire through my chest."

"You have what we call a pneumothorax!"

"What?"

"You have air in your chest cavity. In medical terms a pneumothorax is basically a collapsed lung. Normally, the outer surface of the lung meets the inner surface of the chest wall. The lung and the chest wall are covered by thin membranes called pleura. A collapsed lung is what happens when air escapes from the lungs and enters the space between the two membranes. When you punctured your lung, it let air escape into your chest cavity. When you ran from the trees, and when you hefted the axe, etc., you did it again. You have a bubble of air moving around in your chest. Don't worry; it will be absorbed soon. By tomorrow morning, you won't feel it anymore. I'll give you something for the pain, but no more morphine. "Don't worry. From what you've told me and what I could glean from my examination, I'm positive it was only a minor puncture. Come on, the bathroom is just around the corner." Tom helped Mitch to his feet.

"But I should ask: do you still taste blood?"

"No, not this morning," Mitch said.

"That's good," Tom said as he led Mitch down the hall a few feet. Tom opened the second door on the left and turned on the light.

"Can you manage?"

Mitch nodded and gritted his teeth against the pounding in his head.

"Holler when you're finished. It's obvious you're not a whimp, but you've been through hell, Son, and back again. Don't try to go it alone, not for a week or two. If you even think you need help with something you let me know."

"I will. Thanks."

"Don't mention it. And don't feel special. I'd do it for a mangy old dog."

Mitch grinned.

Tom went to the kitchen, chopped up a pound of the bear meat, fed the dog by hand until he refused to eat any more, then left the plate and went upstairs to take his first shower in three days.

He was beat, but he showered quickly, dressed, and was back downstairs preparing the evening meal within a few minutes. He selected two thick bear steaks, tenderized them, and placed them in a dish to marinate in his own secret sauce. Then he peeled two large potatoes and opened a can of corn. He made some coffee and drank two cups while the steak soaked. After an hour he started the steak and potatoes frying.

"Tom?"

He turned and saw Mitch standing in the hall. He turned the burners down and went to help him.

"Are you alright?"

"I can make it."

"Well, I'm going to help you anyway. Put your arm around my shoulder and lean on me." Mitch, though proud and stubborn, did as he was told but still wouldn't give Tom all his weight until it was too late. Just as they made it into the dining room, Mitch's knees buckled and he nearly passed out. Groaning under Mitch's weight, Tom half carried and dragged him into a chair at the table.

Tom sat down across from him, taking a minute to catch his breath. Breathing heavily and painfully, Mitch said nothing, just leaned on the table with his head in his hands. Then as Tom rose to take care of supper, he said, "Do you know anything about amnesia?"

"Not much," Tom said over his shoulder "It wasn't my specialty. Why?"

"I just stood a long time in front of the mirror, staring at a total stranger. Everything about me seems to be borrowed. I know nothing about myself. It's like I've lost my mind and changed bodies with someone."

"I'm just a family practitioner who's been retired for twenty years. I'm not well-versed in the mental health sciences, but I can try to answer any questions you have."

"OK, how bad off am I?"

"You want the skinny or the fat?" The look in Mitch's eyes answered the question for him.

Tom thought a minute, delving into the recesses of his mind.

"Damage to the brain can produce retrograde amnesia, which is memory loss of events that occurred just before the damage, or posttraumatic amnesia, which comes after damage. Most amnesia lasts for only minutes or hours, depending on the severity of the damage, and then it disappears without treatment. In fact, there is no treatment I'm aware of. With severe damage, amnesia can be permanent.

"You're exhibiting signs of retrograde amnesia. Now is when I'm supposed to tell you that you're going to be fine and that your memory will come back soon, and not to worry about it. But you'd see right through that baloney in a heartbeat, so the fact is...well, you've got some swelling on the brain, Son. But let's not confuse that with brain damage. You're up and walking around, you're not slurring your words, you've got an appetite, and you don't seem to have lost any physical abilities, although your mind *was* wandering earlier. But that's probably due to exhaustion and the swelling. Let's put it this way: Whatever hit you, didn't connect completely. You're awake and fairly lucid now, so I'd bet the ranch you'll be fine.

"I know it's not much consolation, but at least you're not alone. What you need right now is what you have here. You have a half-assed doctor to see to your physical needs; you've got my dog and I for companionship; and you're surrounded by God's country."

"I'm not sure if I believe in God. I mean I don't feel

anything there."

Tom started to reply but hesitated, mulling that statement over. Finally he spoke.

"How can you know that if you remember nothing else?"

"All these hours of lying in bed, wondering whether I'd live or die...." He took a deep breath. "One wonders about such things. Logic tells me that when I die I'd go back to where I came from: oblivion."

"That's not a comforting thought," Tom replied.

"Not comforting at all," Mitch said. "But it's all that makes sense to me, not that I ain't open to the possibilities."

"Well, to be honest, Son, there was a time when my scientific mind would have agreed with you. However, in my line of work one sees and experiences events that can only be ascribed to divine intervention. Take my Son, for instance. Jeremy was born prematurely and there were so many complications that he should have died. Yet he lived. I've asked myself why more times than I can remember, and science alone cannot answer that question. With my wife's Christian influence, somewhere along the way I regained my faith. It's as strong as ever now. If you can't find it in your heart and soul to believe in God, just believe in me for now.

"We'll see you through this. This cabin is your home; you are one of the family. You have all the rights and privileges I would give my own son if he lived under this roof. So perk up and loosen your belt. I'm not only a good doctor, I'm the best cook in these parts."

"Ah, I understand," Mitch said. "I get an earful and a mouthful?"

"Are you saying I talk too much?"

Mitch just sat there and remained silent for a few moments, thinking, embarrassed by what he'd just said.

"Naw, I reckon you're lonely and just need to talk." Then he said, "Thank you, sir, but I don't want to be a burden. Soon as I'm able to travel, I'll be on the move."

"And just where will you go?" Tom asked, as he brought Mitch a cup of coffee. "You've no memory, no name, no identification, and it's a long way to any town worth stopping in."

Mitch responded, "By the way, what day is it? And where are we? What year is it?"

"Whoa! Ease back on the questions a bit, and I'll answer them one at a time." Tom said, laughing at Mitch as he returned to the stove. He knew the stranger wasn't himself...didn't even know who himself was at this point. He came back a few minutes later with two plates heaped with bear steak and all the trimmings. Then he went to the cupboard by the sink, took out two tall glasses, and filled them with milk from the fridge. He set them on the table and returned with the coffee pot.

After Tom said a short prayer of thanks, they began to eat. They ate mostly in silence, for Mitch had found his appetite and wasted no time with questions.

"I was hungry enough to eat a bear," Mitch said twenty minutes later as he pushed his plate away. "We must have eaten half of him."

"Her," Tom said. "Someday I'll tell you about that old sow. Right now you must have other things on your mind, so let's sit a spell and you can ask all the questions you want."

Tom left the dishes for later and helped Mitch get comfortable on the couch. He opened the windows on both sides of the fireplace and pulled back the curtains. A pleasant breeze blew into the room.

"My wife made these curtains before she died," Tom

said as he stood staring out the window on the right, the one nearest the door that led to the veranda. The wind brought in a breath of spring. The tangy aroma of pines dominated the air and Mitch breathed in deeply.

"I love that smell," he said, "I always have." Tom glanced at him inconspicuously but didn't say anything.

Tom sat down in his old, comfortable recliner and filled his pipe from a pouch he kept in his shirt pocket.

"I don't know how I know that, but I do," Mitch said. "I also know the bear on the other side of the river could smell me but that it couldn't see me. I think I know a lot about the mountains and the animals, maybe, I don't know." He paused momentarily, then said, "But I know one thing for sure. I've been in and out of it for a few days, maybe more. I don't know how long I was on that cliff before I woke up, but I've seen and heard enough to know that it was the same bear that attacked us."

"That's right," Tom said. "She knew you were hurt and she was on your trail. Tom lit his pipe and puffed on it, relaxing. The breeze pushed the blue smoke lazily about him and around the room; the sunlight shining through the windows danced on the swirling haze and lent a dreamy state to the early afternoon. Before Mitch could get any of his questions answered, he was snoring.

Tom finished his pipe and then got up and covered Mitch with a blanket. Barney woke just then, and Tom sat down on the floor beside him. With his back to the couch, Tom gently petted the top of Barney's head and talked softly to the most courageous animal he'd ever known.

"It looks like you two are going to make it." Barney licked his hand in reply. "I'm sorry to have you wrapped up so tight, but I can't let you move too much. That old sow cut you up pretty bad."

Barney whined and looked anxiously toward the door. Tom carried him outside.

Mitch sat up and through half-closed eyes he watched as Tom helped Barney with nature's demands. He smiled at the wonderful old man he'd come to be with. Contented, he sighed and let his head fall back down and was soon asleep again.

Tom unloaded the wood and stacked it by the side of the cabin near the splitting stump. Soon the forest rang with the sound of his axe. For two hours he worked, while Barney dozed in the sunlight and Mitch slept inside. Work, as Tom saw it, led to cogitation, and he felt that a man who wouldn't work was often lazy in the mind as well.

When he finished chopping, he had a week's supply of firewood, and was sure of two things. First, he was certain the stranger was originally from Texas, or had spent a lot of time there; the accent was unmistakable. Second, Tom was sure he would not stand in the way if the stranger wanted to leave and search for his past. However, Tom had made up his mind that he'd keep him around as long as possible. He liked the man, and it was good to have someone to talk to, someone aside from himself and the dog, though he loved the dog.

Tom rationalized that he was a doctor and could give Mitch the best care. He could report Mitch to the proper authorities and get in touch with his family, if he had any. But Tom argued with himself that in Mitch's state of mind, it might be better if he stayed away from family that he didn't recognize.

Tom knew that the mountains had a healing power. The clean, fresh air and the ruggedness brought out the best in a man. Mitch would fare well here. In the

end, Mitch might hold it against him, but it was a risk
Tom would take...and later come to regret.

CHAPTER FIFTEEN

Sherrie knocked on the door, then opened it and peeked in as Donna came off the couch to greet her. Sherrie had called and said she was coming over.

"Hi! I thought you might like some company."

"Sure, come in. Want something to drink? Tea? Coffee? Soda?"

"No thanks, we just ate. Harold's bowling tonight, and I was lonely and worried about you. Are you alright?"

"No, I'm not, but I'm hiding it well, aren't I?"

"I would be nuts by now," Sherrie said. "It's been six days, and you're doing so well."

"I know, Sher', it's as if they just flew into space. And Barbara won't speak to me; she's blaming Mitch, therefore me."

"That's absurd. She has no right," Sherrie said.

"I'm not going to let it bother me. If I were in her shoes I might feel the same."

"What do you mean, you are in her shoes."

"Nope. Not at all. I know in my heart and soul that Mitch is alive. But everybody thinks I'm nuts. My own son doubts me."

"Where is Steven?"

"He's working. He wanted to take some time off, but I encouraged him to keep at it. He means well, but I'm fine, and he doesn't need to be moping around the house."

"If it's any consolation, I believe you. If you say that he is alive, then he is."

"That means a lot to me," Donna said, hugging her friend. "I love you."

"I love you, too. You're my best friend. Come to think of it, you're my only friend. So, let's talk. Tell me about him. I mean, what are you feeling? What are you thinking? Let it out; I'm all ears."

They sat down on the couch.

"He needs me. That is difficult. For the first time in our marriage, I can't go to him. I can't be there for him. You know, like you, he has questions about the existence of a god, but I pray for him, and that at least makes *me* feel better." Donna stifled a tear and said, "I know he has crashed, he's probably hurt, but he's alive. He will make it. If my husband can still walk, if he can just crawl, he will survive. He never backed down from anything in his life.

"They must be in the thick of the wilderness or we would have found them. Mitch knows those mountains. He's hunted up there extensively, with a camera more often than a rifle, and he's studied wilderness survival for more years than I have known him.

"Mitch can survive in the worst conditions; he's in great shape; he will make it. It might take him days, even weeks to walk or crawl out, or to find help, but he will be home. I'm certain of it. Matter of fact, I'm so certain of it that I designed another block for the quilt. It shows us back together again."

Donna sprang up and practically danced across the carpet to the cedar chest, where she removed a brightly colored piece of cloth.

Sherrie, amazed at Donna's energy and spirit in spite of her hardship, said, "Donna what is it about you? It's almost supernatural the way you cope."

"I told you, I pray. I can do nothing of myself, but I can do all things through Christ who strengthens me. Philippians 4:13. If you weren't so stubborn, you could have it, too." Donna sat back down beside Sherrie and handed her the block she'd soon sew into her quilt.

"I know you believe, but I don't know, it's so, um, I mean, I just can't believe in something so, so vague. I need something I can see and touch and smell. I need proof! When did you do this?"

"Last night. We were exhausted when we got home from searching for Mitch and both of us went straight to bed. I could only sleep a couple of hours, so I got up and worked on this."

"It's beautiful. It's neat what you can do with a needle and thread."

"My mother taught me to quilt, and my grandmother taught her. All the women on both sides of my family made their own quilts and blankets. It's part of my heritage. I grew up with a needle in my right hand.

"You really believe he's alive, don't you?"

"No doubt in my mind."

"Then you've got to find him."

"So do you," Donna said.

"Huh?"

"But unlike you, I don't know where to look." Inside, Donna was fighting not to break down and cry. In spite of her faith, at times she nearly lost control. This was one of those moments. She loved her friend, and like any conscientious Christian, she longed for Sherrie's salvation. Sherrie was mulish though, and like many non-believers, she couldn't comprehend the blessings believed to be inherent in the life of a Christian, though Donna was a shining example.

"We haven't a clue; the authorities are baffled. They will call off the search at the end of the week if they don't find something."

Sherrie gave the cloth back and Donna laid it aside. Then she broke down. Sherrie held her and stroked her hair gently, cooing to her softly until she cried herself out. Then they talked until Sherrie had to leave.

Donna sat by herself and waited for Steven to come home. He arrived at ten, hoping for news about his father but expecting none. Donna told him she'd heard nothing, and once more, he retreated to his room.

The search was canceled four days later. Immediately, Donna hired another pilot and she and Steven searched a grid pattern that they had worked out. Methodically they searched an area one hundred miles wide by three hundred long, back and forth, section by section, finding nothing. Reluctantly they, too, returned home, exhausted and dejected.

As the days passed, Donna's beliefs never dimmed, but Steven withdrew into himself and spent much of his time alone. So much so that Donna insisted they seek counseling. At first, it seemed to help, but after the third session, Steven refused to return. He remained in his room alone when he was home. He rarely spoke to his friends and practically deserted his girlfriend.

Donna finally sat him down one evening, exactly three weeks after his father's disappearance and made him talk to her. He admitted having a recurring dream. He kept seeing his father stumbling through the woods on a dark stormy night, lightning flashing everywhere, rain falling in sheets.

"He must be alive. I feel it, too," he'd said. He cried in her arms for about ten minutes while she cried silently to herself.

Understanding the emotions of a young adult could be difficult, if not impossible, but this time she had no trouble. She'd called his girlfriend and asked her to come over. Donna explained that no matter how much he denied it, he needed her.

Steven was downstairs when the bell rang, and Molly leaped into his arms when he opened the door. Donna winked and smiled, tossing him the keys to her Lexus convertible. She gave him some money and told them to have a good evening on her.

Things started to look up after that, and Steven no longer shut himself away in his room. His father would not have wanted him to waste time grieving. He resumed his life. He got serious about his job again, and he got back into the daily grind of homework. His personality changed, too. He had grown up overnight and took things a bit more seriously, like his relationship with Molly. Losing his father gave him a greater appreciation for life and he wanted more of it. It wasn't long before his nightmares ceased, and they all began to pick up the pieces, deciding to take each day as it came, one day at a time.

CHAPTER SIXTEEN

K urt? Wait up, this pace is killing me."
"Hey, dude, this was your idea," Kurt
said, "you gonna whimp out on me?"
"No, just slow it down."
"Alright, I'm getting tired, too," he lied.

The two teens had just about finished a five-mile hike along the Snake river, around the mountain, and were about to climb a mile to the top. It was a grueling climb, but worth the journey. The fishing on the summit was outstanding. Few anglers had what it took to reach the lake at the timberline, thus few enjoyed the rewards.

Kurt, the high school quarterback, had been making the trip with his father since he was ten. Gary, his best friend and teammate, had spent the winter in the hospital after a skiing accident.

"Stop a minute," Gary said, sitting down on a rock. "I've got to rest. What time did you say the girls were going to meet us tomorrow?"

"About noon," Kurt said. "Hey! Look down there." He pointed to a deep pool downstream. "How about a swim before we head up?"

"Last one there is a homo," Gary yelled as he threw off his pack and ran. Kurt had his off just as fast, but stumbled and fell on the way down. When he met up with Gary he found his friend on his knees, vomit gushing from his mouth. Kurt followed his outstretched arm as Gary pointed to the other side of the pool. What Kurt saw made him fall to his knees, retching.

Floating face up by the bank was a ghastly white and bloated body. Its clothing was ripped and torn, the body battered and broken.

"Oh, God, I'm out of here," Gary shouted as he ran back up the trail. Kurt remained on his knees, vomit dripping from his chin.

The body swirled around in the pool and was almost swept into the main stream, but floated back at the last minute, bumping into a half-submerged tree. It remained there long enough for Kurt to tie it in place with his belt.

Back up the trail, Gary waited beside his pack, pale and sick.

Kurt joined him a few minutes later, and they silently marched back down the trail.

Two hours later, the police in Grangeville, roughly 40 miles northwest of where Tom nursed Mitch back to health, received a report of a floater in the river, west of town. Within minutes, choppers were dispatched, the body was located, and police detectives were on the scene, accompanied by Kurt. Nobody faulted Gary for not returning.

"Is this where you found the body?"

"Yes, Sir. It was floating around in the pool when Gary got here. Then it got caught on the tree and I tied it there with my belt.

"Man, that dude is totally freakin' dead, you know, and I'm going to be sick again. I've got to get out of here."

"I understand, Son. You can go. Do you want your belt back?"

"No way, Dude. I mean no, Sir. I could never wear it again. You know what I mean?"

"Yes, Kurt, I'm afraid I do. Thanks for your coopera- tion. The chopper will take you home."

"Yes, Sir," Kurt said, and ran immediately to the chopper.

♠ ♠ ♠

A reluctant police officer stepped from his patrol car, and after a moment of hesitation, proceeded to the front door of the Gaines' residence. He knocked three times before the door opened. Barbara Gaines stood there in a nightgown, obviously drunk, with a drink in her hand.

"Mrs. Gaines?"

"You found them."

"Not both. Can I come in, Ma'am?"

"Dead," she said, seeing it in his eyes.

"I'm sorry," he said staring at the floor, afraid to meet her eyes again.

"May I come in?"

"Never had a cop in the house," she said, beckoning him to follow her inside. "Come to think of it, I've never had a cop." She giggled, and then asked if he wanted a cup of coffee.

"That would be nice," he said as she bade him to sit at the kitchen table.

She heated water in the microwave and made him a

cup of instant coffee.

"One sugar, please," he said.

She sat it down hard in front of him, spilling a little.

"Sorry, I'm just a little drunk, in case you didn't notice."

"No problem," he said. He sipped his coffee, and waited for the right moment to deal the blow. "Nice kitchen. My father was a carpenter; he specialized in kitchens. He liked to say a house should be built around a kitchen."

"Where was he found," she said, ignoring the small talk.

"His body was found in the Snake River, a few miles north and west of Grangeville."

"His flight plan had him flying east of there closer to the Salmon River. Are you sure it's him."

"Identification was intact. But to be sure...."

"You need me to identify the remains."

"I'll drive you there as soon as you can get ready." He sipped his coffee, letting his eyes stray to her cleavage, which she blatantly offered. She bore an uncanny resemblance to Ann Margaret. She noticed him looking and teased her hair, smiling at him. Blushing, he averted his eyes. She reached out and touched his hand.

"I never loved my husband. I'm alone, been alone for a long time. I was never faithful. It never bothered me when he was alive. It won't bother me now."

A good cop, Officer Reynolds pulled his hand from under hers, finished his coffee, and resumed his duty.

"Mrs. Gaines, you need to prepare yourself. Your husband's body traveled a long distance after being badly damaged when his plane apparently went down."

"Apparently, my ass!" Barbara spat. "You know damned well he crashed his plane. The fat son-of-a-bitch probably had a fuckin' heart attack. Alright, you've done your duty. You ain't gonna make a pass at me, so just get the hell out."

"Ma'am, I'm just doing my job. I'll go, but someone will be back to pick you up in an hour. Please be ready."

She led him to the door and slammed it after him. The sound rang in his ears all the way back to the station.

Donna was sewing when the phone rang. Startled, she jumped and stuck herself with the needle. Sucking on her injured thumb, she reached for the phone on the table beside the couch.

"Hello?"

"They found Greg. He's dead. They found him in the Snake River, west of Grangeville. They said they didn't find both of them. They just told me. I just told you. Now you know. Ain't gonna be no funeral. I'm gonna burn the son of a bitch."

At first, Donna didn't say anything. She stared at the carpet. Then she found herself speaking.

"Barbara, I'm so sorry."

The phone clicked and Barbara was gone. Donna stared at the receiver until Steven came down the stairs a minute later.

"Was that about dad?"

Donna stared at the phone.

"Mom, what's wrong?"

"That was Greg's wife," she said, finally hanging up. "His body was found in the Snake River west of Grangeville. There was no sign of your father or the plane."

After a few minutes of emotional turmoil and the flowing of many tears, a light suddenly shone in Donna's eyes. She gathered their charts and maps and spread them on the kitchen table.

"Greg's body was found here on the Snake River."
She pointed at the map. "Their flight plan had them flying about fifty miles west of Riggins, over the Salmon
River. Right here," she said, pointing at the map. "That
has to mean the plane crashed into or beside one of the
rivers, or in one of the creeks that flow into them.
There's no telling how far Greg's body floated in the
swift current. OK, let's think. The Salmon flows into the
Snake south of Grangeville. OK, Yes!" She was getting
excited, talking fast. "We'll start where Greg's body was
found and work upstream, south and west. If we don't
find the plane near either of the rivers, then we search
all the rivers and creeks that flow into them. If we are
thorough we stand a good chance of finding your father."

Ignoring pleas for them to stay home while profes-
sionals returned to the search, Donna hired the pilot
again, and their hunt was on once more.

Every bend in every river and stream was searched
repeatedly, but to no avail. After almost a month of
painstaking search by hundreds of personnel, on the
ground and in the air, the operation was officially
closed. Mitch was listed as missing and presumed
dead.

Nonetheless, Donna never gave up hope, but instead
grew stronger in her faith; she knew someday she'd be
reunited with her husband.

CHAPTER SEVENTEEN

BACK WITH TOM AND MITCH,
THREE WEEKS EARLIER...

Tom stopped chopping for a moment to mop sweat off his brow with his red bandana. It was warm for this early in the year and he was perspiring heavily. Nevertheless, he enjoyed the work, and in spite of the unusual temperatures, it was a beautiful day for it.

Only a few clouds dotted the sky, and a light breeze skipped through the treetops. A cottontail watched from beside a stump at the edge of the woods as Tom worked. It also watched Barney, expecting to be chased at any moment. Barney wanted to give chase, but could only watch. He wanted to scratch too, but he resisted the urge. He was still heavily bandaged and immobilized. It was better to lay and itch than scratch and fall.

Tom was an observant man by practice and by trade. He missed none of this, nor did he miss the buck feeding at the back of the cabin. The deer were used to him and were relatively unafraid. The front door was open and Tom heard Mitch close the bathroom door.

"About time to call it a day," he said as he drove the axe into the chopping block. He gathered an armful of what he'd just split, stacked it on the porch, and then took Barney inside.

Mitch was just sitting back down when Tom walked in. Tom laid Barney beside him, then slid into his recliner and filled his pipe and lit it.

"Warm today," he said, puffing the pipe to life. "Too warm for this early in the spring, but I'm not complaining."

"You sure know how to keep busy."

"Habit," Tom spoke around his pipe, "been working all my life. If I stop now, I'll just get old. Wouldn't want that to happen, would we?"

"I reckon not," Mitch said with a grin.

"I'm going to head into town tomorrow. I need to pick up the rest of the meat and get groceries and bandages. You'll need some clothes and personal things, too."

"Thanks, but I can't allow you to spend money on me."

"Ah, don't worry about that. Money is the least of my worries. I got your sizes from your other clothes before I burned them with the rest of the trash."

Mitch looked over at him and laughed with a slight grimace of pain.

"I'm surprised you had enough left to burn."

"Well, it made good tender." He smoked a few minutes. Mitch scratched Barney behind the ears. They watched the fire.

"How're you feeling?"

"Like a truck ran over me."

"No, I mean what's going on in that head of yours?"

"I'm alright, I suppose. I'd be lyin' if I said I was doin' any better. I've got a knot in my stomach; fear I guess, like a fire in my gut. Sometimes it just smolders, at other times it's like a big wind comes along and fans the flames." Mitch paused, staring into space. A log fell, sending up sparks. "I hate to admit it, but I'm scared, Tom. The other night I woke up and didn't know where I was. It took a few minutes to remember. Has that ever happened to you?"

"Yep. I'm sure it happens to everyone now and again."

"Well, in general, that's what happened to me. I woke from nothingness a few days ago and still don't know who I am."

The fire crackled and popped. Tom wondered about the days to come, Mitch guessed at what came before. Barney sat in the middle, blessed to be living in the moment.

As the sun left the sky and the wind ceased to blow, the forest fell softly silent. All was still and calm.

"Nothing like the quiet of the forest," Tom whispered reverently. "When the snow is covering the ground, I can go out in the woods where the wind is still, and it is so purely silent that I swear I can hear my heart beating. The whisper of my breath, the rustle of my clothes against my body as I walk softly in the snow becomes an offensive noise. There is no sound like the silence of a forest to calm a man's soul." Tom paused a minute to smoke his pipe thoughtfully. The blue-gray smoke drifted and swirled around his head.

"Don't worry about the cost of clothes and things. I'll work it out of you as soon as you're well enough." Tom grinned around his pipe. "Which might be sooner than either of us expect, the way you're coming along. I tell you, Son, you amaze me. When I first laid eyes on you back under those trees, I thought I'd be digging you a hole instead of feeding you. That might have been easier, now that I think about it."

Mitch chuckled.

"In answer to your earlier questions, today is Tuesday, the 8th of April, 2009. We're in the mountains of Idaho, a hundred and thirty miles due north of Boise. East of us is some of the wildest country south of Canada. The river out back is named the Salmon, or—or as some call it—The River of No Return." It feeds into the Snake River, just south of Grangeville, which in turn feeds into the Columbia River.

"And, unless I miss my guess, you're originally from Texas, and you were here on a hunting trip."

Tom rose from his chair and walked over to the fireplace. He gazed lovingly at his late wife's photo on the mantelpiece. He asked her forgiveness for what he had done. Then he picked up Mitch's knife and cigarette lighter.

"How do you know that?" Mitch asked.

He turned and handed the items to Mitch.

"Those were in your pockets. Do you smoke?"

"Don't have a craving for it."

"So the lighter must be for starting a campfire, and that is a hunting knife with a heavy, locking blade. Not a toy, very sharp and strong.

"It makes sense," he said as he turned the knife over in his hands, opening it and closing it, testing the sharpness of the blade.

"What makes you think I'm from Texas?"

"I've done a bit of traveling, and I attended medical school in San Antonio. Folks in the Lone Star have a quality about them that you'll seldom find elsewhere. It's nothing that makes them better or worse, just different. They are proud and strong. The state is very self-sufficient, producing and growing all they need. They don't back down from anything. I see that in you. I hear it in your voice. You have the accent to go with it; pure Texan."

"Then Texas is where I'll go when I get on my feet."

They talked for most of an hour. Barney slept on the floor at Mitch's feet. Tom was aware of a bond growing between the two, but he was wise enough to understand, and he encouraged it.

What bothered Tom was the realization that somewhere, someone had to be missing this man and most certainly looking for him. It had been a long time, however, since anyone had been around for him to talk with. Along with Barney, he felt a strong attachment to Mitch. It was as if they had all been thrust together for a reason.

Tom thought it best to keep silent, to keep his thoughts to himself. Mitch might be better off not dealing with it at this time; however, the more he thought about it, the more it bothered him.

"Son?"

Mitch looked up.

"Do you make anything of the initials engraved in the handle of your knife?"

"No, they mean nothing to me." The knife was a folding hunter, time worn and well used. The initials on each side were nearly worn off but still legible. "L.C." was engraved in both sides.

"It's as if it belongs to someone else."

For several minutes, both men were silent, deep in thought. Then Tom's tongue cut loose.

"Son, I can see that you've been wracking your brain for an answer to all this. We don't know what actually caused you to lose your memory, accident or not, and it won't do any good to worry over it. You and I both know there is a chance your memory may never return. I'd advise you to begin to accept that, and to just take each day as it comes. On the other hand, you might wake up tomorrow and everything will come back to you.

"You can try to find your past, your family, friends, but if you do, and you have no memory of them, then it could be worse for you and for them. Son, wounds heal quickly in this high country, and Lord knows you have a lot of healing to do. It's a big, lonely place up here, and it's been this way for much too long. I could help you find your past right away, if you want. We can call the authorities if you want. Or you can stay here and rest.

"Perhaps I should just drive you to the hospital right now and let things go through the proper channels. Barney and I would welcome your company, but I leave it up to you. I'm sure you have family looking for you."

Mitch fingered his mustache, spreading it across his lip, and then he sighed.

"Alright, you've talked me into it. To be honest, it scares me more to go out there than it does to sit here and wonder about it. I think I'd like to hang around if you really want me to stay here." Barney nuzzled him and looked up, begging attention. Mitch grinned and stroked the dog's golden fur.

"Yeah, dawg, I'm stayin'."

"Are you sure?"

"I'm sure."

"Ok," Tom paused and sighed, relieved. "That's settled, now we need to settle on a name for you. Let's see, there must hundreds of names that start with L."

"It doesn't matter what you call me," Mitch said, "just don't call me late for supper."

"I'm getting a mite lonesome for something to eat my

own self." Tom laughed heartily; he felt good. "How about some more stew?"

"Whatever suits you tickles me plumb to death." Tom said as he high-stepped it into the kitchen. Mitch remained with Barney on the couch, watching the flames dancing with the shadows around the room. He thought about the initials on the knife and ran some names through his head, but none rang any bells. He needed something to spur his mind.

He got up slowly and then hobbled around the room, checking books and magazines for names, hoping he'd recognize his own. Having no luck, he stopped by the window that Tom had gazed out of earlier. He watched two chipmunks scurry industriously among the pines. Barney whimpered behind him and Mitch turned to look over his shoulder.

"What is it, dog?" he asked as Barney whined again and looked down at his water bowl.

"Thirsty?" Mitch turned from the window, walked over, and knelt beside the dog.

"Hey, I haven't taken the time to thank you." A lump rose in his throat as he knelt down beside Barney. "You saved my life. I'll never forget that." Mitch held Barney's head in his hands while Barney licked his face.

"It took courage to do what you did."

Tom watched from the dining room. He'd been on his way back in when he heard Mitch's tender words.

"He's not the only one with a measure of courage. I've seen men twice your size turn and run at the mere sight of a bear, but you were about to go at the meanest of them with an axe. You couldn't have cut a toothpick, the shape you were in, but you were there to back me up. And I appreciate *that*."

"I was out of my head, Tom; I didn't know what I was doing."

"I don't believe it."

"Barney's thirsty," Mitch said. "I'll get him some water."

"I'll get it," Tom said. "You rest. How about a glass of iced tea?"

"Sure," Mitch said, sitting back down, "I haven't had a glass of tea since, since I can't remember when." He laughed and suddenly clutched at his chest. "Ouch! Guess I'd better stay away from the jokes; I can't handle the punch lines."

"I'll get the tea and bring you something for that pain," Tom said as he picked up Barney's water bowl. "Do you like it sweet?"

"Been craving something sweet."

"Hm? Sweet tooth," Tom said as he returned to the kitchen, "That makes two of us."

Tom filled Barney's water bowl, and got them some tea.

"Thanks," Mitch said as Tom handed him one of the glasses and two small red capsules.

"This is Ibuprofen. It's an anti-inflammatory drug for arthritis, muscle aches and pains, etc. It will help with the swelling, and shouldn't upset your stomach if you take it with food."

Tom put his tea on the end table beside his chair and strolled to the fireplace. He put two more logs on the fire and stirred the coals. Sparks exploded around the logs and rose up the chimney as flames sprang up and died. He shoved the coals up close to the logs and stood back. The flames tried again and caught hold of the wood. The cabin was tight and well insulated, but in spite of that, the day had begun to take on a chill.

"Another month or so and we won't need the fire, except at night, now and again."

"How cold does it get? Do you get a lot of snow?"

"I've been snowed in a few times. I've seen it three, sometimes four feet deep. I have a tractor with a blade just in case it gets bad. Keep it down by the horse corrals."

"You've got horses?"

"I've got two Appaloosas on a ranch east of Boise. Matter of fact, it's about time to bring them back up. I leave them down there during the winter. It's easier on them, and on me. They get plenty of good feed and exercise, and it doesn't cost me anything; they earn their keep."

"You asked how cold it gets. Minus thirty is about the coldest I've seen yet."

"I think I'll go after the horses next week. I didn't bring them up last year and I'm anxious to see them again. By then, you'll be able to travel. Want to tag along?"

"If I won't be in the way."

"I doubt that. I've a hunch you'll be a big help, and the trip to town might do you some good. You think about it. We'll talk it over again in a few days."

"No need to think on it. I'll go."

"That's the spirit," Tom said as he rose from his chair to check on supper. "More tea?"

"Please," Mitch said, holding up an empty glass.

While Tom was working in the kitchen, Mitch hand-fed Barney the rest of the bear meat Tom had left. The dog finished it all and looked for more.

"I'll see what I can dig up," Mitch said, taking the plate and rising painfully to his feet. He made his way slowly into the kitchen with the empty plate. Tom met him halfway. He gave Mitch a stern look as he took the plate.

"Here's your tea, you stubborn fool." Mitch took the glass and winced inwardly, but Tom didn't say anything more.

"I've got some TV trays. We'll eat in there. This big meal will make you sleepy; you'll be close to your bed." Tom's tone made it clear to Mitch that Tom wasn't happy with him.

However, a few minutes later as Tom was serving supper, he made a joke and they had a good laugh to break the awkward silence that had fallen between them. Then they ate a quiet supper in front of the fireplace and Mitch, full as a tick, fell fast asleep on the couch, as Tom had expected.

The weathered old man sat up for awhile, smoked his pipe, and talked to his dog, as was his evening habit.

"I've got a feeling about that young man. I've a hunch he's here for a reason. There's something going on here, something important. I don't know how I know. It's just a feeling. He's strong, Barn', very strong, and I don't just mean physically, but he's just as mule headed, too.

"I think his memory will return. It may take awhile, but he'll be himself again.

"Did you see his reaction when I mentioned the horses? I bet he knows horses.

"I know it's selfish of me, but, though I'll do what I can to help him find his other life, I hope his memory doesn't come back too soon. Don't get me wrong, but your company just isn't enough. I'm lonely for someone to talk to, someone who can talk back, share ideas and thoughts."

Tom grew suddenly silent and then his bottom lip began to quiver.

"I really miss her, Barney. God, how I miss her." Tom cried a little, and his cheeks shone with the glistening tears of his loneliness and grief.

The fire crackled and popped.

Tom sat up for a few more minutes and then he retired to his bedroom. He lay awake for an hour, thinking about Natalie, holding her to his chest in memory, before drifting off to sleep. He rose early the next morning as usual. When Mitch stumbled sleepily into the kitchen at six, led by the aroma of freshly brewed coffee, breakfast was waiting. After they ate, Tom removed both Mitch and Barney's stitches. It had been a week since Barney had found Mitch. They were healing fast. He changed their bandages, made them comfortable, and then he drove to town.

He bought clothes and toiletries for Mitch, then bought groceries and picked up the bear meat from the butcher.

It was raining when he got back to the cabin. Mitch met him at the door and helped him with the packages, then sipped a cup of coffee while Tom put everything away. The coffee was fresh, and Tom brought a box of doughnuts to the table and joined Mitch.

"How are you two getting along?" Tom asked as he opened the box and pushed it across the table. He noticed that Mitch had tidied up the house, and his tone told Mitch he wasn't happy about it.

"I'm fine, but the dog's been restless," Mitch said as he reached for a doughnut.

"I'd best take him outside," Tom said.

"We just took care of that."

"You're going to overdo it, Son!"

"Just doin' what needs to be done," Mitch said as he dipped a doughnut in his coffee.

"Does that include *ruining* the coffee?"

"What do you mean? It's better than yours!"

"Oh, you think so? You want to do the cookin' too from now on? Wash the clothes? Mop the floor? And chop the wood?"

Mitch sipped his coffee, tasted it thoroughly, and then said, "It is a little weak."

"I thought you'd see it my way." Tom laughed and yawned in the middle of it. Mitch refilled their cups and passed the doughnuts back.

"I've been looking around; you've got quite a place here. Whoever built this cabin sure knew what he was doing."

Patient and knowing hands had built the house. All the floors were polished hardwood. All the ceilings followed the rooflines and were overlaid with tongue-and-groove pine. Huge polished timber joists crossed overhead in every room.

"My father built it. I remember helping after school and on weekends. Dad wanted me to be a carpenter, but I chose to be a doctor."

"Lucky for me and the dog. I appreciate all you've done, Tom."

"My pleasure, Son." Tom finished his coffee, leaned back in his chair, and almost fell over when Barney yelped loudly from the other room. Both men scrambled to their feet and ran quickly to his aid. Tom arrived ahead of Mitch and found Barney lying beside the couch, asleep, and kicking his free legs frantically.

"He's just dreaming," Tom said, "probably fighting the spotted bitch again." Mitch hobbled up, dragging his right foot. Out of breath, he staggered to the couch and tried to sit down, but he passed out and fell face first against the wooden arm of the couch. He rolled off onto the floor. Blood ran from his nose.

"Dammit, Boy," Tom said as he turned Mitch over and stretched him out. He jerked a pillow off the couch and placed it under his head. He ran to the linen closet in the hall and got his traveling medical bag and some towels. He had been one of the last doctors in Idaho to actually make house calls. Kneeling beside Mitch, he wiped blood off his swelling face. Mitch's shirt and the floor where he'd fallen were splattered with it.

His nose was badly broken.

"You damned fool. You just had to play it tough."

Barney was awake and trying to crawl to Mitch. "Lay still, Barn'," Tom said as Mitch moaned and opened his eyes. His first reaction was to reach for his nose.

"No you don't. I haven't set it yet."

"Set it? Huh? What happened?"

"You broke it when you fell on your face, after you ran in here, after you cleaned the kitchen, after you carried the dog outside and back, and after Lord knows what else you did that you should not have been on your feet doing. Lay still and *do not move*." He handed Mitch a towel.

"Hold that under your nose."

Tom walked to a roll-top desk in the corner and he took two pencils out of the middle drawer.

"I'll let the coffee slide, because to be honest with you, it wasn't that bad. However, the rest is *intolerable,* for a patient, anyway. Son, it's not that I don't appreciate your help, I do, but you are not well enough yet to do so much." Tom wiped more blood off Mitch's face and then he said, "Sit up and lean against the couch." With a sigh, Mitch released the pent up anger that had boiled up in him after Tom's barrage of reprimands. He scooted back against the couch.

"Better go ahead and sit *on* the couch. You might pass out again here in a bit." Tom paused a minute to catch his breath, then said, "I've got half a mind to roll up a washrag, stick it between your teeth and do this the old-fashioned way." He paused a second, then said,

"But I've got some Novocain going to waste. I might as well use it."

"OK," was all Mitch could manage at the moment.

Tom opened his bag, searched through it a minute and came out with a syringe kit and a clear bottle of liquid. A few minutes later, Mitch wasn't feeling much where his nose used to be.

In spite of the numbing affect of the local anesthetic, Mitch moaned a little when Tom set his nose. True to Tom's words Mitch nearly passed out again, but managed to stay conscious.

"Guess I didn't use enough anesthetic."

Barney barked loudly and Mitch groaned again.

"Shut up!" Tom said. Then he frowned at himself. "I'm sorry, Barn', I didn't mean that." The dog seemed to understand and grew silent, but remained tense in his posture as Mitch moved and groaned painfully again. Mitch started to reach for his nose but Tom stopped him.

"Easy, Son. Don't you dare touch that nose. You just leave it alone."

"I feel like I kissed a train. Aw, fuck! It hurts like hell."

"It ain't nothing like the hurt I'll put on you if you keep up the foolishness. And, if you use that language in my house again, you'll find your ass hoofin' it down the road.

"Now listen up . . . and listen well. Do not move any faster than a slow walk for the next three days. You think you're tough, but you're in worse shape than you know. I have a mind to take you straight to the hospital and let them handle you." Tom stopped ranting a minute to gently wipe blood off Mitch's face.

"Do not bend over. Do not pick up anything heavier than a glass of tea or a book. From now until I say dif-

ferent, you take it easy. You got that, Mister?" Tom
looked hard at Mitch, trying to appear mean, but Mitch
couldn't miss the kindness in the old man's eyes.

"Y-yes, S-S-Sir," he stuttered. "Whatever you say,
Doc. I swear I won't even strain to fart without your
permission." Tom doubled over. He laughed until his
eyes filled with tears and his belly ached. Barney
yapped excitedly, and even Mitch managed to chuckle,
but he didn't laugh. To laugh was to hurt, and he'd felt
more than his share of pain in the past few days.

"You're right, Tom." Mitch said after Tom regained
his composure. "As soon as I change my shorts, I'll lie
down and be a proper patient."

"You'd better." Tom said, "I'd hate to have to carry
you outside, too."

A half hour later, drugged and relatively comfortable
but thinking too much, Mitch watched the flames
dance around the logs in the fireplace. In spite of Tom's
hospitality and Barney's friendship, he was frightened
and lost. So many questions ran through his head and
sped so fast that it nearly made him dizzy. With each
question came a new jolt of fear, until his head
throbbed and the agony drove him to his knees, where
he beat the floor with his fists in anger and frustration
until Tom went to him and held him like a father would
hold a son.

He held Mitch and cursed fate for the torment that
he was suffering, for the obvious depression and anxiety he was feeling, and he cursed himself for not calling
someone. Tom knew it wouldn't take much to find out
who the man was and where he belonged, but Tom also
had to consider that Mitch was physically and mentally
damaged. Tom felt that Mitch wouldn't be able to handle the pressures of dealing with the public and a family he didn't know. He battled with his conscience, his

sworn duties as a doctor, and his loneliness while he tried to comfort the man and ease his fears.

Once again, his conscience won out.

"I'm taking you to the hospital tomorrow. We'll get you some help. We'll find your family."

"No! Not yet. I'm not ready."

"But someone must be looking for you."

"Then they are looking for someone else. The man I was doesn't exist. How can I go back?"

"I don't know, but don't you want to try? Your memory may come back if you see someone you know. Hold on a minute." Tom got up and went to the fireplace. He brought back the billfold that he'd found by the river.

"I found this downstream from Sampson's Ledge. It could be yours." He averted his eyes guiltily as he handed it to Mitch.

"There's not much in it, just some photos and a lot of money. I'm going to take Barney into the kitchen and redo his cast. See if those photos ring any bells."

Tom groaned as he picked up Barney and carried him to the kitchen table. He laid him down and removed the old cast. He was pleased to find a clean wound. The swelling had receded and Tom was able to examine the break more closely. He was satisfied that the leg would mend well. He cleansed it and made a new, slimmer cast. When it dried, Tom put him on the floor and Barney immediately took advantage of his new mobility and hobbled slowly outside to take care of business on his own. Tom sighed with relief and rubbed his sore back.

When Barney hobbled back in a few minutes later, Tom was sitting Mitch down at the dining room table. The dog watched anxiously but remained silent while Tom worked on his friend.

Professional, stone-faced, and serious, Tom probed

Mitch's swollen face. Mitch sat stock-still as Tom worked. The painkillers were taking effect, but not completely. Although he didn't utter another sound, tears from his watering eyes coursed down his cheeks and mixed with the blood that dripped from his nose and off his whiskered chin. Mitch's face had swollen until his nose was almost lost in it, making it tough for Tom to feel the position of the shattered bones and crushed cartilage.

"I'm sorry, Son. I know this is hurting something fierce, but unless you want to go to the hospital, or have a crooked nose...."

Tom let it lie as he felt Mitch jerk under his hands. Convinced he'd done all he could, he taped the mound that once was a nose.

Sitting down opposite Mitch, he said, "I did what I could. Only time will tell. We'll look at it again in a few days."

"Forget it," Mitch said. "If it ain't straight now, I'll live with it. I've had enough pain."

"You've had more than your share and taken it better than most. Sorry I had to put you through that." Tom heaved a big sigh and pulled himself wearily to his feet. He got them both a tall glass of iced tea...and some tranquilizers for Mitch.

"Don't touch your nose. Don't blow it for three weeks, and for Christ's sake, don't sneeze. The pain would knock you out, and Lord knows what else you'd break. The Valium will help ease your mental state. Natalie had anxiety attacks...."

Mitch nodded his head groggily in agreement and blinked his eyes sleepily. The medication Tom had given him earlier was about to put him down. Tom made his two patients comfortable and then retreated to his bedroom to rest.

Two hours later he was up again and preparing Mitch's room down the hall. He changed the sheets and opened the window to let fresh air in. He put Mitch's new clothes in the dresser and laid out toiletries in the adjoining bathroom. Before leaving the room, he stood at the open window and gazed out at his forest.

♠ ♠ ♠

Early evening found Mitch waking to the delicious aroma of homemade chili. He smiled, rolled over, and swung his feet off the couch. For a second he thought he might be sick, but the feeling passed and he made his way to the bathroom before going to the dining room to eat.

After a hearty supper of chili and beans over rice, and some good conversation, Mitch excused himself and returned to the bathroom to shower and shave. Afterward Tom re-taped his ribs and changed his bandages. He gave Mitch some more medication, and they all retired to bed early.

When Mitch awoke in the morning, Barney was sleeping on the floor beside his bed.

The next several days passed quickly and without incident. Both Barney and Mitch were healing fast and Tom was busy caring for them. Barney was never far from his new friend's side. Tom didn't really mind that Barney had taken to Mitch. It was enough to know that they were both alive and getting well. Tom didn't have time to be jealous, and when he thought about it, he realized that he was happier than he'd been since the death of his wife.

After five more days, Tom moved Mitch upstairs, knowing the climb would help to rebuild his stamina. When Mitch limped down the stairs the first morning,

Barney was waiting at the bottom. The second day Barney met him halfway, and on the third morning, Mitch awoke to find the dog beside his bed again. Mitch carried him down and continued to carry him down until one day Barney ran down by himself.

When Tom moved Mitch upstairs, he also allowed him to take short walks outside and each time out he returned with an armful of wood. Barney hobbled out onto the deck and watched as Mitch moved about.

Mitch and Tom had many long talks out there on the porch. They discussed politics, religion, philosophy, and, of course, the wilderness. Tom found Mitch to be quick-witted and intelligent. Mitch relished Tom's stories and words of wisdom gleaned from a lifetime in the mountains. Tom was impressed to find Mitch knew the names of most of the plants and trees around the cabin, including what was edible and what was good for medicine. But Mitch's old self wouldn't surface, and Tom found no more insight into his past via subconscious leaks.

They had talked about the photos in the billfold. Mitch didn't recognize them, but he kept the billfold handy and looked at them now and then, somehow drawn to the photos.

CHAPTER EIGHTEEN

I know you're out there, Honey. I know you're alive." Donna stared out the window at the snow-capped mountains. "I'll never give up on you. I hope you know that."

Donna had been standing at the window for half an hour. She stood there everyday, staring up at the mountains, praying, thinking, and longing for her husband. As she stood, entranced, she alternately turned her wedding ring around her finger and held Mitch's, which hung on a gold chain around her neck. Mitch never wore jewelry in the woods, not that he often wore his ring to begin with. He took care not to wear anything that would draw attention to him, nothing shiny, that is. She liked to tease him, saying that she knew he could have more fun without it.

She was so lost in thought that she failed to see her pastor drive up. She didn't see him get out of his car, didn't even know he was at the door until he knocked. Even then, it took a second to register. He knocked again as she opened the door.

"Hello, Donna. I hope I didn't come at a bad time."

"Good morning, Richard. Please come in; I wasn't doing anything."

"It is so quiet," the preacher said as she shut the door behind him.

"The house has been unnaturally quiet without Mitch. It seems like it is just sitting and waiting, like me. Would you like something to drink?"

"No, thank you; I have only a moment. I need to get back to my office and prepare Sunday's sermon."

"Well, I'm going to pour myself some coffee. Make yourself comfortable. I'll be right back." Donna whispered to herself as she turned and walked into the kitchen rather quickly, "God, I don't want to hear this sermon twice." She poured herself a cup of coffee, then picked up the phone and dialed Sherrie's number.

"What's on your mind, Richard?" Donna asked the aged pastor as she sat down beside him on the couch a minute later.

"Donna, I, ah, we, I mean the Church thinks you should consider going ahead with memorial services.

"No!" Donna cut him short. "I'll not have it."

"But it's been nearly a month, and with Mr. Gaines' body having been found, well, you must face it: Mitch is gone."

"Richard, I know he is gone, but that does not mean he is dead."

"People are beginning to talk. To put it bluntly, they think you've lost your mind"

Donna stood up. She walked over to the window.

"I couldn't care less."

The pastor looked at the carpet and sighed.

"Donna, you need to be thinking more about your-self, and of Steven. It may not seem like it now, but life does go on without those we've lost."

"Would you come here?" she asked, without turning around. He rose from the couch, stood motionless a moment. Debating with himself, choosing his words he walked up and stood beside her.

"I have a lot of experience here, Donna. I know...."

"What do you see out there?"

"I, ah, trees, cars. What am I supposed to see?"

"Look at the robin in the neighbor's yard. See the blossoms on the trees and bushes? Can't you see it? It's spring and everything is alive," she exclaimed, waving her arm across in front of her. Then she looked him in the eye. "And so is Mitch! Just as I can see it out there, I can feel it in here," she said, pointing at her heart. "I feel it with every beat. I don't care if people talk. I'm not crazy," she hissed. "I am grieved, but I am not disturbed. Mitch is alive up in those mountains." She pointed and looked north. "Somewhere up there, my husband is surviving, and I'm down here surviving. I shall have no more talk about services for the dead." As Donna's anger flared, she turned away from the window. "He is alive!" He backed away from the strength in her voice.

"OK, I'm sorry; I didn't mean to upset you."

"I'll be fine," she said as she sat back down with her coffee. He sat down beside her and decided to take a more subtle approach.

"I was wrong, talking you into something I knew you weren't ready for." He paused a moment to gather his thoughts. Donna sipped her coffee and glanced casually at her watch, then at the front door.

"I'm all ears if you want to talk about it," he said after a minute of awkward silence.

Donna heaved a big sigh.

"I'm sorry for shouting at you. I'm on edge these

days. It's just lonely without him."

"I know, dear. I know it must be hard on you. Let's talk about that. I've counseled hundreds of people who have lost family or loved ones. You should be terribly grief-stricken, yet you are the picture of confidence and strength. What is it that keeps you going?"

"Why, preacher, I am surprised at you. *Faith* is what keeps me going. It is my faith in God."

"Yes, I know, but I have never seen it so strong, never in all my life."

"I found it years ago, and I dare not lose it. My faith is what keeps my two men and me going. Wherever Mitch is, he needs it; he needs me to be strong. I cannot let him down anymore than God would let you or me down. "I'm going to make you a promise. I give you my word. You watch the entrance to the sanctuary. Keep a watchful eye on it because before those new leaves outside turn gold, Mitch will walk with me through those doors."

The front door flew open and Sherrie blurted, "Are you ready?"

"Oh my gosh! I forgot. Richard, I have to go. Sherrie and I have a racquetball court in fifteen minutes," she said as she looked at her watch.

"Sher', let me change quickly. Forgive me. Thanks for stopping by. She turned to Sherrie. "Would you see the preacher out for me?" She ran up the stairs, stopping halfway. She looked down at Sherrie and the bewildered pastor.

"Richard, you never did tell me what Sunday's sermon is going to be about."

He stopped with his hand on the doorknob.

"I was going to preach on faith."

CHAPTER NINETEEN

EARLY MAY

T he sun hadn't yet begun to push away the darkness when Mitch opened his eyes. The birds still had their heads tucked beneath their wings, asleep among the bushes beneath the pines.

He stared into the darkness, listening. All was quiet. It was the first time he'd awakened before Tom. He rolled onto his side and turned on the reading lamp. Barney looked up at him from beside the bed and then yawned.

Mitch sat on the bed a few minutes, thinking. Tomorrow they would be going down to get the horses. That excited him somehow, but the thought of going to the city made him uneasy.

"Mornin', dog," Mitch mumbled. "Feeling frisky today?"

Thumping the floor with his cast, Barney jumped to his feet, wagging his tail enthusiastically.

"So am I. Let's fix breakfast this morning; give Tom a break." Barney answered by running quickly out the door and down the hall. Mitch heard the thumping of plaster against wood as the dog ran down the stairs on his own. He hoped it hadn't wakened Tom.

Barney was waiting at the side door off the kitchen. Mitch let him out and stood at the threshold taking in the crisp freshness of the pine-scented morning. He wondered where his real home was and hoped it was at least half as wild and wonderful.

Barney returned from his rounds, and Mitch closed the door quietly behind them.

"Lie down and be quiet now. We don't want to wake Tom." The dog jumped up on the couch and flopped down.

Mitch built up the fire. The thermometer at the back door registered 36 degrees, and it was a bit chilly inside. In a few minutes logs crackled, the chill was in retreat, and Mitch was heating vegetable oil and peeling potatoes for frying. He laid out ten slices of bacon and set the flame on low as he'd watched Tom do. Then he put on a pot of coffee and fed the dog.

In a few minutes, the aroma of fresh brewed coffee floated around the kitchen and stealthily down the hall, eventually steeling its way into Tom's room.

Tom's eyes fluttered open and he checked his watch. His moustache bent in the middle as he caught the smell of coffee. He walked into the kitchen twenty minutes later, freshly shaved, just as Mitch was cracking the last egg into the pan.

"Mornin'," Mitch said with a grin. "You didn't specifically say I that couldn't cook."

Tom sat down in his chair. Curious and amused, he watched, silent, as Mitch finished at the stove.

"Enjoy," Mitch said, handing Tom his breakfast, "I'll

bring the coffee."

Mitch sat across from Tom and poured them a cup, then bowed his head while Tom gave thanks. The blessing said, Tom picked up his cup, gazed at Mitch from under bushy eyebrows, and then carefully sipped his coffee. Mitch leaned back in his chair as Tom's penetrating gaze bored into him. He wondered if he wasn't about to see another side of Tom. He jumped and winced when Tom set his cup down too hard, spilling coffee on the checkered cloth. Tom glared at Mitch, causing him to wonder whether he should have stayed in bed.

"This coffee," Tom roared, "*if* you can call it that... ain't bad at all." He grinned. "If the rest of this meal is as good, then you're hired. Let's eat."

Mitch beamed, knowing it was going to be a good day.

After breakfast, Tom hiked to the barn with Barney limping at his heels. Mitch cleaned up in the kitchen. He was feeling good. His head seldom hurt now and his side bothered him only when he rolled over in his sleep. Except for his nose, his outward appearance was that of a healthy man. On the inside, however, he was not feeling as well. Granted, Tom and Barney had become family, and Mitch was glad that he'd accepted Tom's hospitality. Tom was like a father to him, and he knew that Tom was fond of the position. For now, Mitch was happy, but he knew it wouldn't suffice for long. He was aware of an emptiness deep within. As much as he'd come to care for Tom and his beautiful, brave dog, Mitch knew that he'd soon be leaving.

Finally finished with the inside chores, Mitch decided to get some fresh air. When he thumped onto the veranda, he heard Barney barking down at the barn. He breathed deeply of the mountain air, rubbed his face, and limped down to see what was up.

The barn was a hundred yards downhill from the cabin, and he wondered if he could make it back up; Tom's land was not exactly flat. In fact, it was quite steep in places. The slope behind the cabin was no exception.

The building was taller than the two-story cabin and more than twice its length. It was situated on a flat spot angling from the northeast to the southwest. Mitch could see the open doors of the loft on the northwest end as he approached from the north. The main doors to the barn were on the northeast to his left, and he could see they were also open. As he drew close, he saw a little brown-and-white ball of fur speed out with Barney hobbling clumsily after it. The dog abruptly forgot the chipmunk when he saw Mitch coming down the hill. He jumped up and down, yipping gleefully, oblivious of the cast on his leg.

"What's all the excitement about," he heard Tom yell. Then Tom stepped out of the barn, saw Mitch, and waved.

"What's up?" Mitch asked.

"I'm cleaning water buckets and feed troughs. Then I have stalls to prepare."

"Can I help?"

"I tell you what. It's apparent I can't keep you down. So from now on, you're on your own. Just don't complain to me if you overdo it again."

"Thanks; I've got cabin fever. If I don't get out and do something I'll go nuts."

"Start by cleaning out the stalls. Get them down to fresh dirt. They need to be level and flat. When you get them that way, throw in about eight inches of sawdust. There's a shovel and rake in the tack shed at the west end."

"I'll get right on it," Mitch said, eager to get to work. He was ready to make himself useful. He took stock of the barn and its layout as he made his way to the tack shed. A familiar feeling flooded his heart and soul.

"Just the first two stalls on the side nearest the river," Tom yelled, "the others have never been used."

Mitch nodded and hobbled down the length of the barn. Separating the two sides of the barn and running the length was an indoor arena. Mitch noticed a truckload of sawdust had recently been dumped in one corner. Friendly smells of straw, old wood, horse manure, mice, and grain enticed him. Birds chirped in the rafters overhead and something scurried softly across the plank floor of the loft. Halfway down the isle between the arena and the stalls Mitch suddenly stopped and stood quiet, strangely feeling that he'd been there before. He bent and scooped up a handful of dirt and let if filter through his fingers.

The tack room awaited him. It called to him. Suddenly he couldn't wait to get inside. He opened the door, took one step and froze in his tracks. A pair of beautifully handcrafted western saddles graced the back wall. Behind the saddles, hanging on pegboard, were numerous bridles, halters, spurs, chaps and ropes. The air was saturated with the smell of oiled leather and horse sweat. It was a pleasant smell in any western man's opinion.

Goose bumps rose on Mitch's skin and he was overwhelmed by it. He leaned against the doorjamb, feeling quite homesick, but for what, he didn't know.

Then he felt Tom's strong hand on his shoulder.

"Are you alright, Son?"

Mitch replied. "I walked in, saw all this, and felt like I'd found an old friend. I feel homesick, Tom. Everything is familiar. I know I've worn chaps. I've had spurs on my boots. I have raised horses, and I've worked cattle. I can tell you how to imprint a horse, how to raise him up healthy, and to love the company of human beings. I can train for roping and cutting; for reigning and team penning; for trail and western pleasure. I know these things. I've used all this equipment, I know all this, but I can't remember a single day of it."

"Be patient, it'll come."

"Man, I hope so. I sure hope so."

"I'll be in the corral if you need me," Tom said. "Don't overdo it. If you get tired, just leave it for later."

"I'll be fine."

Mitch spent some time in the tack room, running his hands over the saddles, fingering the bridles and the halters. He held the spurs in his hands and spun the rowels. They seemed like old classmates at a high school reunion, with faces he remembered, but names he couldn't recall. He hung the spurs back up and then got to work, for once wanting to forget something, to shake the homesickness.

He worked hard, and in no time he had both stalls leveled and raked smooth. By then, Tom was finished out back and came to help.

Mitch scarcely knew he was working as he and Tom labored most of the morning getting the barn and stables in order. Tom kept a concerned eye on Mitch as they worked, and by the time they were finished he was certain that the work was not new to his friend. Also, Mitch's ease with the tools and his *apparent* lack of weariness were good signs that he was on the way to a full recovery.

They finished a little after ten and made their way up the hill to the cabin. Tom let Mitch set the pace.

"Whew! I'm beat," Mitch said as he fell onto the couch. "Guess I'm still not as fit as I used to be."

"Chop some wood," Tom said a split second after he noticed how Mitch referred to his past health. His life was there, almost ready to come out. It would come soon, but selfishly, he hoped not too soon.

"Do what?"

"An hour or so a day at the chopping block will build up every muscle in your upper body and some in your legs as well, especially if you alternate and swing the axe from both sides. It might seem awkward at first to chop left-handed, but you'll get used to it. I've enough wood to keep you busy for a month, and I'll be cutting some more as soon as we get back from Boise. I'll even pay you for what it's worth."

"I can't take your money after all you've done. But you're right. If my memory doesn't return, well...I suppose I'll just have to go after it."

Tom laughed heartily.

"You sure have a way with words, but let's cross that rickety bridge when we get to the crick. Are you hungry?"

"Does a skunk stink?"

"Yeah," Tom said, "but not nearly as bad as you. Where's the deodorant I gave you?"

"Deodorant? I thought that was air freshener; I stuck it under your bed."

"You can eat raw bear meat with the dog; I'm going to fry me up a thick beef steak." With that, Tom turned and left the room. Mitch laughed and said, "I like mine medium-rare. Pink, but not bloody."

Mitch said just loud enough for Tom to hear, "I bet he doesn't even know how to cook a decent steak, Barney," Barney jumped up on the couch beside him. "Reckon I should show him how?"

Suddenly Mitch leapt off the couch with a high-pitched howl as Tom poured ice-cold water down his back.

"You ornery old coot!" Mitch shouted. "What'd ya do that for?"

"Ornery? Ha! You don't know ornery yet. You keep bad mouthin' my cookin' and I'll show you a side of ornery you've never seen."

"You old devil," Mitch exclaimed, shivering. "I'll get you for this. You better watch your back, old man, because I'm layin' for ya."

"Go take a shower, you ungrateful pup. Like I said, you stink."

"Dawg, how do ya put up with that crazy, mean, old, flea-bitten, sad excuse fer a doctor? If he weren't the main cook in this here house, I'd shoot him and put us out of our misery." Mitch thought a second, caught his breath, and then said, "Naw, that'd be a waste of gunpowder. Then we'd have to bury him. So I guess we're stuck with him."

Tom turned his back on the two of them and highstepped it into the kitchen, laughing all the way. Mitch followed and offered to help. Tom said he didn't need any greenhorn telling him how to cook. So, Mitch took a shower, suggesting that Tom do the same.

"Barney, that youngster should have been my son," Tom said a few minutes later. Tom gazed at a photo of his late wife that hung in the dining room. "What do you think? Wouldn't he have made us a fine son?" Barney, sensing a sudden mood change in Tom, crept from the room.

"Damn you, Jeremy!" Tom cursed loudly. "Why'd you turn bad? Nat', what did we do wrong?"

Overhead, not yet in the shower, Mitch heard every word. It left him proud, sad, and puzzled.

"That was a fine meal, Tom," Mitch said an hour later. "I can honestly say that was the best steak I can remember eating."

"You're worn out, aren't you?"

"A little," Mitch admitted.

"In a week or two you'll feel as good as new. Get some rest; I'll clean up in here."

Mitch pushed back from the table and retired to the living room, where he pulled off his boot and stretched out on the couch. Barney fell out on the floor at his feet, and within minutes both were sound asleep.

Tom finished in the kitchen, showered, then sat in his recliner and smoked his pipe. It wasn't long before the pipe went cold in his hand. A dozen species of birds twittered and flew about outside as a doe and her fawn trotted silently across the yard. Tom snored while Mitch and Barney slept in silence. In the kitchen, a mouse dined on a crumb it found beside the stove.

An armada of clouds sailed lazily across a powder blue sky while the pines swayed in the cool breeze. Inside, the three rested from the morning's work, while outside, the forest was alive and busy. Bees gathered nectar from the wild-flowers and roses bursting forth from the fertile earth. The squirrels and chipmunks gathered pine nuts as butterflies fluttered everywhere.

The fawn, never out of his mother's view, playfully pranced stiff-legged across the meadow that was Tom's front yard. He arched his back like a bucking horse and crow hopped over to the forest's edge, where he stopped before a blackberry bush and stretched his shiny black nose toward a butterfly that was exercising its large wings in the crisp mountain air. The fawn licked his nose and tentatively leaned closer, stamping his right hoof, bobbing his head, mocking his mother, trying to fool the insect into moving.

The butterfly remained still, except to flex its wings. The fawn's curiosity urged it forth; his inquisitive nature prompted him to action. He touched it and then jumped two feet in the air when the butterfly flew from its perch in retreat.

An hour ticked by, then another. The sun, like a large apricot floating in the sky, reached its zenith and began a downward trek toward the horizon. Barney awakened beside Mitch, sat up, and sidled closer. Laying his muzzle lightly on Mitch's shoulder, he huffed softly in his ear. Mitch opened his eyes and turned his head as Barney looked toward the front door. After letting the dog out, Mitch returned to the couch, put his boot on and limped quietly onto the veranda.

Tom re-lit his pipe.

Mitch carried an armful of logs to the chopping block. He split several logs right-handed, then, as Tom had suggested, he switched to his left and tried to chop another. It was so awkward that he immediately switched back to his right. From the window where he watched, the old man laughed. Swinging from his right the axe moved easily in Mitch's hands. He soon found an easy rhythm and began splitting logs cleanly with one stroke. He worked steadily for almost an hour, while Tom read a magazine. Then, finally winded, Mitch sat down on the veranda to take a break. Barney ran from where he'd been watching in the shade at the side of the house and sat down beside him.

"How ya doin', fella?"

Barney answered with a wag of his tail.

"I know, I'm still sore in a few places my own self." He looked over the dog's healing cuts, and his mind wandered back to the day Barney found him. Had it been fate? Was he destined to arrive there, from wherever he came? Were the three of them thrown together for a reason? He rubbed Barney's ears, and Barney pushed against his hand. Mitch laughed and roughed him up. The dog rose up on his hind feet and nipped at him playfully.

Tom chuckled, watching from the window. Mitch threw a stick for Barney who ran clumsily after it and picked it up. He promptly brought it back but wouldn't give it to Mitch, who wrestled it from him and threw it again. As he returned it a second time he saw Tom in the window, dropped the stick, and barked loudly. Mitch turned, saw the curtains fall and a second later Tom stepped outside to join them.

"You've found a friend."

"I've found a couple."

"You handle that axe pretty good, right-handed, that is."

"Why, you old coot. You set me up so you could have a good laugh."

"Maybe," Tom said, unable to stifle his laughter."

"Go ahead; laugh it up; your turn is coming."

"I bet you are just as good with a rope."

"Only one way to find out," Mitch said as he stooped to pick up a stray chunk of wood by the porch, throwing it over by the chopping block.

"I'm not a cowboy like you," Tom said, "but I like to ride. I haven't ridden since Natalie died. We used to ride most every day."

"I'm not sure I'm s*till* a cowboy, but it feels right, in some respects. Then again, I get this feeling there's more to me than that." He carried an armful of firewood to the veranda. Tom had enough firewood to last a month. By then summer would be on the way and he'd need less each day, but he was preparing for next winter. He'd spend the next two months of pleasant weather gathering, splitting, and drying the next year's supply.

Tom pitched in and they had it all stacked in just a

few minutes.

Barney even tried to help, dragging a chunk of split wood up onto the steps. Mitch took it from him and threw it on the stack.

"I wonder if we could teach him to cook," Tom suggested.

"I wouldn't. He might want to eat at the table."

"Might as well," Tom replied, "he's got to have better manners than we do. Come inside; I've got a fresh pitcher of tea; figured you'd be thirsty."

"Yes, Sirree!"

Mitch leaned back on the couch and drank deeply of his tea as Tom stood at the window and sipped his. Barney rested outside, yearning to run through the forest.

"He misses having the freedom to chase those critters. I don't let him get away with it much. I like having them around."

Mitch sucked on a piece of ice and wondered about Tom. What he'd said earlier bothered him but he didn't pry.

"The wife used to bake a dandy chocolate cake," Tom said suddenly. "I have the recipe, and I've got a sweet tooth. Sound good to you?"

"Sounds great to me," Mitch said, thoughtfully fingering his mustache.

"I'll get it in the oven, and later, while it's cooling we'll run into town and I'll treat us to supper at the café."

Mitch's face grew taught, and he began to pace the floor. A sudden uneasiness turned his stomach and he broke out in a cold sweat. Part of him wanted to scream, part of him wanted to run, but he forced himself to breathe deep and within a few moments he calmed himself down. He walked outside and stood on

163

the veranda, watching the pines swaying at their tops, breathing their tangy fragrance.

"You, OK?" Tom asked from the doorway.

"I'm just a little anxious about going to town."

"If you'd rather stay here, we can do that, but I thought it would be nice to get out."

"No, I'll be fine. It'll do me good to get around other people. I thought I was prepared; was looking forward to going with you to get the horses, but when you get right down to it it's pretty damned scary.

"But, I've got it to do. Might as well climb down on this bronc and let her buck."

He sighed.

"And I want this doggone cast off my leg. The itching is driving me nuts." He stepped down off the veranda. "I'm going for a walk."

Mitch headed for the woods. Barney jumped up from where he'd been lying and followed. Tom turned and went inside; knowing what was coming, but not yet ready for it.

An hour and a half later, the cake was cooling on the dining room table and the two men were halfway to town.

"People are going to be curious about me," Mitch suggested. "Have you thought about that?"

"We'll say you are a family friend, up from Texas, recuperating from an accident."

"Sounds fine with me, but I need a name."

"Hadn't thought about that much lately," Tom said. "The initials on the knife, do they ring a bell? What's the first name that comes to you?"

"Nothing comes to mind."

"Well, I've been thinking and I've got a nickname for you. What would you say if I called you, Steel?"

"Steel?"

"Yeah," Tom said. "Like the blade of that knife, you've yet to be broken. It fits you."

"And if need be, you can take Natalie's last name: Freeman.

"I guess it'll work," Mitch said, liking the sound of it.

Mitch sat quiet, thinking, then said, "I guess that'll work, but I don't feel much like a free man. I'm trapped, Tom. I'm trapped outside of myself. Some nights I lie awake staring at the ceiling, trying to remember, but my mind is as blank as the ceiling is dark. I'm vacant, empty; tapped dry."

He fell silent.

"Maybe you shouldn't try so hard. Stop trying to force it, just let it come back of its own accord. Do you want me to give you another Valium?"

Mitch shook his head and continued to gaze at the forest until Tom drove around a corner and the lights of town jumped out at them.

"Riggins," Tom said. "Ain't much to the place aside from a spot in the road. In fact, there are just four hundred and nine of us." He turned right at the first stop sign, the radial tires squealing on the pavement, and then turned left into a small lot beside an old but well-maintained diner.

"This is the Around the Corner Café. Best eatin' around here, except for my own, of course. Don't tell Clara I said that. She'll run us out with a broom. She's been known to do it for less."

Tom chuckled as he stepped out of the Suburban. "I'll never forget the tongue-lashing she gave this guy one day as she swatted him out the door. That feller'd just as well been shot, and all he did was complain that there was too much pepper in the gravy."

"Sounds like a real nice lady."

"Whoa! Don't jump to conclusions. She's not lady-like, she's, well, you'll see."

"Well, look what the horse shit," roared a large, buxom, rosy-cheeked woman and answered Mitch's question.

"How the hell you doin', Tom?"

"Doin' fine, Clara. What's cookin'?"

"What's cookin'?" she roared. "I'm cookin'! That's what's cookin'. I'm the best durned cook this side of the mountain. Ain't I, Sam?"

"Uh huh," mumbled an elderly man sipping coffee at the counter. "Hey, Tom, ain't seen ya fer a while. Doin' awright?"

"I'm fine, Sam. You know me and the woods," Tom replied as he and Mitch sat down in a booth by the front window. Clara came out from behind the counter to greet them, handing them a menu. She glanced curiously at Mitch.

"Clara," Tom said politely, "I'd like you to meet Steel. He's up from Texas." He winked at Mitch.

"Hello, Steel." She held out a beefy hand. "That's a unique name."

"Hello, Ma'am, pleased to meet you," he said as he took her hand and shook it once, firmly but gently.

"I hope whoever hit you got what he deserved," she commented.

"He was in an accident," Tom said. "He's up here to recuperate."

"Well, this is the place for it. I'll give you guys a few minutes to look at the menus. Tea for both of you?"

"That'll work for me," Tom said.

"And for me as well," Mitch said.

"You watch out, Steel, don't let that old fart do any doctorin' on ya. Last feller he doctored was buried the next day."

Tom just looked at Mitch and grinned.

"She's a hoot for sure."

"Sounds like she'd be good to ride the river with," Mitch said and wondered where he came up with such a remark.

When she came back with the tea, Tom ordered steak, fries, and salad for the both of them.

"Man, that is a *big* woman," Mitch said.

"And she's as strong as a lumberjack," Tom said around a chunk of ice. "Her husband and her oldest son are both timber men, and her daughter won't be messed with either. None of them are less than six feet tall. Not to change the subject, of course that might be safe, but are you planning on keeping that beard?"

Mitch rubbed his face, and raised a thoughtful eyebrow, thinking that it was none of Tom's business. However, he said, "I don't know for sure. I tried to shave the day you bought me the razor, but my face hurt too much. Now I like the way it looks. I'll keep it for a week or two, see how it does."

"Here's your salad, boys," Clara said as she came out from behind the counter. "I put an extry slice of tomato on yours, cowboy, because yer the best lookin' feller I've had in here this year, even if you do have a broken nose and half a beard." She turned on her heels as his mouth fell open, and she disappeared into the kitchen as quick as she came.

Tom laughed heartily.

"I forgot to tell you, she likes cowboys."

"How could she tell?"

"You don't have to be wearing the garb, Son. A cowboy is like a soldier. It doesn't matter what he wears; you can always pick him out of a crowd. It's more how he carries himself than anything else. It has more to do with bearing, attitude, and character. Son, like you said in the barn, you either are, or have been, a real working cowboy. There isn't a doubt in my mind. And that's a good thing."

Clara walked up with a pitcher of tea and filled their glasses while making eyes at Mitch.

"Your steaks will be done in a few minutes. Steel, what would you like on yours, ketchup or steak sauce? Lot of folks around here like ketchup."

"Just sprinkle it with salt, pepper, and garlic powder, and it'll be fine," Mitch said. "Why spoil a good steak with fancy sauces?"

"Where did you say you were from?" she asked.

"Texas."

"Well, Darlin', if ever I decide to find me another man, that's the first place I'll look, and don't be surprised if I come looking fer you. Tom, you could learn something from this gentleman."

"You'd be surprised at what this feller's been teachin' this old man. Now quitcherjawin' and go fetch our supper; we're hungry."

"I'll get your supper, Tom, but you watch your mouth or I'll send your butt out on the business end of my broom." Clara spun on her heels and was gone. Some big people move with uncanny speed, and she was no slouch. She disappeared behind the counter and came back a few minutes later with their steaks and all the trimmings.

"Have at it boys," she said pleasantly, leaving them to their meal. They had their work cut out; she'd given them the biggest, thickest steaks she had.

Clara was back in the kitchen when they finished eating. They waited a few minutes, then they got up and Tom left a nice tip. He strolled full-bellied to the cash register while Mitch waited by the door, full as a tick.

"Clara," Tom hollered, "are you going to let me pay

for my supper?" He heard her answer from somewhere in back.

"Must be taking out the garbage," Tom muttered.

"Doesn't she have any help?" Mitch asked.

"Can't keep help," Clara said as she reappeared behind the counter as if from out of nowhere. She wiped her brow with a towel. "Whew! It's hot back there. Can't find anybody willing to work as hard as I push and for what I can afford to pay. So I end up working alone most of the time. I really don't mind. I actually enjoy it. Been running this place mostly by myself for fifteen years, and with any luck I'll do it for another fifteen."

She gave Tom the check.

"That was a fine meal, Clara," Mitch said from the door.

"That goes for me, too," Tom agreed as he withdrew his billfold and paid the check.

"Oh my," She said suddenly. "I plumb forgot to ask if you wanted dessert. I just pulled an apple pie out of the oven. Can I cut you a slice?"

"I'm already stuffed to the gills," Tom said, "but thanks anyway."

"Well, how about you, good-lookin'?"

Mitch grinned and let go of the door. He walked boldly up to Clara, took her right hand in his, and kissed it lightly.

"Ma'am, you're a fine cook, and the sweetest woman I've ever met. I'd consider it a pleasure to partake of such a delight, but I'm afraid I'll have to agree with Tom. However, I assure you that I'll be back, and when I do return I'd appreciate it if you would have a slice waiting. Good day, Ma'am." He kissed her hand again, and without further adieu, he followed Tom out the door, leaving Clara speechless. Sam chuckled from down the counter, where he still sat, slowly sipping his coffee.

Outside, Tom said, "Our cake will be better."

"Maybe," Mitch said, as they both burst out laughing. Tom slapped Mitch on the back.

"Damnedest thing I've ever seen. Did you see the look on her face? That woman will never be the same. You have the gift for gab, Son. Wow! I'd give my right arm to see that again."

Inside, still flabbergasted over Mitch, Clara was cleaning up their table and the one next to it. Lying on the seat behind where Mitch had been sitting was yesterday's paper. The headlines jumped out at her.

SEARCH FOR BOISE CITY COUNCILMAN
MITCHELL ANTHONY "MAC" COOPER
HAS BEEN ABANDONED

Clara saw Mitch's picture below the bold print and turned to Sam.

"Hey, doesn't this look like the man who was with Tom?"

She showed the paper to him.

"Maybe a little, but that man had a beard and a different name, and I heard Tom say he was from Texas."

"Yeah, I know, but there's something about this photo." She smiled. "What a gentleman he was, and such a flirt."

"You asked for it," Sam said.

"Yeah, I suppose I did." Clara looked at the photo again.

"I see a resemblance."

"You're just dreaming. That feller's done swelled yer brain and you're seein' things."

"You're probably right, Sam," she said and tossed

the paper in the trash. "But the look in Tom's eyes said that he was up to no good. They couldn't wait to get out of here."

Mitch stayed in the truck with Barney while Tom ran into the store. Tom was scarcely gone before he returned with a small sack of groceries.

"Thanks for supper," Mitch said as they pulled out onto the highway.

"My pleasure! Lord, that was something to see. Where did you come up with that?"

"Heck! I don't know. It was like someone else was talking. I even shocked myself."

"She is a good cook, isn't she?" Tom said.

"Almost as good as you."

"Good answer," Tom said. "If she knew the real reason we declined dessert she'd have run us out for sure."

"She was big enough to do it," Mitch agreed.

"And it wouldn't have been the first time. That old gal used to cook for the logging crews and she ran a sight of those boys off for a lot less. It's a good thing she's mellowed out over the years."

They were quiet for a few minutes, then Tom said, "It's going to be chilly tonight. You'd best get a fire going as soon as we get back. I'll frost the cake and set the table, and then we can celebrate."

"What's the occasion?"

"Barney's anniversary! It just occurred to me that it was four years ago today that he wandered up."

Back at the cabin, Mitch grabbed an armful of wood, carried it in with him, and stacked it in the bin beside the fireplace.

"Tom, where's the hatchet?"

"If it's not in the bin, then it's behind the front door."

The hatchet was not in the wood bin, so Mitch

looked and found it behind the door beside the broom.

"Mitch, Mitch, honey, wake up!" Mitch stood up slowly, his head pounding. His mind reeled with a vision of a woman walking naked through the fog. Then he saw her wielding a broom. She chased him. He felt suffocated, choked with panic. Nevertheless, as quickly as Donna's voice escaped his subconscious, it returned from whence it came. He just stood there, shaking, disoriented.

He yelled for Tom and Tom came running in to find Mitch standing behind the door, pale and shaken.

"My Lord, Son, what's wrong?"

"Didn't you hear it?"

"Hear what?" Tom asked, puzzled.

"I heard a woman calling the name, *Mitch*. She was calling for *me*. Then I saw her, at least I think I did."

"Son, I didn't hear anything. Man, you look like you've seen a ghost. Come in here and sit down a minute."

"No, I'm alright, but I think I just remembered something." Mitch found the hatchet in his hand, turned, and walked slowly and deliberately to the fireplace.

"I have to chop some kindling."

"Are you sure you're alright?" Tom asked, following him, worriedly fingering his mustache, frowning with concern.

"Yeah, Tom, I'm fine. It just happened so quickly. One second I hear a woman calling my name...."

Tom caught his breath and held it as Mitch faltered, took a half step, and then stopped in his tracks.

"She called me, *Mitch*." He spoke slowly, his voice trembling with emotion. "I'm, Mitch. My name is, Mitch."

Mitch turned and stepped to the hearth as Tom released his breath in a long sigh of relief.

"The next thing I know, I see a woman, a naked woman, walking away from me. Then she chased me out of a house, with a broom. Then I felt trapped. It was like I was buried alive. Then it was gone, she was gone. Gone like that. Mitch snapped his fingers.

"Do you know her?"

"No," Mitch said, "but it's the same woman in the photos in the billfold you found."

He removed a chunk of wood from the bin and placed it in front of him. Tom watched as Mitch expertly cut it into thin strips.

Thoughtfully, Tom returned to the kitchen.

Tom had been lonesome to the point of lunacy before Mitch came along. He accepted that Mitch couldn't stay forever, but he wondered if it would be so wrong to do nothing to help him on his way. However, his thoughts were betrayed by his nature. He knew he'd do all he could. He owed Mitch that. He owed him for saving his life.

Tom finished the cake and set the table. Mitch came into the dining room as Tom was pouring them both a glass of milk.

"Have a seat...Mitch." Tom was not yet comfortable with the name. "Let's eat and talk about it." Barney flopped down beside Mitch.

Tom had set three plates and he laid one on the floor in front of the dog. However, knowing chocolate was bad for dogs; Barney's plate was heaped with dog biscuits.

"Happy Anniversary, Mutt. Make yourself sick." Tom sat across from Mitch and said, "I think I'll do the same." Mitch didn't say anything; he made it a point never to talk with his mouth full.

Tom lifted a big forkful to his mouth, closed his eyes, and tasted it slowly. Then he took another bite with ice cream.

"I think I've just died and gone to heaven," Mitch said. "What do you think about all this, Barney?" Barney just wagged his bushy tail and crunched another biscuit.

"Not bad at all, Tom. If you don't mind, I'll have another slice."

"Cut another for me, too," Tom said. Then, "I was right, Mitch, it would have been easier to bury you than it is feeding you."

"You've no room to talk, old man," Mitch said, feeling ornery.

"Yeah, I eat a lot," Tom said, "but that's because I work so hard taking care of you and the mutt. Of course, he isn't near the trouble you are. He knows when to stop hurting himself."

Mitch pretended not to hear, making short work of his cake, but when Tom took a break from razzing him, he took his own shot.

"Why you crotchety old fart, you won't admit it, but you haven't enjoyed life this much in a month of Sundays. You're just rattlin' on because you don't know any better. Keep it up and I'll sue you for malpractice. I'll claim you set my nose crooked on purpose because you were jealous of my good looks. I'll call Barney up as my witness. He saw it all. And if that ain't enough, I'll claim you've been poisoning me with that slop you call stew, even if I do like it."

Tom eyed Mitch sharply at that last remark but finished his dessert without further comment. Mitch finished his, pushed back his chair, leaned back, and sipped his milk, waiting with a silly grin on his face.

Tom drank his milk, and then with jaws tight and a firm mouth, he glared angrily at Mitch.

"Why you big, lazy, ugly, bum. I ought to get my ra-

zor strop and tan your ornery hide. Didn't your mother
teach you to respect your elders? Oh, I forgot, you don't
have a mother. A buzzard crapped on a fence post and
the sun hatched you out."

Mitch lost it and the room filled with their laughter
and the joyous barking of a beautiful golden dog.

"Did you hear that, Barney?" Mitch said, clutching
at his belly, "That flea-bitten scoundrel called me an
overgrown buzzard turd. Well, for all we know he could
be right."

"Smells like rain," Tom said a half hour later over
his *Western Horseman* magazine. He'd been reading a
short story about pioneer life in Wyoming, written by a
young man from Texas by the name of Mike Lamb.
Mitch sniffed the air as he set aside Tom's worn copy of
"Walden," by Henry David Thoreau.

"Mm, it sure does," he said. "Old Henry must have
been tough to live like he did, completely relying on
what he could find and trade for to build his shack,
and brave the elements like he did without any of the
modern amenities of his day."

"He was different; ruggedly independent. Few in today's society could do as he did."

"Well, you're not that much different from him. I noticed you don't have a television or radio, at least I
haven't seen any around the place."

"We didn't watch a lot of television. I have a small
set up in our room. I keep track of the news and that's
about it. I might watch a movie from time to time but
there's not much on the air that intrigues me, except
perhaps the Discovery and History channels."

Tom removed his reading glasses and set them on
the oak end table beside his chair. He rubbed his tired
eyes thoughtfully for a second, then packed and lit his
pipe. He puffed on it a moment, then called Barney to

his side. The dog hobbled sorely over, the worn and dirty cast thumping noisily on the hardwood floor, and placed his chin on Tom's left knee, wagging his tail contentedly. Tom petted him with a loving hand.

"The news these days is bad enough; but other than the Discovery-type channels, most of the crap on TV doesn't cut the mustard with me. What they call Prime Time is nothing but sex and violence. We used to have a big set down here but I gave it away after Natalie passed. She enjoyed craft shows and such."

He grew silent again, remembering.

"As for a radio, I don't have one down here, but I like music--country, classical, the old rock & roll. Well, I take that back. When it comes to country, I like some of it. But I can't abide cheating songs. Natalie loved singing along with the radio. She had a beautiful voice. She kept a radio in the kitchen, but I put it away because every song reminded me of her." Tom's bottom lip quivered and tears misted his eyes. His voice shaking, he said, "I can bring the TV and radio down if you want to use them."

"No, I don't need them," Mitch said. "I'm sorry. I didn't mean to upset you, I was just curious."

Barney whined and pulled away from Tom, limping to the door. Tom pushed himself out of his recliner and followed to let him out. Mitch got up and met them at the door, giving Tom a friendly pat on the back.

"Keep your grief if you need it, but when you are ready to let it go, I'll be here."

"Thanks, Son, I know."

"I think I'll take a walk, Tom. I need to stretch my legs and think about some things. Mind if I take Barney?"

"I reckon it's alright, Mitch, just don't overdo it."

"I like that name," Mitch said as he donned a light

jacket that Tom had given him. Tom watched as they wandered into the woods toward the east. Barney danced clumsily around Mitch. He watched until the forest closed its arms around them, then he wiped the mist out of his eyes and turned from the door. He eased his old bones back into his recliner, sighed heavily, put on his reading glasses, and picked up his magazine.

Mitch and Barney only walked two hundred yards or so before tiring. Mitch sat down and leaned against a tree. He picked up a dry pine needle and picked his teeth. Barney rested his head on his lap.

"Tom's a wonderful old man, Barney." The dog looked up and swished his tail across the mat of needles that covered the ground beneath the tree. They sat in the midst of the forest, listening to the crickets, the wind, and the song of the whippoorwill. Mitch thought about the woman who had called his name. The sudden vision had startled him, but then he'd been living in fear since he'd awakened at the river's edge. As happy as he was living with Tom and his dog, not a day went by that he was not trembling inside, afraid to wake, afraid to sleep. As much as he wanted to remember, he was as much afraid of what he might discover about himself.

Was he a good man, or bad? Was he a criminal? Was he married, divorced? He had no wedding ring, but he could see and feel the faintest suggestion of a worn channel around his finger where a ring must have been at one time. Could he have lost the ring? He wondered if the woman in the vision was his wife.

He sat quiet, thinking. His mind drifted back to that cold, painful, and haunting morning when his world began. He recalled the awakening, and wondered if the terror that he'd felt on that day would ever be forgotten.

Tom said it could have been the head injury that

had induced his memory loss, or some traumatic event before that. Could it be both? They had talked about the possibility that he'd fallen off the cliff. Somehow, Mitch didn't believe he'd fallen off. The feeling was strong that it had been something much more extreme.

The more he thought about it, the more certain he was that it hadn't been an accident, at least not in the sense that he'd stumbled and fallen. No, it had been more than that, much more.

All at once, another picture flashed into his mind. It was so sudden and so frightening that he jumped to his feet and ran back to the cabin in a panic. Barney yelped in surprise and jumped back. He paused for an instant then hobbled after him, whining in response to Mitch's sudden mood change.

Tom was just about to open the door and join them when Mitch rushed in.

"Whoa! What's going on?"

Mitch didn't answer, but ran instead to the kitchen sink where he turned on the cold water and thrust his head under the flow.

"Mitch, are you alright? What happened? What's the matter?"

Mitch leaned over the sink and moaned in anguish.

"No!" was all he said.

Tom waited with a towel in hand, as Mitch shook his head under the cold water.

"No, no, no," he muttered repeatedly, trembling and shaking.

Finally, he raised his head from under the water and turned off the tap. Tom handed him a towel. Mitch took it and covered his ashen face, then leaned over the counter with his elbows resting on the edge.

"Talk to me, Mitch. Tell me what's wrong," Tom said, placing a comforting hand on his shoulder.

Mitch stood up and faced him. Droplets of water dripped from his hair and ran down his face. He wiped himself off and turned shakily toward the dining room table.

"I need to sit down," he said, walking unsteadily to his chair. He fell into it as Tom sat down across from him. Barney stood beside Mitch and rested his head in his lap.

"I was sitting under a tree, thinking, trying to sort things out, when I-I got this feeling. Tom, I didn't fall off that cliff." He looked Tom in the eye. "I think I was thrown." He looked down at the dog and said, "I was thrown, or maybe pushed, but I know I didn't fall. I may be a lot of things, but I ain't clumsy." The look in Mitch's eyes sent a chill down Tom's spine.

"And that's not all." Mitch took a deep breath, let it out, and continued slowly. "Tom, I-I saw myself falling, but it wasn't off the cliff. For a split second, I was reliving my past. No, it seemed more like a dream from the past. I was reliving a nightmare!

"I was falling down a hole. No, it was a mineshaft, or a well, or something like it. The walls were wet." His voice cracked. "It was so strange." He shook visibly. Tom raised his eyebrows and seemed to sit back in his seat a little.

"Whatever I fell down or through wasn't solid, not like rock; it was...alive, Tom. The hole, or well, or whatever the hell it was...I fell through it...no...I fell into it... punched into it like a meteor hitting the earth. This feeling, this memory or dream, whatever it is, is from my past. This much I know; this much I feel. And it's got something to do with me being here."

Mitch's knuckles were white where he gripped the edge of the table. Barney backed away from him and crept to Tom, whimpering, suddenly afraid of Mitch.

179

Mitch saw it and his heart broke.

Confused, afraid, and so ashamed at his unbridled emotions, Mitch collapsed onto the table and cried angrily. Tom pushed Barney toward him and then he rose from the table. Barney looked up at Tom, Tom pointed to Mitch, and Barney tentatively placed his muzzle in Mitch's lap. Mitch raised his head and Barney jumped up and placed his forepaws into his lap and proceeded to lick the tears off Mitch's face. As Mitch hugged his new canine friend, Tom said, "I'll be right back; I know just what you need." Mitch sat back in his chair as Tom's words hit him. They echoed in his ears, only it wasn't Tom's voice speaking the words, it was Donna's.

Tom came back with a cold six-pack of beer and handed one to Mitch, noticing that he was a shade paler than when he'd left him. Mitch wiped his face with the towel and opened his beer. He took a long pull, then another. He wiped the foam off his mustache and sighed deeply.

"Son, I'm not what you'd call a regular drinker, but every once in a while, especially after a hot day's work, I enjoy a cold one. Drink up!"

Mitch managed a smile and hugged the dog that had almost crawled into his lap. Mitch took another deep breath and shuddered as he let it out.

"I felt close to remembering something, but after what I saw I'm not sure I want to. What if I'm running from something, the law for instance?"

"I doubt you're on the lam, if that's what's worrying you. I wondered about that myself in the beginning, but you needn't worry. Barney would have run you off by now if that were the case. That dog hates salesman and insurance peddlers; he's eaten three already. We place them right alongside crooks and lawyers."

The beer seemed to be working; Mitch laughed. The

color was coming back into his face and he was feeling better. Barney felt better, too. And, as if the idea had suddenly struck him the dog jumped off Mitch's lap and proceeded to attack his cast with his teeth. Tom opened two more beers and handed one to Mitch. Soon they were joking again and making light of things, but not before Mitch said he thought the dream had meaning; that it was trying to tell him something; that it was a clue to what had happened to him.

Barney had begun to chew through his cast so Tom removed it and the dog limped into the living room where he jumped up on the couch and licked at his leg. Then Tom reminisced about Natalie while he worked on Mitch's cast.

"She was quite a woman. She'd work right beside me, cuttin' wood or mendin' fence, and she'd get just as sweaty and dirty but she never lost her beauty."

"You'll have to show me some pictures," Mitch said.

"I haven't even looked at them myself. I've left her things alone for the most part. Her clothes are still hanging in the closet; her things are still in the bathroom." Tom's voice began to shake and his hands began to tremble as he cut the cast down the front with heavy scissors.

"I should give her things to someone who could use them." The alcohol had loosened his emotions and suddenly his grief came to a head, too. He fell into his chair, and then it was his turn for release. He cried quietly at first, and then the tears and sobs came like a tidal wave.

Mitch just sat there, sipped his beer, and let him cry. A full five minutes later Tom's tears abated and he said, "I miss her so much. We had it so good," he sobbed. "She left so suddenly. There was no warning. She was just gone." The tears came again, cascading down his worn and weathered cheeks and onto his denim shirt. "I loved her so much, Mitch. I loved her as I never loved anyone or anything. I know she loved me just the same. I've never told anyone until now, but I hurt her. Oh Lord, I hurt her." Tom cried even more, and then said, "There was another woman. It was years ago, when we were still young. She was one of my nurses. It just happened. I knew it was wrong; I knew I had screwed up. I was about to break it off and fire her, just to get her out of my life, when Natalie found out. She left me. She was away for a year, and then she forgave me and came back. Now she's gone, Son, she's gone, and I feel as though I've never made it up to her."

Grief stricken, Tom leaned over the table with his head on his arms and wept convulsively. It was the first time he'd told anyone about his guilt and the first time he'd let himself cry over his wife since the funeral.

Mitch could only sit and look down at his hands. He could say nothing. He'd no life experiences to draw from in order to console Tom. Finally Mitch stood up and placed his right hand on Tom's right shoulder.

"It'll work out," he said.

Mitch then walked to the bathroom, and returned with some tissues, a warm washcloth, and a towel. He handed them to Tom and sat down across from him.

"Thanks."

"Don't mention it," Mitch said.

"I'm sorry, but I couldn't help it; I've been holding it in for a long time."

"In Vino Veritus," Mitch toasted with his beer can.

"Wine brings out the truth in a man," Tom agreed. Then he inhaled deeply and shuddered as he exhaled, and then laughed at himself. Mitch grinned in a lopsided, rugged way.

"Thanks, again," Tom said.

"Aw, I didn't do anything."

"You did more than you know, and you've been doing it ever since you stumbled down the mountain." He heaved a big sigh and said, "Whew! I've needed that for a long time. I guess it's time I let her go."

"You don't have to let her go," Mitch said, unwittingly drawing on his wife's psychology training. "You don't have to let go of your grief until you're ready. And she will always be with you."

"I suppose," Tom agreed. "Now let me finish removing your cast."

"Please! The sum-bitch is driving me up a wall."

Tom chuckled, wiped his eyes, and picked up his heavy-duty scissors. He removed the cast, examined Mitch's leg carefully, and was happy with his work.

"You're as good as new. Now I'm going to leave you two to stretch out the kinks, and I'm going to bed. It's been a long day, and tomorrow won't be any less. I'll see you early in the morning."

"G'night, Tom."

"G'night."

CHAPTER TWENTY

The heavy tires on Tom's truck crunched gravel as he pulled off the county road, waking Barney, who had been asleep on the front porch. The dog met the truck halfway down the drive and followed it to the barn. Weary from the long trip down to Boise and back, the men wasted no time unloading the horses and getting them settled in. The sun finished its trek across the sky as they drove back to the cabin. It set the western sky on fire, painting the clouds orange, gold, and pink.

The horses were nearly identical Appaloosas. Each was satin-black with four white stockings and a mottled nose and rump. They were fine-looking animals. They both had the same sire and dam and appeared to be twins. They were often called that, but Jasper (a gelding) and Dallas (the mare) were a year apart, Jasper being the elder at nine.

After a quick supper, Tom and Mitch sat at the table for a relaxing game of Rummy. Tom dealt the cards and showed Mitch how to play. Mitch won the first hand and then gathered the cards to deal the next. He shuffled the cards and cut the deck as he'd done on the airplane before crashing into the mountainside. Tom watched in wonder for a few moments and then said, "Where did you learn that?"

"I taught myself. It helped to pass the time... when...." Mitch looked up and Tom could see excitement on Mitch's face. "When I was goin' down the road chasin' rodeos." Mitch grinned. "I'm remembering something...something...I'm riding in an old pickup, can't picture who's at the wheel." Mitch leaned forward and put his head in his hands. "I see rodeo grounds, stock pens...somebody's hollerin' at me through the window, calling my name...said I drew Hell-to-Pay in the second go-round. That name rings a bell, but I can't, I can't...damn it, that's it. It's gone." Mitch sat back and sighed, disappointed.

Breathless, Tom waited, but Mitch just shook his head, dismissed the thought, and dealt the cards. Tom remained silent. He didn't push, and he waited.

"Well, Tom, I guess you were right about me being a cowboy. For a minute I was right there. I was livin' it."

Suddenly, the cabin's relative calm was shattered as the almost forgotten telephone came to life. Tom started as if someone had poked him in the back. Then he got up slowly, his age telling on him, and crossed the room to where the phone hung on the wall in the kitchen.

"Hello?"

Mitch watched Tom, unable to contain his curiosity.

"I'm fine," Tom said with an odd flatness in his voice. "No, I don't need anything. How is Sally?"

A long pause ensued, and then Tom shouted so loudly Mitch jumped.

"Dammit! No! I haven't considered it, and I'll be

damned if I will. NO! That's final! Listen, Son, this is
MY land. I'll do as I damned well please where it's concerned. NO! Don't waste his time, nor mine." Another
pause followed. It was an awkward silence. Tom's face
became a furnace, and Mitch could feel the tension
mounting. "Damn it all to hell! NO! I will not talk to
him." Barney crawled into the living room and hid himself in a corner of the couch.

Tom gritted his teeth and listened to the voice on the
other end of the line. Disgust mixed with bitter sorrow
fell down his face, crawled down his body, and soon engulfed the room.

"The hell you will," Tom shouted abruptly. "I'll never
give it to you. I'd just as soon torch it. I'm surprised
you had the balls to say that. You generally have your
wife do your dirty work. Dammit, boy, when are you going to wake up and see what kind of ass you have become? To hell with me! Well, to hell with you, too." Tom
slammed the phone so hard against the receiver the
whole unit ripped from the wall and fell to the floor. A
photo on the wall slipped from its nail and crashed
against the floor. Shattered glass skittered across the
kitchen and dining room. Tom ignored it and stormed
out of the room, crunching glass shards beneath his
boots. Mitch sat in stunned disbelief and waited for the
rebound.

What he heard was the heavy thud of the axe splitting wood. With each powerful stroke, Tom released a
barrage of curses into the night, insulting the pristine
calm. He took his anger out on the logs until the sweat
soaked his shirt and his gloveless hands became red
and sore. Thirty minutes later, spent, his anger drained
away, he drove the axe deep into the chopping block.
After a brief respite to catch his breath he returned to
the cabin.

"I thought that was my job," Mitch said as he hand-ed Tom a tall glass of ice water. Tom drained half the glass and then dropped heavily into his chair, slamming the glass down on the table.

"Where were we?" he asked.

Mitch drew a card and said, "Sounded like somewhere between hell and the Mojave desert." He thought over his cards a minute, then pulled one from his hand and discarded it. "I'm all ears?"

Tom wiped his brow with his bandana and then spoke.

"I don't understand it. We did everything we knew to raise him right. He was our only child and we gave all we had for him. We gave him a good education and taught him to be a good man. We loved him and told him so." He paused and stared into space a few moments, remembering another time. Then he continued, "Everything was fine until he left. He said he'd come back, but he never did, at least not the Jeremy I raised. He's greedy now, and all he thinks about is wealth and how he can make more, and spend more.

"I paid hard-earned money to get him a university degree. He worked hard; I'll give him that. He became a big executive with an investment firm in Salt Lake City.

"He has a house down there that would make this place look like a tool shed. He has every convenience and gadget you could imagine. He even has a damned robot vacuuming his floors."

Tom picked up a card and laid another down.

"All he cares about is money, and more of it, and especially mine. Not that I'm rich, but the trees on this land are worth a fortune, and he wants it. I've told him a thousand times if I've told him once that I'm not selling. Nevertheless, he keeps pushing. He wants to bring a buyer out tomorrow to look it over. He wants to sell off all the trees and maybe develop the land. Says he has an idea to bring "Big Business" to the mountains. He's got some hair-brained idea and wants to finance it with the lumber on this land. Something isn't right and I don't believe his story. When I told him no, he had the gall to tell me he'd get it when I die.

"He's got a long wait coming. I don't plan on leaving this world for quite a while yet, and even if I do, he's not in my will." Tom's face grew redder with each word he spoke. He finished the water, glancing at the broken glass on the floor. The photo had been of himself, his late wife, and their son. He shook his head in disgust.

"After she died, I stayed with him and his wife, Sally, for a couple of weeks. I overheard them talking one evening. Jeremy was telling her that when he got my land they'd sell the timber, get filthy rich and move to Europe. Can you believe that?"

"That would be hard to swallow."

"I'm about to choke on it, Mitch. I have never been so angry in all my life." Tom stared blindly at his cards and then said, "I'm sorry, but I'm just not interested in this game anymore. I'm going to sit and smoke my pipe for a bit and then I'm going to bed." He retired to his re-cliner. Mitch put away the cards and took Barney out-side.

The night was calm but not quiet. From somewhere out back behind the barn, Mitch heard a chorus of bullfrogs. He surmised there must be a pond or small lake Tom hadn't told him about. In a roundabout way, Mitch ended up down at the barn, let himself in, and was greeted by a suspicious snort from one of the hors-es.

"It's just me, guys; nothing to worry about." He filled their water buckets and threw them each a flake of hay. Dallas nudged him and then laid her head on his shoulder. He scratched her neck until Jasper tossed his head and stomped his feet in the other stall.

"You want some, too? Pardon me, Ma'am, while I oblige your jealous brother." Mitch moved to the next stall and scratched Jasper under the chin a minute. Then he called Barney and headed back up the hill to the cabin, having heard thunder rumble in the distance.

A gentle, rain-scented breeze blew from the northwest. The moon, adorned with a fuzzy halo, dodged its way around threatening clouds as it followed them along their way. The wind picked up and as the tops of the pines began to sway, it whistled a sinister tune and lashed at the needle-clad branches. By the time Mitch reached the cabin, the wind was blowing his hair awry and throwing icy rain. He turned up his collar, gathered the wood from around the chopping block, and stacked it on the porch out of the rain. He carried the axe inside, noticing that it needed sharpening. He put it aside to work on later, and built a fire to ward off an encroaching chill. Lightning struck close and Mitch flinched. Thunder boomed overhead like a cannon shot and Mitch jumped again as Tom spoke from behind him.

"I've felt that storm coming for three days," he said, standing there in his pajamas and bath robe. "Sure took its time." Tom eased himself into his recliner and reached for his pipe. "I didn't mean to startle you."

"Yeah right," Mitch said, glancing at Tom sideways. Grinning, Tom knocked his pipe out into a heavy walnut bowl he kept on the end table. With tobacco-stained fingers he refilled it and packed it.

"Did you check on the twins?"

"Sure did," Mitch replied as he moved a log around with the poker, stirring the coals and sending sparks floating up into the chimney to be snuffed out by the rain and wind.

"I watered them and gave them each a flake of hay."

"Thanks," Tom said around his pipe as he lit it and puffed it to life. "I had planned on doing it myself, but I got side-tracked."

Mitch nodded and stood up from the fire.

"Tom, I think we can only do so much for our children, and then it's up to them." He sat down on the couch. Barney jumped up beside him. "It's up to them what they make of themselves, and we can't be to blame if we have done all we could. And even if we could have done better, the past is done; we can't go back and change things. We let them live their lives and make their mistakes." He paused; thinking over what had tumbled unbidden out of his mouth. "I know that may sound strange coming from me in my present state of mind, but I think it's true. I have family somewhere, you know, a wife and children," he said with more than a hint of melancholy. "It's just a feeling, Tom, not certain knowledge." He leaned back with his arms behind his head and studied the fire. Tom smoked his pipe and Barney fell asleep with his head in Mitch's lap.

"Tom," he said, continuing to stare into the dancing flames, "I guess you know I'll be leaving in a week or so." Rain pelted the windows, driven by the wind. The old man didn't reply to Mitch's statement immediately. After a few minutes Tom did speak, weariness clouding his voice. "I know, I've been expecting it." He spoke slowly as if it hurt. "Wish you could stay, but I know you have to go."

Mitch heard a tremor in his old friend's voice, and he couldn't help but notice the pain. They sat quiet for a few minutes, and then Mitch got up, walked over to

Tom and rested a hand on his shoulder for a moment.

"See you in the morning. I'm going to bed."

"G'night, Son."

Mitch walked around behind him and headed for the stairs. Tom smoked his pipe and spent some time staring into the flames before going to bed. He decided to spend some time in his den before actually going to sleep. He sat down at his desk and began to write:

Nat, I just don't know what to do. Jeremy called tonight. It wasn't a pleasant conversation. He basically told me he was waiting for me to die so he could get our land, cut the trees, get rich and move to Europe. The madness of this world has gotten to him. He has changed so much. Could we have done anything different?

The injured man we found is named, Mitch. He's starting to get his memory back. Physically, he is doing very well now and so is Barney. He misses you. I miss you. I miss you so much I feel like I'm going as mad as the world I find myself in. If not for Mitch and Barney, I might do something foolish at this point, for without the son I had hoped to cherish in my old age, I would have only memories now.

Sometimes I wish something cataclysmic would happen, something so violent and extreme that it would wipe the human race from the Earth. It seems to me that we've done nothing but rape it anyhow. Oh, I know as a species we've done some miraculous things, but as I see it we've done more damage than good. Nonetheless, I must remain hopeful that we can rise above our petty differences, our greed, and our arrogance. We have potential, but our technology has outdistanced our capacity to use it wisely.

I sense a change; my life is not ending as soon I had once wished, but instead, with Mitch in our lives now, there is reason to go on. Lord knows where he came from and where he will go, but I have a feeling that even if he does go in search of his past, he will return. He belongs here on this mountain.

On another note: Your roses are doing well this spring. I need to plant some more next to you. I need to clean out the fireplace and carry the ashes down there. You might not know it, but I've learned a lot from you. When you didn't think I was paying you any attention I was so into you. Hon', I am so sorry for what I did so long ago. If I'd known how much I truly loved you, as I do still love you now, perhaps I wouldn't have failed you. And let's hope the human race will someday wake up to its failures and feel as I do about the Earth. From the ashes of the damaged trees I cut and burn to keep this home warm come your beautiful roses.

Earth's time is coming. I feel it in my bones. There's going to be a purging, a figurative burning, that is, a fire that will burn to the quick. My hope and prayer is that from the ashes of this world's madness comes something as precious and rewarding as your roses. Yes, let's hope and pray that something good can from the ashes of madness.

Love, Thomas

CHAPTER TWENTY-ONE

Tom and Mitch woke the rooster the next morning, and before the sun could spread dawn across the horizon, they had the horses saddled and were riding toward the river. They spent the early hours catching trout and enjoying the forest in all its glory. Spring had reached its summit, and Mitch was swept away by the raw, unspoiled beauty of Tom's mountain ranch.

Time passed slowly, and in the days that followed, Mitch gave up trying to force his memory back. Instead he put all his energy into living each moment as it came, and much to Tom's pleasure, he decided to put off leaving until he had somewhere to go.

The days lingered; time seemed to stand still for Mitch. Over the past two years Tom had neglected maintenance, and much work was needed around the place. Mitch was no slouch; he worked hard and soon found himself back in top shape. However, he and Tom only worked when they could spare precious time from their ever-present and extremely important need to keep the freezer stocked with fresh trout from the river and bass from Tom's pond down the hill from the barn.

In the cool of the evening, they set on the front porch and listened to the wind play a symphony in the boughs of the evergreens. Whippoorwills sang in the distance, always in the distance, while crickets chirped in cadence with the blinking stars in the heavens. Mitch was happy to be alive but no closer to the answers he'd soon be forced to seek.

One hundred thirty miles south, his wife hung onto his memory and prayed for his safe return. She continued to work part time at the day care center, and Steven stayed busy at the service station after school. Life was a constant struggle, but they had their friends.

Steven hadn't the faith of his mother, nor the inner voice, which told her that Mitch was more than just a memory. He was beginning to accept the fact that he may never see his father again and he was making plans to get on with his life. Granted, he was young, but he'd always been levelheaded and mature for his age. He was finished with his childhood and eager to grab hold of adulthood.

CHAPTER TWENTY-TWO

Steven rubbed the sleep from his eyes and sat up in bed. He stared at the calendar on the wall across the room that he'd conservatively furnished. His room was neat, clean, and organized. A personal computer and a few reference books occupied his desktop. A picture of his girlfriend, another of his mother and father, a change dish of solid walnut his father had carved for him, and his wristwatch rested on his dresser. All of his books (he had hundreds), mostly nonfiction, were arranged library style in a bookcase that he and his father had built together.

He didn't have a television. But he owned a CD player and enjoyed a variety of music, ranging from Bruce Springsteen to Tanya Tucker, jazz to classical. A Taylor acoustic guitar stood in one corner. The frets were worn from many hours of practice; he was a good guitarist with a flare for fast licks, and was equally adept at slower rhythm and blues. Talented as he was, his ability was unknown outside of his immediate family, and

Molly.

He was modest and played simply because he enjoyed it. He hadn't touched the instrument since the day his father disappeared.

He rose from his bed and put an X across the twenty-eighth of May. He counted the days. His father had been gone six weeks.

Downstairs, Donna sat at the kitchen counter on a bar stool, sipping coffee, waiting for her son to come down to breakfast. She was clad in a faded blue denim shirt and dirty jeans, and her normally silken black hair was natty and unwashed. Dark circles hung like half-moons under her eyes. Sleep ran from her like rabbits from the hound.

As Steven left the bathroom and entered his bedroom, Donna slothfully poured herself another cup of coffee and then put in a teaspoon of honey and a little cream, clanking the spoon noisily against the side of the cup. Carelessly, she threw the spoon into the sink, breaking a glass. She shrugged it of. She'd stopped caring.

Pushing herself off the stool, she shuffled sluggishly to the refrigerator and opened the door. She immediately slammed it shut with a curse and with such force that Steven heard it upstairs. He quickly finished dressing and ran down to find her crying over her coffee. It was the third time in as many days.

"We're out of eggs," she said between sobs. "Fix yourself a bowl of cereal if you're hungry."

He shook his head, declining breakfast, and asked, "Another bad night?"

"I barely slept, as usual, and when I did I had nightmares."

"What about?"

"Can't remember," she lied, wanting to forget. Donna

had dreamed she was back in San Antonio, at the River Walk with Mitch. Only Mitch was dead and the police were dragging his battered body from the water.

Steven changed his mind about breakfast and looked in the refrigerator for the milk, but that was also in short supply. He poured himself a glass of juice and sat down at the dining room table.

"You're not going to eat?" she asked.

"I'm not really that hungry. Don't worry about supper tonight; Molly and I are going out."

"Where?"

"Charlie's for supper, then maybe we'll see a movie. On another note, I'm thinking about asking her to marry me. What do you think?"

Donna nearly spilled her coffee in her lap.

"Huh?"

"I'm considering asking Molly to be my wife."

"Whoa! Just wait a minute. Technically, you are not yet adults. You guys are still kids. Entiendo?"

"I'm not a kid anymore. How can I still be a kid?"

"Is she pregnant?" Donna interrupted.

"No! Of course not!" Steven's face grew red with embarrassment. "Mom, that's our business, OK? I haven't give you reason not to trust me. I need you to trust me now. I feel like I've done a lot of growing up since dad left. I don't see things the same way. And I've been doing a lot of thinking lately. I want Molly in my life. Professor Warren said there are two kinds of men. One has the novelty gene and seeks out many mates. The other has the opposite kind of gene and those men are monogamous. I think I am the latter. I don't look at other women. In fact, I don't even think of other women. Since I met Molly, she's been the only one in my life, and she's the only one I want. A hundred years ago she'd be considered an old maid. Physically she's been ready since she was twelve years old. Why does society want to leash and hold back what nature as already deemed appropriate? I don't understand it."

Donna sipped her coffee and followed it with a bite of dry toast. She chewed thoughtfully for a moment, never taking her eyes off his. Then she swallowed and asked, "Thought about this long?"

"Almost a year; I'm sure she's expecting it of me."

"Women don't think like men. What about college?"

"We'll go together."

"Are you going to wait to get married until you're out of high school?"

"She wants to start college next fall, so I'll take dad's advice and do the same. If she agrees, then we can be married this summer."

"Steven, I trust you. Now, I know I've not been my-self, but I'm still your mother. I'm still older and, hope-fully, wiser. I want you to talk this over with Molly and get her take on this. I agree with you. You have done some growing up. I'd be remiss as a psychologist if did-n't try to talk you out of this. As a mother, I'm con-cerned that you are acting too quickly on your desires. In light of recent events, I also think you may be at-tempting to get on with your life as a means of dealing with your father's disappearance. I'm not saying that is a bad idea. I think you should take life one thing at a time right now. Finish high school first. Take the sum-mer off and go traveling with Molly. Spend three com-plete months with her and then see if you still feel the same. Then attend college together for a year. By then you will know for sure. There really is no rush.

"I'd like to see you wait, but I'm not going to tell you what to do. A lot can happen between now and then." She sighed. Steven sat there like a rock. She could see the steadfastness in his eyes. She knew he had made up his mind. "Ok, ask her. But as long as long as you are being old fashioned about it, ask her father first. Your dad would appreciate that."

"I did yesterday. He approves. In fact he's excited about it. He considers me one of his best friends. How can this not work?"

"I can give you dozens of reasons. Number one, statistics show that first loves seldom last, especially in today's climate. But I can see you won't be swayed. You may not be your father's natural son, but you've sure got his grit and determination. Even so, he'd tell you the same thing I'm going to tell you. I will give my blessing and permission on one condition. You agree on a two-year engagement. If, after two years from today, you still want to proceed, we'll cover all your wedding expenses. If you decide to go ahead with it sooner, you're on your own. How does that sound?"

Steven didn't answer right away. He got up and walked to the living room. He opened the door and stood facing north. He stared up at the mountains. Suddenly he began to cry. He leaned against the door jamb for support. Donna ran to him. She pulled him to her chest. But he pulled away, wiped the tears from his eyes and started talking.

"I miss him so much, Mom. He's gone. He's dead and he's not coming back. You've got your faith, and you think he's alive and that he's coming back. That's good for you. I need reality. He taught me to be a realist. He taught me not to waste time wishing things would happen. He taught me to make them happen. I have to move on. It's the only way I can deal with him going away." He sniffed and wiped his nose.

He hesitated and looked back at the mountains. "OK. Two years. I'll give *you* two years. But I give Molly and me the rest of our lives. I have to get to school."

He kissed her on the cheek and left, shutting the door behind him.

Donna walked to the kitchen. She reached for the phone and dialed Sherrie's number. She answered before Donna heard it ring.

"Hello?" Sherrie said.

"What are you doing, sitting on the phone?"

"What?"

"I didn't hear it ring on my end," Donna said.

"It didn't. I picked it up to call you, and here you are."

"Oh"

"Donna? What's wrong?"

"Can you come over? I need a shoulder," Donna mumbled.

"Be right there."

Donna was still holding the phone to her ear when Sherrie ran in. Sherrie took it gently from her hands and hung it up.

"Come here." Donna fell into her arms, and Sherrie had to struggle to hold her as she cried. Donna could hardly stand by herself.

"It's going to be alright. You'll be fine."

Sherrie smoothed her friend's hair and pulled it back and away from her face. "I'm here, nobody's watching, nobody's listening, just cry your heart out."

"I need to sit down," Donna said after a bit. Sherrie walked her into the living room, where Donna collapsed onto the couch.

"I need my coffee," Donna said.

"No, you need to rest," Sherrie replied. "Get some sleep; I'll be here when you wake up. Then we'll talk." Sherrie spoke softly, crooning to Donna until her friend closed her eyes and dropped heavily to sleep. Sherrie called her husband.

"She's worn to a frazzle, Harold. It looks like she hasn't slept in days, but I've got her sleeping now and I'm going to stay with her." She paused to catch her breath and let her husband respond.

"Thanks," she said after a moment, "I knew you'd understand. I love you. Later."

Donna had let the household chores slide. Her friend spent the morning catching up on them while Donna slept. When she finally awoke, Sherrie made a fresh pot of coffee, and they sat together on the couch and talked.

"What's on your mind, Kiddo? Spill the beans."

"I don't know where to begin," Donna said.

"You've wanted to tell me something since Mitch disappeared, but you've kept it back. Donna, we've been close for a long time, and we've shared all our secrets. It's time you quit holding out on me."

Donna just sat there silently staring off into space for a moment, then put her head down, saw her reflection in her coffee, and slowly began to speak.

"Well, you know I had the feeling," she paused once again to release a heavy sigh, "that something bad was going to happen?"

"Yeah, you mentioned it. Go on."

"Well, Mitch told me he'd stay if I wanted him to, but I let him go. I've been blaming myself. I think he had second thoughts, too." Her hand shook as she lifted her coffee to her lips. She took three big sips, burning her tongue but needing the lift.

"Why did he have second thoughts?"

Donna set her cup down and wrung hands that hadn't seen lotion in weeks. Her once perfect nails were now chewed to the quick. All that remained of the once vivacious and charismatic woman was a stuttering, nail-biting, emotionally wrung-out, half-starved bag of bones on the edge of a nervous breakdown.

Sherrie reached out and took those nail-bitten hands in hers.

"Donna, you know I love you and that I would never do anything to hurt you. You have to tell me about this. It's eating you up inside. You have to get it out of your system no matter how bad it hurts."

"I know, I know," Donna said, pulling her hands away to rub her puffy face. She massaged the sleep and confusion out of her eyes, took a deep breath, another sip of coffee, and continued.

"There isn't much to tell. Not really," she yawned and stretched. "Mitch hadn't slept well the night before, too excited about the trip, or so I thought. He had hardly touched his supper, and later in bed he tossed, turned, and didn't fall asleep until almost four in the morning.

"I woke first, as I usually do, and tried to wake him, but he was dead to the world. I knew he needed his sleep, so I didn't try very hard. Later, after I'd showered, I was brushing my teeth, and...." She inhaled abruptly as she sat up straight. "I haven't brushed my teeth in three or four days. I'm such a mess."

She began crying once more. Sherrie started to reach for her, but Donna waved her away this time.

"I'll be alright."

Sherrie poured them some fresh coffee and found her friend a tissue.

"I heard something hit the floor in the bedroom," Donna said after a few minutes. "I looked around the corner and saw Mitch tangled up in the blankets on the floor. I helped him back in bed. He was soaked in cold sweat. He was as pale as the sheets and he was scared.

"He said he'd dreamed that he was falling." Donna took a deep, shuddering breath, let it out, and said,

"Sher', I-I think his dream came true, and, and, I-I, c-c-could have stopped it."

Like sisters, they held each other and cried together, one giving comfort, the other receiving.

"It's not your fault," Sherrie said. "You can't blame yourself. Don't forget, Mitch *is* alive, unless you've been lying to me, and to yourself and everyone else."

"He's alive, but God knows where he is and why he won't come home, or why he can't come home."

From across the room the grandfather clock suddenly chimed, and the dull bong echoed forlornly throughout the house. It was Mitch's clock, passed down from his great-great-grandfather.

"Oh no! What time is it?" Donna asked, turning to look at the big clock standing against the front wall beside the cedar chest.

"Twelve-thirty!"

"Damn! I'm late for work. The house is a mess. I'm a mess. Oh, God, what a mess. Sher'? What am I going to do?"

She started to rise from the couch.

Sherrie stopped her.

"No you don't. You're not going anywhere, except out to lunch with me. I called in for you, and you have the rest of the week off." Sherrie saw an aura of relief suddenly blossom around Donna. "I've already cleaned the house. Your only concern is to take it easy for a few days."

"Thanks."

"It's nothing. Go get cleaned up; I'm hungry and we're going out to lunch."

Donna hesitated, searching for the strength.

"C'mon', it'll do you good to get out and stretch your legs and catch some rays."

"I'm not sure I have the energy," Donna said as she

slowly rose from the couch.

"Alright, give me a few minutes. While I'm getting ready, think about this: Steven is asking Molly to marry him. He told me this morning."

CHAPTER TWENTY-THREE

That's right, you get the papers worked up and I'll supply you with a name later. Of course I know what I'm doing. Yes, I've given it quite a lot of thought, and I'm positive it's exactly what I want. Thanks, Phil. I'll get back to you later. Bye." Tom hung up the phone, satisfaction shining brightly on his face.

"C'mon, Barn', let's go help Mitch.

Tom got his gloves and hat and strode out of the cabin, walking briskly down to the barn. Mitch was working on the roof, replacing tin that had been blown off by the storm two weeks earlier.

"How's it going?" Tom yelled. "Do you need more tin?"

"Yeah," Mitch hollered down. "Stack up three more sheets and bring me up another pound or so of screws."

Tom pulled three fourteen-foot lengths of roofing tin off the flatbed trailer hitched to the truck and leaned them up against the edge of the roof. He picked up the coffee can that Mitch had thrown to the ground and filled it with screws. He pulled up his gloves, realigned his battered and sweat-stained Stetson with his head, and climbed the ladder to the roof.

Mitch was halfway down the northwest side, facing the cabin.

"I'm just about finished here, Tom. We've three more sheets to replace at the ridge on the other end. I've removed all but a couple of screws in each. I was waiting for you to help me get them down. I've checked for loose screws everywhere and replaced what tin was missing. You need a case or two of good roofing caulk to fill the cracks here and there, and then she'll be weather-tight again.

The barn consisted of two rows of stalls on each side, a low sloping roof over each, with a high loft in the middle between them, covering the spacious indoor arena. The loft was a vertical fourteen feet in height. A moderately pitched roof topped it off. Stacked hay covered the floor below.

An hour and a half later, after they had driven in the last screw with a cordless drill, they sat on the ridge, forty feet up, and gazed out across the forest.

"Some view, huh?" Tom said. "Just over that ridge," he pointed west, "is the town of Riggins. Look south and a bit west. See that winding line of emptiness in the trees?"

"Yeah, that's the Salmon River, right?"

"Yup! Over there," Tom said, pointing west and more to the south, "is where Barney found you. Sampson's Ledge, where you were trapped, is northwest of there about a mile and a half. Now look way off to the northwest. See those hazy hills way out there?"

"Uh huh."

"That's Washington. You can see the Wallowa Whitman National Forest due west, in Oregon, with Hell's Canyon between here and there. A hundred miles north we are bordered by Canada, and east about the same distance you'll find Montana. South and east is Wyoming, and to the south is Utah. We are right smack in the middle of God's country.

Mitch smiled and asked Tom how much rope he had.

"I've probably got two hundred feet or more in the tack shed. Why?"

"I'm going back down the cliff."

CHAPTER TWENTY-FOUR

As Donna stepped down into the living room dressed in jeans and a faded blue denim shirt of her husband's, she asked where they were going for lunch.

"Wherever you want," Sherrie replied generously.

"Let's eat in the deli at the Food Emporium; I need to get some groceries."

"That'll work," Sherrie agreed as they took off in her mini-van. "Harold and I are having my special spaghetti tonight. He suggested you and Steven join us."

"I'd love to, Sher', but Steven's going out with Molly tonight. He and I need to have a serious talk."

"My Lord, Donna, I thought you were out of your mind when you said that. You're not pulling my leg are you?"

"Nope."

"Are you going to talk him out of it?"

"Yeah, right! Like I really have a chance there. He's too much like Mitch. When he makes up his mind to do something, it's done. All I can do is offer motherly advice and pray for a long engagement so they can both know for sure it's what they want."

"They make a sweet couple," Sherrie said.

"I know, and he says they've been in love for a long time. Nevertheless, I keep thinking about my first marriage. What a mess that was."

"What about mine?" Sherrie said.

"Yeah, I suppose you're right. Besides, you two were younger than they are. I just wish Mitch was here to talk to him."

They didn't say anything more until Sherrie pulled into the shopping center and parked.

"Are you going to brush your hair?"

"Huh?"

"Donna, you didn't brush it and it's a mess."

Donna grabbed the rearview mirror and turned it toward her.

"Oh, Lord. Why didn't you tell me?"

"I just did."

Donna searched through her purse but couldn't find her brush, so Sherrie offered hers. Donna brushed her long hair back and away from her face. Throwing it over her shoulder, she said, "That'll have to do."

They took a seat in a back corner, away from all the school kids on lunch break, and talked until the waitress took their orders.

"I'll have a club sandwich and a medium Diet Coke," Sherrie said.

"And how about you," the girl said to Donna.

"I'll have a double-cheeseburger, a large order of fries, and a large Dr. Pepper."

"How do you want the burger?"

"Medium, and drag it through the garden."

"Do what?"

"Put everything on it."

"Oh, duh!" the waitress said, giving them a silly grin.

"Wow, a double-cheeseburger?" Sherrie asked, in disbelief.

"Sher', I'm catching up. I haven't eaten in three days and the smell of food is making me hungry as a horse."

"And I'm beginning to seriously worry about you. You haven't been eating, not sleeping, and now you are overeating?" The unthinkable suddenly struck her, and she shot Donna a hard look. "You missed your hormone shot, didn't you?"

Donna tried to avoid her friend's penetrating stare by looking out the window.

"My God, girl. No wonder you're such a mess. As soon as we finish here I'm taking you to your doctor. What's the number?"

Donna mumbled it off and Sherrie scribbled it down on a napkin.

"I left my cell phone in the van. I'll be right back. Don't eat my lunch, too."

When she returned five minutes later, lunch was on the table and Donna was well into her burger. Sherrie sat down and took a sip of her Coke.

"He wants to see you right away. What do you need for the frig?"

"The basics: eggs, milk, bread, a head of lettuce, uh, tomatoes."

"I'll get it. Have the waitress wrap mine up; I'll eat it later." Sherrie left Donna her keys.

"I'll meet you in the van."

"Thanks, Sher'. You're the best."

"Somebody's got to take care of you," Sherrie said as she hurried away.

Donna ate her lunch and tried to get her mind together while her normally ditzy friend showed a side of her character seldom seen. By the time Donna finished her lunch, Sherrie had the shopping done, and a little more, and was hurrying back to the deli.

"Let's go; the doctor is waiting."

She ushered her friend to the van, loaded the groceries, and then hungrily tore at her sandwich as she drove the five miles to the doctor's office. She was finishing off the last bite when she pulled into the parking lot. Sherrie locked up and walked Donna inside. She signed her in and sat down beside her. Donna already had her head buried in a magazine but she barely had time to read the first paragraph before she heard her name called. A tall, very skinny nurse held the door open as Donna walked wearily out of the waiting room and into a well-lit hallway adjacent to the front office and reception desk.

"Step up here," the nurse gestured toward the scale. "Let me get your weight.

"Donna, you're too tall to be so thin." As if I should talk. "Put on some weight or shorten your legs. You've lost fifteen pounds since your last visit; uh let's see, six weeks ago." Donna nodded and managed to let a sheepish smile pierce her weary frown as the nurse led her to a room.

"The doctor will be right in. He's been waiting."

"Thanks, Gail."

Time was becoming a leech, sapping her strength, and leaving her weak. Each minute added to her weariness. For all the good lunch had done, it had its side effects; indigestion and drowsiness assailed her. She trudged into the cold, white room and fell down on the hard table. The paper covering rustled noisily underneath. While she waited, she scanned the walls. Norman Rockwell prints adorned the room, along with numerous certificates of completion in specialized areas of medicine. Several frayed magazines stood in a rack by the door.

As she fought drowsiness, appraised the artwork, and read the certificates, she listened to a child cry in the next room as a nurse administered what must have been a tetanus shot; she heard the mother tell the child that if he'd been wearing shoes he wouldn't have been poked by the nail. Donna frowned at the mother.

"Lady, shoes won't stop a nail like the sharp eyes of a watchful mother."

"My thoughts exactly, Donna," her doctor said as he walked in and closed the door behind him. "But I am more concerned about you. What is this nonsense I hear about you missing your hormone shot two weeks ago?"

"I forgot. It's easy with all I've been going through."

"You are going through tough times, I'll grant you that, but that is no excuse for letting yourself go like you have. What would Mitch think about the way you have lost concern for your health? Open your mouth." He inserted a thermometer under her tongue. He took her blood pressure, listened to her heart and lungs, and then read her temperature.

"I know I'm doing the nurse's job, but I wanted more time with you. Donna I've known you since before I delivered Steven, and I've been treating you all these years. This is the first time since your hysterectomy that you have missed a shot. You have never even been late.

"I'm not going to talk you out of believing that Mitch is still out there, somehow alive, but honestly, you should begin to look ahead. You can start by taking better care of yourself. For him, when he returns, for Steven, but mostly for you."

"I know, I know. It's just been so long without him.

So long, and I, I just don't know how long I-I c-c-can h-hold on. Oh, God, Ben, why, why? What have I done to deserve this? I-I can't...."

Something inside Donna gave way. She felt herself falling and then felt the doctor's strong hands catch and hold her.

"I'm so scared," she screamed hoarsely. "Hold me, Ben. I'm afraid." She clung to him and cried convulsively. He held her without reservation, and was reminded of his own loss not too many years ago.

He could think of nothing to say. Probably couldn't speak if he had the words, so he just held her, remembering that when a woman cries that is what she needs most. He caressed her hair, smoothing it across her shoulders and patted her back. He held back his own grief, a loss of which her tears had reminded him.

He gathered strength and gave it to her.

He'd almost made up his mind to hospitalize her, fearing a breakdown, but then she seemed to change. It was subtle, but he sensed a resurgence of the Donna he knew and admired so well. It was enough to change his mind.

It seemed like he had held her for a long time, but it had only been a few minutes. Then Donna pulled away and leaned against the table with her hands behind her back. Ben handed her a box of pink tissues and pretended to look through her file folder, ignoring the wet spot on his shoulder as Donna cleaned her face and caught her breath.

"I'm sorry," she said.

"No need," he said, checking his watch. He had another patient waiting.

"Can you talk?" he asked. Donna nodded. "Alright," he said. "Would you like a glass of water? Let me get you some water."

Before she could answer, her doctor was out the door and down the hall. In just a few moments, he was back with a glass of water and two pills.

"The pills will help you sleep."

"I don't need—"

"Yes! You do. Go home and straight to bed. Sherrie told me what she knew. I can surmise the rest."

Donna heaved a sigh and was overcome with the shudders. Ben laughed and Donna smiled meekly.

"Whew," she said, "I haven't felt one of those in years. I'm sorry for putting you through that."

"Don't apologize. I understand. I lost a son, remember?"

Donna did remember.

Six years before, Ben's son had been killed when his Air Force jet suddenly and mysteriously exploded during a practice mission over the Florida Keys. His body, or what would have been left of it, was never found. A few bits of shredded clothing and one empty boot was all that turned up. Ben had been devastated, and his career had faltered. He had been overcome with grief during one of Donna's visits, and she'd been *his* strength.

Donna took the pills and drank some water while her doctor leaned against the door, took off his glasses, and rubbed his eyes, sneaking a peek at his watch.

"Except for your hormonal imbalance and lack of sleep, not to mention exhaustion, you are fine. Listen, I have another patient waiting so I have to leave you. Get some rest. Eat right. Exercise! You know the drill. Gail will give you a shot to get you back in sync, and I'll write you a prescription to help you sleep. See me again next week."

"I will. I promise," Donna said. "Thanks."

"And one more thing," Ben said as he turned to

leave, "if anyone could survive up there, it's Mitch. He's the fittest man I know. Don't give up on him. He's alive until someone proves otherwise. Keep your chin up, Sport."

"Thanks, Ben."

CHAPTER TWENTY-FIVE

M itch had explained his need for answers and how he thought the cliff would be a good place to start, so Tom suggested they saddle the horses and make a day and a night of it. They packed up and left immediately. With Tom in the lead and Barney running ahead, behind, and between the horses, the trio started up the mountain. They were headed deep into the woods, to a private and secluded fishing hole. It was also where Natalie was buried.

Tom usually drove the distance and hadn't walked it in many years. Even on horseback it was slow going through the dense forest until they could find his old trail, or what was left of it.

"Haven't been up this way in a long time, but there's a trail here somewhere."

"Can't we just follow the river?"

"Wish we could," Tom said, "but it's not that easy. Two creeks flow into the river between here and the cliff, and one of them can only be crossed at a certain spot. This is rough country. The only other way is to take the county road and then cut back toward the river on a seldom-used dirt road."

A blue jay squawked in the trees above them. Mitch rode tall and easy in the saddle, as though he was born to it. Dallas had given him a little trouble when they first started out, crow hopping and spinning with her back humped beneath the saddle, but Mitch had just laughed and instinctively pulled her head around to his left knee and made her stop, riding easy and in control. Once she knew who the boss was she settled down and behaved herself.

Mitch shifted his seat, centering the saddle. The sound of squeaking leather was pleasant to his ears and was somehow familiar. At a widening in the trees, he urged Dallas ahead and caught up with Tom. They rode side by side and talked while Barney nosed around in the brush.

The forest was thriving; birds chirped and whistled among the branches of the trees and shrubs. Squirrels, rabbits, and birds scurried out of harm's way. Ahead Mitch heard the soft rustling of water flowing over moss-covered rocks and polished gravel. He nudged Dallas with his spurs, and she trotted quickly past Jasper. When Tom caught up, Mitch was kneeling by the stream.

"You just found one of my old fishin' holes," Tom said. "I used to spend hours fishing here. The waters around here are full of fish."

"Is the hunting as good as the fishing?"

"You'd be surprised, Son. Then again if you were in your right mind you might be telling *me* about the abundance of game in these woods."

Mitch started to rise but stopped when he saw something shining in the creek bed. He reached down into the clear, cold water and brought out a handful of silt and gravel abundant with specks of white crystal laced by hues of gold.

"Probably fool's gold," Tom said before Mitch could ask."

"Fooled me," Mitch muttered as he threw it back and rinsed his hands. He remounted and followed Tom upstream a few hundred rugged yards before they found a place to cross. Dallas stepped gingerly across the stream while Jasper jumped and nearly spilled Tom. The commotion scared up a mule deer buck sporting one heavy antler. Mitch stared in awe as the heavy-bodied deer bounded away, scaring up another smaller deer. A half hour later, after encountering several more deer and a small black bear, they pulled up at the cliff and tied the horses by the leaning pine.

After looking down to make sure, Mitch said, "This is where I climbed out. Let's go up the hill and see if we can find where I went down."

Mitch untied his horse and led the way uphill on foot. When they had gone the length of a football field they eased to the edge of the cliff and looked down.

"This is it," Mitch said. "On the other side is where I saw Patches."

"Another good fishin' hole," Tom said. He wrapped his arms around a tree and leaned over the side. "It's a hundred feet to the bottom," he said. "I'm getting dizzy just looking at it. Are you sure about this?"

Mitch nodded and said, "The water is down about ten feet."

"And it's still twenty feet deep," Tom said. "You're one lucky son of a gun. If you had landed in the water, you'd be...."

"Fish bait," Mitch said, stepping back from the edge. He looked for a suitable tree to tie off to. He found it ten feet downhill and close to the edge. He tied three fifty-foot ropes together, fastened one end to the tree, and tossed the loose end over the side.

"You don't have to do this," Tom said.

"Yes, Tom. I do. It's the last place I remember; it's the first place I know to look. I'm going to scout around. Maybe I can find a clue as to how I ended up down there." He thought a minute. "I doubt if I fell, so either I was thrown, pushed, or I jumped."

"You didn't jump. A man who has fought so hard to live wouldn't throw his life away. And if indeed you would, then why out here all alone?"

"Well, let's see what we can find."

Not knowing what they were looking for, they searched the area for thirty minutes, but found nothing out of the ordinary.

"Whatever you are looking for isn't here," Tom said.

"I probably won't find anything below either, but I have to look. Are you ready?"

"Hey! Don't look at me. I'm not going down there. Not on the end of a rope."

"No guts, no glory," Mitch replied, and without further discussion he donned his gloves, turned his back to the river, and with the rope around and under his seat he jumped backward and disappeared over the edge. Tom gasped at the suddenness of Mitch's descent and dropped to his knees to peer over the edge.

"Scare ya?" Mitch asked only a few feet below where he was leaning back on the rope with his feet braced against the sheer face of the cliff.

"You aged me ten years, you young pup."

Mitch laughed and let a few inches of rope slide through his hands.

"Don't worry, Doc, I know what I'm doing, I think."

He pushed away with his feet and was gone and down with a series of backward leaps. In the blink of an eye he was past the belly in the cliff and out of sight. The rope went slack.

"I'm down," Mitch yelled up.

Tom released his pent-up breath and drew deeply of the crisp mountain air. He cussed himself for being old, then lit his pipe and leaned against a tree to wait.

The horses swished their tails at the irritating flies and dozed beneath the trees while Tom smoked and watched a bald eagle soar overhead. Barney sat on his haunches and peered over the edge cautiously, whining for Mitch.

Mitch retraced the steps he'd taken after coming back from oblivion weeks ago. All traces of his fire had been erased; the massive pile of tangled driftwood had been swept away, and even the largest of the boulders had been moved by will of the river

He stood at the place where he'd first awakened and looked up at the cliff. He studied the shelf again and noticed how narrow it actually was. Peering back up at the cliff, all his ideas of how he'd come to be there vanished. He couldn't have fallen from the top of the cliff without landing in the water; the outward curve, the belly in the rock would have impeded his fall and forced him out past the ledge. He shook his head, bewildered.

Doesn't make sense, he thought as he took a last look around. Then he grasped the rope and started back up. The rope made the climb easy *in comparison* to his first ascent, but he still had his work cut out for him. He half expected to hear the roar of the bear behind him, and he even glanced over his shoulder at the rocky beach but saw only a couple of birds chasing water bugs at the river's edge near a jagged piece of thin white aluminum resting between a boulder and a piece of driftwood. If he had seen the numbers on the other side of it, he might have recognized the identification numbers of Greg's airplane. When he reached the upper shelf he stopped to rest, grinning mischievously as he yelled up at Tom.

"I'm resting on the upper ledge; be up in a few."

"Take your time," Tom yelled back sleepily. "I'm taking my beauty nap up here."

Mitch didn't rest; he immediately began working his way along the face of the cliff, following his earlier escape route. It was easier this trip, but he was spooked to think he'd been out of his mind the first time—and near dead, too. The shelf under his feet was only two feet across at its widest point, and in some places as narrow as eighteen inches. At least it was straight and didn't deviate from its angle of ascent. It appeared the mountain had cracked through and the upper portion had fallen back from the river, leaving the narrow path that ended in the trees a few yards ahead.

He stepped slowly and carefully, laughing at his recklessness, leaning against the cliff for balance. Below, the river taunted him again and he chanced a glance. The swiftly moving water had a hypnotic effect, and suddenly he found himself swaying and feeling dizzy. He closed his eyes and leaned tightly against the rock. When the feeling passed, he pressed on more carefully, his eyes on the path ahead. Then he was on top and sneaking through the woods with orneriness on his mind.

He kept close to the trees and their soft carpet of needles. He moved with a woodsman's grace and ease, but he was not clever enough to fool the horses. He spotted Dallas through the thick trees and brush. She was looking directly at him, her ears forward, nostrils distended, ready to blow.

"Easy there," Mitch whispered, watching for Jasper. Before Dallas could let her breath out and give him away, he was at her side and stroking her neck.

"Easy now; don't spoil my fun." Dallas relaxed and let her breath out in a long sigh, tossing her head playfully. Neither Tom nor Barney was in sight, but suddenly Jasper stepped out of the woods trailing his lead rope. He whinnied loudly before Mitch could stop him. Then from behind him, much to his surprise, he heard a chuckle and the strike of a match. He turned so swiftly he nearly tripped over his big feet.

"What do you take me for, Son?" Tom asked and laughed as he scratched his dog behind the ears. "Think I'm some kind of greenhorn or tenderfoot? I grew up in these woods!" He puffed his pipe thoughtfully. "You ought to be ashamed of yourself, trying to sneak up on an old man. You could have given me a heart attack." Tom didn't give Mitch a chance to reply. He just kept talking as he walked toward the horses.

"I waited a bit, and then I called down. When you didn't answer, I knew what you were up to." Tom caught Jasper. He'd released him, sabotaging Mitch's plan.

"Like I said, I was raised in these woods."

Mitch stood, tongue in cheek as Tom tightened the girth on his saddle.

"What's the matter, Son," Tom asked as he swung astride Jasper. "Did I startle you?"

Dallas nudged Mitch in the back with her nose and whinnied softly.

"You devious old scoundrel," he said under his breath as he succumbed to the fact that he'd been beaten at his own game.

"Uh, what's that? What did you say?" Tom grinned. His arms were crossed over the horn, his right hand loosely fingering the reins. His Stetson was thrown back on his head, the wind ruffled the hair over his sweaty brow, and the sunlight showed amusement in his eyes.

"Nothing," Mitch said. He tried unsuccessfully to hide a sheepish grin as he untied Dallas. He glared at Tom as he tightened the cinches of his double rig saddle and said under his breath, "Sneakin' old varmint!"

Tom chuckled past his pipe. Then, with eyebrows lifted, head raised and cocked slightly to one side, Tom said, "Come again?"

"I said you're a sneakin' old varmint," Mitch yelled.

Tom leaned back in his saddle and roared. Mitch could hold it back no longer; he busted out, too, but his laughter trailed off when he saw that the rope he'd used to go down the cliff was coiled and hanging neatly on Tom's saddle horn. He looked from the rope to Tom and back.

"That's right. Two can play this game," Tom said.

With the quickness of a striking snake, Mitch launched himself at Tom, trying to push him off his horse. However, thanks to excellent training, one light touch with a heel and Jasper sidestepped out of the way.

Mitch fell on his face.

"You ornery old coot," Mitch cussed as he jumped to his feet and scrambled to climb into the saddle.

"I'll get you for that!" he yelled as he hit leather. "If I catch you, I'll, I'll."

Tom was already gone.

Mitch gathered the reins and spurred Dallas. They took after Tom with Barney barking excitedly at their heels. They raced downhill for fifty yards, dodging trees and brush. But then he suddenly pulled Dallas to a halt as he looked back uphill over his shoulder. Dallas had been trained well and one tug on the bit was all she needed. She stopped so suddenly that Mitch was pitched forward over the saddle and nearly busted his nose on the back of her head. He settled back into the saddle, reminded himself he was not riding a green broke horse, and turned her back uphill. Barney hesitated, undecided as to whom to follow, then ran after Mitch.

Mitch was forcefully drawn back to the top of the cliff, manipulated like a puppet, defenseless against a nameless, relentless feeling that he must return. Once there, he stepped out of the saddle and stood at the edge, staring down at the river. Then came a feeling of impending motion, as if he stood on the end of a gangplank, knowing at any moment he'd find only air beneath his feet. Then the Earth trembled, a rushing of wind whistled past his ears, and he was falling again. Hot blood coursed through his veins, tearing through his heart, thundering in his ears. The air was thick and stifling. His breath hardened and caught in his throat like a cement plug as the Earth opened, becoming a hole that sucked him violently down. Darkness descended and the Earth closed around him.

CHAPTER TWENTY-SIX

By the time Sherrie had driven Donna home from the doctor's office, the medicine had taken its effect and Sherrie virtually carried Donna upstairs and put her to bed.

"Sher'," Donna mumbled groggily, "leave a note for Steven, please."

"If I can find something to write on."

Donna motioned to her purse.

"Just let him know...what's up, and tell him to have a good time."

Donna's head fell to one side and her eyes rolled back in her head as her exhausted mind searched for what she knew she needed to say.

"Uh, have him...wake me...when he gets in."

"Is that all?" Sherrie asked as she sat on the edge of the bed scribbling on a note pad. "Geez, Louise! I hope he can read this. I can't, and I wrote it." She looked over her shoulder. Donna was sleeping soundly. Sherrie added a line to the note, telling Steven to have Donna call her in the morning. She stuck the note under a magnet on the refrigerator and put the groceries away. Then she roamed the house, looking for anything she might have missed earlier while she was cleaning. She noticed the cedar chest was partially open. Happy and high-spirited as usual, she danced across the soft carpet and opened the chest. Folded neatly atop several blankets was Donna's quilt. She spread it out on the carpet and sat down on the couch to appraise it. Captured by its beauty, she slipped off the couch and knelt before it. She reached out and touched it. She felt the shapes. She ran her fingers along the stitching, tracing a life story from their meeting in San Antonio to their Colorado honeymoon; from his proposal at the River Walk to the birth of their son. The story unfolded, square by square, until it rested after the disappearance of Mitch, waiting for a new chapter to be stitched.

She sensed the good times; the hard times; the struggle in the beginning to make a life; the eventual success; the love; the caring; and the family. Toward the end, where Donna had sewn life after the crash, she sensed the tragedy and the hope; the grief and love; the strength and faith of the artist. She was drawn into the quilt. As she gazed upon it and ran her fingers over the last two blocks Donna had created, she was captivated by its energy. She lived their lives in a moment, understanding and feeling the meaning of true love.

Next to the last panel was a detailed rendering of an airplane flying over a mountain pass. Goose bumps rose on her skin as she ran her fingers across the last block Donna had finished. It was Mitch, Donna, and Steven, together again. Smiling to herself she wondered about Donna's heritage and the stories her Spanish ancestors must have told.

CHAPTER TWENTY-SEVEN

Dallas trembled at the smell of fear coming from the man standing before her. The odor struck Barney, too, and the dog dashed into the woods with his tail tucked between his legs. Dallas grew taut as she strained against her training, divided by the urge to bolt and the discipline to obey the reins in Mitch's hand. Her fear was strong; she bunched her muscles and readied herself to turn and run.

Mitch groaned as if punched in the gut, and then he passed out as his knees buckled and he fell toward the edge. Dallas forgot her training. Rearing in panic, she threw back her head and turned to run. As her hooves cut the earth, her twelve hundred pounds of flesh and bone pulled against the reins, which, as luck would have it, were wrapped twice around his right hand. When Dallas lunged away she pulled Mitch with her, jerking him away from the cliff edge, but throwing him beneath her wildly flailing hooves.

♠ ♠ ♠

Tom slowed Jasper to a walk, waiting, listening. Mitch should have been right on his heels, but Tom heard nothing except the river and the soft chop of his horse's hooves on the carpet of pine needles and grass. Jasper's ears were also tuned to the trail behind. Tom stopped and waited for a few minutes, then finally reined the horse around and headed back up the trail, fully expecting Mitch to be planning something devious.

Barney had barely penetrated the darkness of the woods when his love for Mitch overcame his sudden fear of him. Sensing that Mitch was in danger, Barney catapulted himself back into the clearing as Mitch fell under the frightened horse.

Once again, Barney threw himself in the face of death. Prepared to give his life, he launched himself between Mitch and Dallas's iron-shod hooves. Mitch hit the ground with a grunt as Barney's 80 pounds rammed Dallas square in the chest, throwing her off balance and over onto her back. Barney fell beside Mitch and crawled dizzily to his side, whimpering and licking his face. Mitch moaned and blinked his eyes, unaware that he'd narrowly escaped death again. For a second he had been reliving the nightmare and the dark horse, the omens that had preceded the plane crash; the robbers which had stolen his past and killed his friend. He rose shakily to his feet and grabbed the leaning tree for support.

"Guess I overdid it again," he said as he dusted off his clothes and cursed his luck.

He shuddered as he remembered the feelings that had overcome him before he passed out. He tried to shake it off as he coaxed Dallas to him and gathered the reins. He was just about to swing into the saddle when he heard Tom approaching. Mitch plucked a dangling pine needle from his brow as Tom rode up.

"Something wrong?"

Tom dismounted, concern showing on his furrowed brow.

"Naw," Mitch shrugged, "just...thinking."

"I waited down yonder for you," Tom said as he scratched Barney on the head, noticing a trickle of blood running down his left ear.

"What happened to you, Dawg? Get tangled up in the briars?" He switched the reins to his left hand and sidled up beside Mitch.

"What's up? Hey! Are you alright? You're white as a fish belly."

"Tom I have a funny feeling. Something is happening, or is about to happen."

He stared across the river again, as he had before he blacked out and nearly fell over the edge.

"I feel a change coming. I can't put my finger on it, but I do know something for sure."

"What's that?"

"When I was down below I looked up, and I couldn't see where we're standing now. The cliff bows out in the middle like a fat man's belly. Anybody falling off here would have landed in the river."

Tom inched forward and peered over the edge as Mitch gazed across the canyon.

"It didn't start down below. It started across the river, or upstream. You mentioned that you had fished over there?"

"Yeah, but it's been a few years."

"How do we get there?"

"There's a road takes you most of the way, but then you have to hike a mile to the river."

"Would you take me there tomorrow?"

"I suppose so."

"Right now," Mitch said, "I just can't make any sense out of all this. I wake up one morning half-dead, my feet dangling in the river. I'm soaked to the bone, the sun is blazing down on me.... Wait a minute! The shelf was dry except for a small pool back up against the base of the cliff. Why was I wet? Why was everything within a few feet of me wet? Why was the rest of the shelf dry?" Perplexed, Mitch bit his bottom lip and chewed on it.

"Tom took out his pipe and lit it. He smoked and pondered what Mitch had said.

"It hadn't rained or snowed for several days before you came to. As a matter of fact," Tom said around his pipe, "it had been unusually warm during the middle of that week. We had storms that week, but the rain missed us."

"Snow!" Mitch said with conviction. "That's it! I'm sure of it. I was lying in snow. That's why I was wet." He was excited. "What if I had landed...why am I saying that? Landed from what? From where? Certainly not from up here." He thought a minute.

"I had to have fallen or been made to fall. It's the only explanation. The river wouldn't have deposited me down there. It would have swept me on past. Assuming I was in the water to begin with, but the current was too strong. I would have drowned had I been in the water, or I would have been bashed against the rocks. I would have been dead. No! I fell! But from where?" He stooped to pick up a pine needle and stuck it between his teeth.

The wind blew the hair sticking out from beneath his hat. The river below seemed to laugh at him, to mock him. It cursed him for he'd escaped.

"Maybe I was in a snowdrift. Could that be it? Could I have landed in a snowdrift? Maybe that's what saved me. What if that drift broke loose and slid down the shelf into the river just before I woke up? There was a spot of snow here and there, now that I think about it.

Tom chimed in, "If the snow was deep enough it could have softened your landing. Now you have *me* saying it. But how you survived is not the question. The question is what you survived. It's beginning to look like you just fell out of the sky."

Mitch glanced up and rolled his eyes at Tom. Then he shook his head and said, "Come on." He centered the saddle and checked the cinches, then he swung into the saddle as easily as if he'd done it all of his life. Tom knocked his pipe on the bark of the leaning tree and followed suit.

"The answer lies over there somewhere," Mitch said as he pointed across the river and into the distant trees. "The feeling is strong in me. Something happened over there. Tomorrow we're going to start putting the pieces together."

But tomorrow would find him nowhere near Tom's mountain ranch.

Where the trail allowed, they rode side by side; where it narrowed, they rode single file with Tom in the lead and Barney bringing up the rear. They rode in silence, thinking and just taking it easy. The only sounds were those of the forest, the river, and the squeaking of saddle leather. The breeze turned cooler and whispered melodiously through the pines, cedars, fir, and spruce. A pair of jays squawked in the branches above and followed them as they rode. Aside from Mitch's frustration, he was happy as a lark. They were outdoors nine thousand feet up the mountain.

A chipmunk sat on an old stump and nibbled on a

pine nut, watching as they passed, seemingly uncon-
cerned. Now that Barney was free to chase he chose not
to, as if it were suddenly beneath him.

Tom reined up.

"Hear that?"

"Hear what?"

"Nothing," Tom said proudly, "nothing but the wind
and the river and the forest, and what God filled them
with. It's the sound of Mother Nature in the nude; unbridled, unhindered, and unpolluted. Praise God for the
glory of it."

He led off again and Mitch followed, smiling blissfully. The smile hadn't yet faded when Tom stopped at his
lunch spot by the river, where he stepped off and un-
saddled Jasper. He turned the horse loose and encouraged Mitch to do the same with Dallas.

"They won't go far. They know this place," Tom said.
"This was Natalie's favorite spot on Earth. She and I
used to sit down here and while away many an afternoon, just talking, fishing, or making love." Mitch
looked up in surprise from where he was unsaddling
Dallas.

"You did what?"

Tom laughed.

"Takin' advantage of a lady in the woods? Why you
ought to be horsewhipped," Mitch joked.

"Me? It was her idea! Both times!" Something about
that struck Mitch's funny bone and he doubled over
and had to hang on to the saddle to keep from falling.
Saddle, saddle blanket, and Mitch tumbled to earth.
Dallas stood her ground and swung her head around to
stare at him. Mitch looked over the top of his saddle,
which was now on top of him, and saw Tom through
the space under his horse's belly. Tom was laughing so
hard that tears rolled down his cheeks.

Mitch tossed aside the saddle and jumped to his feet. He dusted his hind-end off and turned Dallas loose. His lopsided grin splayed across his face as he humbly accepted the sandwich Tom offered. Tom was still laughing and wiping tears off his weathered face.

"You're good at fallin' down. Did you break anything this time?"

Mitch said nothing. He couldn't with half his sandwich stuffed in his cheeks. He looked like a squirrel with a mouth full of acorns. Still chuckling, Tom sat down on the log. Mitch watched as he and Barney went through their ritual. When Barney ran to the river to drink, Mitch followed.

At the river's edge he stood, captivated. The river, menacing in the canyon, was jubilant now and seemed to be laughing with Tom as it bustled on its way. Lush vegetation grew along the banks. Blackberries were abundant, and he made a mental note to collect some to take back with them. Horsetails, skunk cabbage, and ferns also graced the forest floor, along with wildflowers in a rainbow of colors. A dipper, a small water bird, darted about in the shallows in search of minnows and water insects. Ladybugs adorned the tall grass, crawling up and down in their hunt for microscopic aphids.

"Ladybug, ladybug, fly away home," Mitch said, wondering where he'd heard that. The river was three times as wide there as it was up near the cliff and it moved more slowly. It was cold and clear, not as stained with mud and silt as upriver. He knelt down and scooped up a mouthful.

"Here, drink from your canteen," Tom said, suddenly standing over him. "That water only appears clean. It probably *is* safe to drink, but these days you never know."

For several hundred yards in either direction along the river the trees were sparse. It was a good area for casting.

"You're right," Mitch said.

The weather was perfect; they had a light breeze, mild sun, and partly cloudy skies. Mitch ruffled his hair. Time for a haircut, he thought, and found himself thirty-two years back in his past.

"Sit still, Mitchell," a young woman said.

"Mamma, it's gettin' in muh eyes."

"Easy, Son," the barber said, "I'm almost finished."

"Mamma, can I have an ice cream cone after?"

"Well, I guess so. But you have to promise not to make a mess in your daddy's new pickup truck."

"OK, Mitchell, I'm done; you can step down." The barber folded the apron and lifted it off the boy's lap. Little Mitchell jumped out of the chair and ran to the door, then ran back to the barber.

"Whatcha do with the hair ya cut off everbuddies' heads?"

"Well, Son," the barber winked at the boy's mother, "if it's long enough I sell it to the man across the street at the pet shop."

"Wha's he do wid `em?"

"That will be fifty cents, Mrs. Cooper. Mitchell, he soaks the hair in warm water, and all those little hairs turn into snakes. He sells the snakes to the farmers. They keep the mice and rats away."

"Wow!" Mitchell said. "Mamma, did ya hear that?"

"Yes," she said with a frown. "Sam, you ought to be ashamed."

"Mitch? Mitch?" Tom put a hand on his friend's shoulder. Mitch turned to Tom with an odd look on his face.

"What's wrong, Son?"

"I know my name. It *is* Mitch. It's Mitchell Cooper. I remembered getting a haircut when I was about six. I was with my mother. She called me Mitchell and the barber called her Mrs. Cooper. We were going to get an ice cream cone." His eyes glistened with distant memories.

"It's coming back."

"I knew it would," Tom said and then prayed a silent prayer of thanks as he opened the door of a small shed at the edge of the clearing. He removed two fly rods and two tackle boxes.

"It doesn't make much sense to haul them back and forth, so I keep them and a few supplies down here." He handed a rod and box of tackle to Mitch and pointed him toward the better fishing upstream.

With skill he didn't know he had, Mitch studied the insects flying and crawling around him, then selected a fly from the box and tied it on. With confidence born of experience, he stepped onto a rock and from that to another, and then one more until he was twenty feet into the river. He balanced carefully on the moss-covered boulder, and with clear, vociferous water rushing and swirling around him, he worked the rod deftly, pulling and casting line, then softly landing the fly upriver to his left, above a rock jutting out of the water. He held the rod lightly but firmly in his right hand, feeling for that tell-tale tap. He fished and wondered about that little boy behind the dark curtain of his mind, while downstream Tom fished below some rapids. Barney stretched out in the grass and slept.

On Mitch's second cast, he saw a silver streak dart out from behind the jutting rock, but the fish missed. He saw it again on the third cast, but again it missed the fly. The fourth and fifth cast yielded nothing as well, so he cast farther upstream and guided the imitation grasshopper right in and around the rock where he had spotted the fish. Suddenly his rod was nearly wrenched from his hands as the lunker headed across the river, peeling line off the reel. Then the line went slack.

Mitch raised the rod and reeled feverishly; the fish had turned back, but then it turned again and made a mad dash upstream. The line sung as it grew dangerously taught and once more screamed off his reel.

Mitch lost his balance and slipped into the icy water. The water was so cold it took his breath away. He fought to regain his balance but went under. Spitting, sputtering, and screaming at the frigid water, he burst above the surface still clinging to a rod that was bent double under the extreme pressure the fish was handing him. He quickly abandoned the river and made his way to land.

Tom heard Mitch yell and headed upstream. He saw Mitch running with the fish. Mitch kept steady pressure on the line, running fifty yards before the big fish tired, slowed, and finally stopped at the bottom of a deep pool.

Tom watched as Mitch played the fish with care and intensity. He played the trout out of the hole and almost had his hand under its belly when it took off again. Mitch held his ground, giving and taking line for another three minutes.

Panting from the exertion of running upstream, Tom leaned against a tree to watch. Barney yipped excitedly and ran up and down the bank. Mitch once again eased the fish into the shallows, then he gently lifted it out of the water with both hands under its belly, holding it at arms length.

"Whoa! Would you look at that," Tom said.

Mitch beamed, and raised the fish higher.

"That's not the biggest brown trout I've seen taken out of this river, but it's the biggest I've seen in a long time." Tom took the big German Brown trout gently from Mitch and held it out in front of him to judge its weight.

"Twelve pounds if it's an ounce. Go-o-o-d fish!"

"Let me see it," Mitch said. He very gently removed the hook from the gristle in the lower jaw, then knelt in the water and quickly let it go. At first the trout just rested, pumping its jaws for the breath of life, then slowly swam a couple of feet, turning as if to look back at them, and then shooting off into the deep.

"You were right, Tom," Mitch said as he turned and walked back upstream. "This *is* a good spot."

"There's more in there like that, too, but they're wise and hard to catch. They get bigger, too. The state record is just a hair over twenty-six lbs, but I've been fishing this river all my life and that's the one of biggest brown I've seen caught here yet."

Tom laughed and pushed Mitch playfully.

Mitch laughed and pushed back.

"Hey, Dawg. Betcha Tom *never* caught a fish *that* big."

"Bull," Tom said. "Didn't I tell you about the time Nat' and I went down to the gulf. We used bait bigger than that."

"I'm hungry, but not for tall tales," Mitch threw back at him with a grin. "Let's catch some more for supper."

Tom and Mitch poked fun for the next hour and a half as they fished side by side. They caught several more fish, but none near the size of the big one Mitch had turned loose. They released all but four pan-sized rainbows and when the sun began to sink below the treetops, they gathered their catch and made their way back to camp, where Mitch hunted firewood and Tom unpacked their gear. The twins, though untethered, stayed close as Tom said they would. Barney just lived a dog's life, watching, scratching, yawning, and generally getting in the way.

As the sun descended and the light faded, the stars began to dance in the heavens and sparks from the fire floated toward the sky. Smoke curled lazily up through the pines as Mitch peeled potatoes and Tom prepared the fish for frying. Butter sizzled invitingly in a cast-iron skillet over the fire beside a pot of steaming coffee.

"Sure smells good," Mitch said over a hot cup. As the moon rose, crickets began to make their music, and frogs croaked noisily but not unpleasantly. A bird twittered softly in the pine boughs overhead. The twins stood a few feet beyond the fire, side by side and head to tail. Every few moments one of them whinnied softly or leaned on a different leg. Barney raised his ears inquisitively every few moments. Mitch sipped his coffee. Tom turned the fish.

"Mitchell Cooper. That's a good name," Tom said.

"I wonder if she's still alive."

"Your mother?"

"She was pretty. Hair into snakes? Right, and the short pieces became worms, I suppose."

"What?" Tom asked, giving his friend a puzzled look. Mitch told him what he'd remembered.

♠ ♠ ♠

Across the miles, Donna's eyes darted open. She smelled smoke. She jerked upright in bed, looking around the room, listening, grasping at her surroundings with every sense.

She rose swiftly and ran out of the bedroom. She checked upstairs and down but found nothing burning or smoking. Whatever had been in the air, if anything, was gone now. Had she imagined it? She checked the time. It was after seven and she was hungry.

Donna turned from the living room and ambled into the kitchen, where she found the note Sherrie had left for Steven. He'd written a note on the bottom telling her he'd be home by ten.

She made a sandwich, poured herself a tall glass of milk, and then went into the living room. Before she could sit down, a knock sounded on the door and Sherrie peeked in.

"You OK?"

"I'm fine, Sher', come in."

"I saw the lights; wanted to check on you."

"I'll be fine. I just woke up. I thought I smelled smoke, but it was nothing. It was probably in my dreams. I vaguely remember dreaming about Mitchell and the mountains."

"I'll look around."

"No, that's alright. The smoke detectors didn't even go off. Have a seat. Hungry?"

"Nah, we just ate. Did you get enough sleep?"

"For now. I'll go back to bed after Steven gets home. He said he'd be home by ten."

"You talked to him?"

"No, but he came home. He left a note."

The television remote control was lying on the couch beside her. She punched a button and the big-screen television came to life.

"Wanna watch a movie?"

"Sure, let me call my hubby." Sherrie went to the phone in the kitchen. Donna couldn't quite hear what she was saying but knew by the tone that Sherrie was in a bit of hot water. Then a long silence ensued, followed by a soft click.

"Something wrong?" she asked as Sherrie returned.

"No, nothing," Sherrie said.

"Liar."

"Huh?"

"Break a date?"

"You know me too well. Yeah, we were supposed to go see a movie but we can see it tomorrow. I'll make it up to him later, if you know what I mean." Donna shrugged her shoulders and just stared blankly at the screen. Sherrie cursed herself for her thoughtless words, knowing how much Donna missed Mitch and their lovemaking.

Across town Steven and Molly were approaching the theater.

"How's your mom?" Molly asked as they pulled into the parking lot.

"Not so good. This morning I found her crying alone in the kitchen again."

"Again?"

"Third time this week. She cries herself to sleep at night, too.

"Gosh, Steve, that's terrible. I would have totally died by now. What's going to happen? I mean, what if your father doesn't come back. What if he's dead? Sorry, but I had to ask."

"Don't worry about it. I've asked myself the same question but I'm not ready to give up hope. I have to be strong for mom. She's about to break."

"It's been so long; shouldn't you be thinking ahead?"

"I am. Dad's business is prospering and it will continue to do so. He planned ahead. He hired the right people and built the business to a point where it could function without him. This is the worst-case scenario, but he wanted us to be taken care of should anything happen to him." He checked his watch. "The movie starts in five minutes. We better get going."

♠ ♠ ♠

Back at the river, Mitch and Tom were comfortably fattened on fresh trout, pork and beans, fries, and canned peaches. They drank steaming coffee from tin camp cups and watched the flames disappear into the night while the horses grazed contentedly in the meadow behind them.

"It was a good thing your father did, saving this land. What'd you say it was that spurred him to it?"

Tom smoked his pipe thoughtfully for a moment, noting the western influence in Mitch's speech.

"I guess he realized that if we kept raping the forests, it wouldn't be long before virgin forests were gone. In his later years in the logging industry, as I've already told you, dad planted where he cut, but even then he knew he couldn't replace the natural forests he'd wiped out. He hoped others would follow his lead but he knew the greed that drove them—the same greed that is decimating the rain forests of South America. Granted, we cannot presently do without lumber, but we must find ways to cut down our use. In some areas of Malaysia, only ten percent of the forests remain.

"I read recently that it takes 75,000 trees for one edition of *The New York Times*."

"Wow, that many trees? You've got to be kidding"

"It's what I read recently, and I looked it up to be sure. I was just as dismayed as you are. But that's just one newspaper, in one nation. We have six percent of the world's population and produce half of the world's garbage. We cut and burn, burn and pollute, take and rarely give. Maybe you are better off without your memory; they say ignorance is bliss. I wish I didn't know some of what I do. Want another shock? Our great nation, so I read, dumps two billion gallons of raw sewage and toxic waste into our oceans every year.

"Two billion gallons?"

"That's what I read a few years ago." It makes me sick to think about it. Son, we have all but written our epitaph. Global warming isn't just a myth. Human beings have become a geological presence on this earth. We've messed up. Personally, I think we've caused irreparable damage. The trees are Earth's lungs and we've ripped them out. I think the human race is doomed, and damned if we don't deserve it."

Mitch was speechless for several minutes. Tom stared into his coffee and regretted opening his mouth.

Finally, Mitch said, "It's easy to see why you like this place. I wonder why your father didn't build down here."

"He almost did, but then chose wisely to build closer to the county road. Natalie wanted me to build down here and rent out the cabin, but we never got around to it. The storage shed yonder is as far as we got. I sometimes wish we had built a home down here. At least she's buried here. That's her grave yonder."

"Figured as much," Mitch said with respect. "Seems right."

"Often wondered myself what draws us here," Tom said.

"Does it matter?" Mitch asked, "Does one need a reason to love something?"

Tom smoked thoughtfully a moment.

"No, I guess not," he said.

Mitch stirred the fire; sparks flew skyward. He added more wood and listened to the sap pop and sizzle. The twins wandered down to the river to drink, then came back to stand behind the men. Dallas nudged Mitch with her nose. He scratched her under the chin and listened to the rustling of the river.

"What was she like?"

Tom glanced sideways at him. His eyes caught the firelight and sparkled in the glow. A faint smile broke the bitterness that had ruled his face, and he sighed.

"She was beautiful, even in her old age. She liked yellow dresses, horses, old movies, and roses. She planted this bush three years ago. She planted those at the cabin and cared for them like they were her children. In a way they were, after Jeremy took off.

"She enjoyed life. She never complained. She was as fresh as a breath of spring. She was a Christian woman and she believed she'd go to a better place. Sometimes, like you, we all have moments when we're not so sure about that, but I'm inclined in my old age to believe like she did. Sometimes I can feel her presence here. It's as if she comes back from time to time to check on me.

"When she died I thought I would die as well. I thought I had lost everything, but you have shown me different. I often wonder if you weren't sent here for a reason."

"Or," Mitch suggested, "could be that He sent you and the dog my way."

"We may never know," Tom said.

Suddenly Barney leapt to his feet and gazed guardedly across the fire, whimpering. Then abruptly his mood changed and he barked inquisitively, trotting to the other side. One of the twins snorted and pawed the ground.

Mitch got up and cautiously followed Barney.

"What is it, Barn?" Tom asked as he got up and followed. Mitch knelt beside the retriever, where the light from the fire blended with the dark of the forest. Barney sniffed and scratched at the dirt, then whined and sniffed the air.

"He's sure acting strange," Mitch said, feeling uneasy as he also sniffed the air.

"What is it, Son?"

"Beats me," Mitch said, turning back to the other side of the campfire. He picked up his cup and filled it from the pot that rested on a flat rock beside the coals.

"Did you smell anything?" he asked.

"Yeah, but I can't say what I thought it was without appearing addled."

"Perfume?" Mitch asked over his cup.

Tom nodded. "Yeah," he said.

He sat back down on the log, shaking his head.

"Strange," Mitch said as he stepped around the fire again, peering into the darkness. After a few minutes of pacing back and forth, he returned to the log. For the next two hours he listened while Tom reminisced about Natalie and his father, while back in Boise, Steven and Molly sat side by side, hardly close enough, and watched the movie while sipping Cokes and sharing a bucket of popcorn.

"I liked the older ones better," she said later as they left the theater with the rest of the crowd.

"Me, too, but I still enjoyed it," he said as he opened her door. He waited until she was seated then shut the door and walked around to his side. He climbed in and gazed longingly at her sitting there like a princess, so attractive in her blue jeans and white blouse, her long, dark hair contrasting so beautifully against the red interior of his truck.

She scooted over next to him and put her arms around him, pressing her full breasts hard against his chest, kissing him passionately. Taken aback by her abrupt show of affection, Steven felt himself go spinning inside and kissed her back hungrily. She pulled away. She was breathless, her heart pounding.

He looked into her eyes as his own heart pounded with passion. She returned his gaze and neither had to say a word.

"You know I love you, Steve."

"You know I love you," he said. This was where he had intended to pop the question. But during the movie he had thought over his conversation with his mother. He had realized that she was right. Life was short, but not that short.

"I'm going to marry you someday, Molly," he stated instead.

"I know," she said without hesitation. "But after college. Don't ask me before then. If you do, I'll say no." She kissed him and then told him to take her home before her father called and told them to get home. He grinned and kissed her back. He sighed deeply, knowing that everything was in its proper order. He counted his blessings and told himself to thank his mother when he got home. His only regret was that he couldn't share this moment with his father. He started the pickup and drove her home.

"Mom? You up?" he said as he entered the kitchen from the garage a few minutes later.

"In here, Steven," she hollered from the living room. Steven walked in and sat in his father's recliner, leaning back with his hands behind his head. Donna and Sherrie looked at him expectantly.

"Well?" Donna asked.

"Well what?"

"What did she say?" Sherrie said.

"I didn't ask her. I thought about what you said, Mom. You are right, of course. No, I didn't ask her. I told her. I told her I was going to marry her someday.

She agreed, but told me not to ask her before we finished college, or she'd say no. You're right, mom, women *are* different. I wish dad was here so I could tell him. He almost started crying and it showed. He jumped up and walked briskly to the kitchen.

"I'm hungry," he said over his shoulder. "Anything in the frig?"

"Look on the top shelf. There's some sliced ham. Make you a sandwich," Donna said. She turned to her friend.

"I'm so proud of him. Here he comes. There he goes."

Steven ran up the stairs with a sandwich in one hand and a glass of milk in the other. When he reached the top, he turned on the landing, and then walked halfway back down.

"Thanks, Mom. Love ya. See you in the morning. Have sweet dreams."

The women turned to each other in unison as he ran to his room.

"He isn't a little boy anymore," Donna said.

"In case you haven't noticed, Dear," Sherrie said as she looked after Steven, "he's all man, and there's nothing little about him."

"Sher'! You better watch your mouth. I can't believe you said that about my son."

"He's a hunk, dear, and speaking of hunks, I'd better get home to mine. This movie stinks, and you need to sleep." She got up to leave.

"Yeah, I know. Thanks for coming over."

"Good night, Steve, you good-looking thing," Sherrie yelled upstairs in spite of Donna.

Donna saw her friend to the door and then, after making sure her son hadn't left a mess, she wearily climbed the stairs and returned to bed.

An hour later, Steven woke with a start. The smell of

smoke was strong in the air. He jumped out of bed, pulled on his jeans, and ran down the hall. He saw nothing indicative of a fire, but the smell was strong just the same. He made a beeline to the end of the hall and started down the stairs, stopping short when he heard his father's voice coming from his parent's room.

He burst through their door.

♠ ♠ ♠

Mitch was uneasy after Barney's outburst and the subsequent and simultaneous sensing of the perfume by Tom and him. He sat silent and reserved while Tom talked about his life. Mitch nodded his head now and then, making a comment when necessary, but mostly he just stared across the flames toward the river as if expecting to see something. He watched and waited. The feeling was strong that more was to come as the familiar scent drifted mysteriously through the chilly evening air.

The later in the evening it became, the more anxious he felt. Tom noticed and suggested they break camp and head for the cabin instead of spending the night as they had planned. Nevertheless, Mitch wanted to stay. He stirred the coals, added more wood, filled his cup, and then sat back down. As he sat down Barney stood up and began to whine. The twins both pawed the ground and snorted. Mitch looked across the fire and froze. Tom dropped his cup. Barney barked crazily. Mitch sat there, unable to move or speak, as the twins bolted and ran.

♠ ♠ ♠

Steven saw his mother sit up in bed as he flew through

the door. The room was filled with the odor of smoke but empty of the real thing.

"What's going on?" Donna cried.

"I smell smoke, and I-I heard dad's voice in here."

"Me, too! But...."

Her voice caught in her throat as both she and her son witnessed a blazing fire at her feet, floating above the floor. Donna started to scream, but the scream was cut short when suddenly she saw her husband, an old man, and a large golden dog looking at her through the flames.

"Dad!" Steven yelled.

"Mitch, my God, Mitch," Donna said as she reached out for him.

♠ ♠ ♠

Through the flames Mitch could see a bed floating above the ground. Then a figure approached the bed as another sat up in it. Then in unison, they looked straight at him. Mitch didn't feel the hot coffee spilling down his pants and onto his boots.

"Dad!" exclaimed the young man by the bed.

"Mitch, my God! Steven, it's your father. Mitch?"

As quickly as it came, the vision vanished and left two silent and shaken men staring wide-eyed and slack jawed across the flames.

"Mitch?" Donna reached out for him but as she leaned forward, they disappeared into the shadows, her husband, a silver-haired old man, and a large golden dog. Steven stared blindly into the shadows where the image of his father had faded.

Mitch trembled. Tom couldn't move, not even to swat the mosquito that was draining blood from his left earlobe. The wilderness was mute and deathly still. The rush of the river and the cackle of the fire at his feet were the only sounds that even dared to scratch the surface of the silence.

"Tom? Did you see that?"

Tom nodded so slightly it was nearly imperceptible.

"It was my wife and son. I knew it. I have a family."

♠ ♠ ♠

Steven came out of it only when Donna streaked past yelling something about a dog. He turned slowly and walked out of the bedroom and down the stairs to find his mother sitting on the couch with the quilt clutched to her breast. Steven fell heavily beside her. Slowly, as if in a trance, he reached for her and held her, rocking back and forth with her as she cried for joy. For the moment, Steven was still too shocked to speak, too stunned to cry. Then Donna mumbled something about an old man and a dog.

"What dog? What old man?" he heard himself say.

"I know where your father is. I finally know where he is. It was there all along."

"I don't understand. Mom? What happened?"

"I can't explain it, Steven, but something just showed us where your father is." She found her strength and took hold of her son. She shook him out of his daze.

"Steven, listen! Remember when we were searching that area along the river, southwest of Grangeville?" Steven nodded slowly. "Remember the old man and the dog sitting by the water?" He nodded again as a light came into his eyes. "It was the same man and the same dog we just saw upstairs, and your father was with them. Look," she told him. "Look at this." She turned the quilt around on her lap until she found the block she'd been inspired to create over two months ago. "See this? It's your dad and that dog. I made this three weeks before your father disappeared. I don't need to tell you what that implies."

♠ ♠ ♠

Mitch began breaking camp, but Tom was still shaken and continued to gaze into the flames. Mitch caught and saddled the horses and packed their gear. He helped Tom into the saddle after dousing the fire. Tom was severely shaken and it worried him.

Two hours later, they sat in the living room, Mitch on the couch with Barney beside him, Tom sitting in his recliner. Tom was unnerved by what he'd seen and hadn't spoken a word.

A fire blazed once more before them, more for the comfort than for the warmth. Upon arrival at the cabin, Mitch had left Tom inside and rode to the barn alone, leading Jasper. On his return, he found Tom standing at the west end of the cabin, looking toward the river and shaking his head in disbelief. Mitch took him back inside, and then built the fire.

Now he leaned forward with his elbows on his knees and peered at the cracks in the hardwood floor. Barney sat beside him, watching intently as Mitch tapped his boots and rubbed his beard, rocking back and forth nervously. An excitement was building in him. He felt an eagerness to act.

"Tom," he spoke suddenly. "It's time. I have to go. I can't wait any longer. Tomorrow I'm heading for Texas."

Tom didn't say anything for several minutes, and then he rose from his chair and walked slowly over to the fireplace. He reached up with a trembling hand and lifted a small wooden box off the mantle. He opened it and removed a roll of hundred dollar bills. He peeled thirty off, replaced the box, and handed the money to Mitch. Here, put this with the thousand in your billfold.

"You earned it. It's yours. You'll need it. I'll drive you into town in the morning. A bus comes through daily. It will take you to Boise. From there you can catch another to Texas." Tom spoke in such a way that Mitch didn't even try to refuse the money.

"Thanks, Tom."

"It's the least I can do. I've been selfish; I've kept you here when you could have long ago been home with your family. We could have found them somehow."

"No. Don't blame yourself. It was my decision; I decided to stay. I was the one who refused to go to the hospital. I'll take the blame for that." Tom changed the subject, embarrassed.

"Never in all my days have I seen anything like what we saw tonight." He walked slowly to his chair.

"I know what it was, but I can't explain how it happened." He started to sit down but stopped and pointed toward the river. "You weren't meant to die out there. I know little about the paranormal, but it's written all over you. I did not heal you. You were beyond help; I figured you a dead man."

Tom paced the floor. The firelight cast his shadow tall against the back of the room. Sparks flew up the chimney as a log fell behind him. Flames leapt up and his shadow darkened in the brightness.

"Son, I've been stubborn in the past, but right this minute, I am a God-fearing man, and right now I'm shaking in my boots. It was He who saved you, He who brought us together, and it is He who is going to bring you and your family back together again. I see no other explanation.

"You are a marked man, my friend. God had His

hand on you from the beginning. Tomorrow you go find your woman and your son." Tom paused abruptly, stared at the floor a few seconds, and then turned to him again.

"Want a beer? I sure could use one after that."

"Yeah, sure," Mitch said with a grin, "why not."

♠ ♠ ♠

Neither Steven nor Donna slept much that night, and by daylight they were fast on their way north. Fearing more flak from family and clergy and the authorities, Donna kept silent, telling only Sherrie about what had transpired and their plans. They hit the road and hit it moving.

CHAPTER TWENTY-EIGHT

Y ou can wait over by those sliding glass doors," the attendant said. "Your bus should arrive any second and will be leaving shortly there- after. We run a tight schedule. Be ready to roll."

"Thanks," Mitch said. He and Tom walked over by the doors and sat down on the hard bench.

"Son," Tom said with more than a hint of regret, "I'll be waiting by the phone. Call me when you get where you're going."

Mitch's bus pulled up.

"Call me if you run out of money. Work can be hard to come by, especially for someone without a history. I'm pretty well heeled so don't worry about asking for money; what's mine is yours."

"I'll keep in touch," Mitch assured him.

"Son," Tom paused and bit his bottom lip to keep it from quivering. "Don't be a stranger. You are family now; my home is your home. When you find your fami- ly, I want you to bring them up here. I want to meet them." he said. In his own way, he had adopted Mitch.

"Count on it," Mitch said as the call came for him to board the bus.

"Well," he said, "I guess it's that time."

Tom followed Mitch to the loading area. Mitch was reticent, but not without emotion. He struggled to rein it in, for he had come to love Tom like a father. He would miss him, and suddenly Mitch had the disturbing feeling that he might never see Tom alive again. He turned to Tom with tear-filled eyes.

"I'll miss you," he said as he gripped Tom's hand firmly, then pulled Tom to him and hugged him to his heart. "I love you, Old Man."

"I love you, too, you buzzard turd," Tom replied hoarsely, then managed a chuckle and then they both laughed in spite of the circumstance.

The bus driver tapped his foot.

"You'd better get," Tom said. Mitch nodded and climbed into the bus. Tom watched as the bus pulled away. He watched as it stopped at the corner and then as it headed south. He watched until it disappeared, then he walked diagonally across the street to the café, took a seat that gave him a view to the south, and ordered coffee.

"Tom, you don't look so good," Clara said. "Something wrong?"

Tom just nodded and mumbled incoherently.

"You look like you just lost your best friend."

"I may have," Tom said as he stared out the window, "I just may have."

His eyes never left the road.

She sensed that Tom needed space, so she let him be but kept a watchful eye on him and his coffee. Tom sat through three cups, speaking to no one except Clara, and then only to thank her for refills.

After an hour of staring out the window between sips of hot caffeine dressed in black, Tom sighed deeply, rose to his tired feet, paid his check, and left without a word. He walked to the store and bought a few supplies. More alone than he'd been in two years, he drove slowly back to his mountain.

"I don't know about Tom," Clara said to Sam a little bit later as she wiped the counter in front of him.

"What do you mean?"

"He was in here an hour ago, ordered coffee, and didn't even say hello or goodbye. He just stared out the window. I'm afraid for him, Sam. He wasn't himself." She paused and thoughtfully sipped a glass of tea. "He did say one thing, though, and strange it was, too. He said he might have lost his best friend. I wonder if he lost his dog."

Donna and Steven walked in the front door of the café.

"Hey, folks, what can I do ya for, an early lunch or a late breakfast?"

"We just need some information," Donna said. "We are looking for an elderly man who might live down along the river. He'd have a large yellow dog, a golden retriever, I believe."

"You just missed him. He was here about an hour ago."

"You know him?" Steven asked.

"Do I know him? Why heck, everybody knows Tom."

"We must talk to him," Donna cut in. "Can you tell us how to find his place?"

"Is something wrong? Tom said something about losing his best friend. Come to think about it, his friend wasn't with him."

Donna leaned against a chair for support as a wave of dizziness hit her.

"What did he look like?" Steven said, fear edging into his voice.

"Tom or his friend?" Clara said, coming around the counter.

"The friend," Donna said.

"Well," Clara said as she cleaned a clean table and rearranged the cups and silverware. "He was tall, dark, dayum good-looking, even with a busted nose. Looked like he'd been in a fight. Let's see, he had the prettiest blue eyes. Tom, that's Dr. Braden, he said that his friend was up from Texas, recuperating from some kind of accident."

"It's him, it's dad." Steven shouted, "It has to be him."

"Where does Dr. Braden live?" Donna pleaded.

"Up that road yonder," Clara said and pointed out the window to the east. "Follow it till it dead ends. That'll be about ten miles. Take the gravel drive to your right. You can't miss it."

♠ ♠ ♠

Tom sat in his chair and stared gloomily into the flames of yet another fire. Despite the warm weather, he had brought it to life as soon as he got home and had been sitting and staring past the flames, his old heart breaking. He was alone again, except for the dog at his side.

Donna and Steven pulled into the driveway. Barney's ears perked up and he barked aggressively and ran to the front door.

"What is it, Barney? Who could that be? I hope it isn't Jeremy. I'm not in any mood to deal with him right now."

Tom rose wearily to his feet and shuffled slowly to the door. As he opened it, he heard the Jeep round the last curve in the drive. Barney ran outside and Tom watched as the Jeep pulled up and stopped beside his truck.

"Dog! Hush! Come here!"

Barney whined but obeyed.

Donna and Steven stepped out of the Jeep. Barney whined at Tom's feet for a moment and then, as if he had seen an old friend, ran to Steven, wagging his tail and barking excitedly. Tom felt himself stepping off the porch, pushed by unseen hands.

"Mom! It's *him*."

Donna nodded and stepped forward to greet Tom.

"Dr. Braden? Thomas Braden?"

"You must be his wife and son. How did you know? I don't understand. We saw you sit up in bed. It was floating above the fire."

Tom turned to Steven who had joined them.

"You were there, too." Tom said.

"We saw you! My dad, too!" Steven said.

"But he's not here, is he?" Donna said, fearing the worst.

"I put him on the bus to San Antonio this morning."

"Then he's alright? He's alive?"

"Oh yes, of course, Mrs. Cooper."

"Donna. Call me Donna. And this is our son, Steven."

"Nice to meet you." Tom shook his hand.

"Yes, folks, Mitch is very much alive. That is his name, right?"

"Yes." Donna nodded slowly. "San Antonio?"

Suddenly it hit her sleep-deprived brain.

"But we live in Boise!"

"Ma'am, I have some really bad news. Mitch lost his memory when he fell. He knows virtually nothing about his past. He doesn't know you or Steven. He only knows his name from a brief memory recalled from his childhood. He didn't recognize you when he saw you last night; he just knew he had to find you."

"Wait a minute," Donna said with a start. Confused, she said, "He fell? What do you mean?"

"Well," Tom said, "we found him down by the river," he pointed south and west, "on Sunday the 13th of April. Mitch said that he had awakened from oblivion two days earlier at the bottom of a cliff. We assumed we fell off it but we questioned that, too. You would have to see the place to understand. We talked it...."

"Dr. Braden?"

"Please, call me Tom," he said.

"Tom, the last time I saw my husband was on Tuesday, the 8th of April. I watched him fly toward Montana from Boise. They found his friend's body in the Salmon River, east of Grangeville, three weeks later. We found nothing of the airplane."

"Oh, Lord!" Tom whispered. "Are you telling me that he crashed? Mitch survived a plane crash out there?"

Donned nodded solemnly.

"Come inside; we've got a lot to talk about."

Tom brewed a fresh pot of coffee and introduced Barney to Steven while Donna called the bus station. Then over coffee, while awaiting news of where Mitch was heading next, Tom told them how Barney had found him, about the bear attack, and everything that had transpired in the past two months. Donna and Steven sat quiet, listening intently, hanging onto every word.

CHAPTER TWENTY-NINE

Here you are, Bud. This is as far as I can take you."

"Thanks," Mitch said as he opened the door and stepped out with his bag. He paid the cab fare and turned away.

"Hey! Mister? It's none of my business, but why didn't you stay on the bus? It's a hell of a long walk to Texas!"

"Don't like buses, I don't have a car, and I have an inexplicable fear of flying. Adios!"

The cab driver just shook his head as though Mitch was crazy, turned the car around, and sped back to town for another fare.

Mitch looked north to the mountains.

"I'll see you again."

He looked south and east toward Texas and whatever awaited him there. The sun shone hot. Sweat beaded his brow and trickled down his sides from under his arms, but a breeze tumbled down from the mountains, riffling through his shirt, caressing his brow with cool fingers, inflating him with its freshness.

Autos and semis passed by on his left. He did not thumb; he just walked. He would walk until he was tired. If by chance he was offered a ride, he might take it, he decided. He felt so good he began to sing.

He started with "As I was out a ridin', a graveyard shift, midnight till dawn, the moon was as bright as a readin' light for letter from an old friend back home," neither knowing nor caring where the words came from. He finished the song and then began another. He walked and sang the miles away. Horses and cattle raised their heads; they listened inquisitively as he passed. An audacious young colt trotted up to the fence on his right.

Mitch crossed the ditch and approached affably.

"Hey, Fella."

The yearling sorrel stallion tossed his head and reared playfully, then raced across the pasture. Mitch laughed as the colt turned a tight circle, raced back, and skidded to a stop next to the fence, tossing his head and mane. Mitch reached through the wire. The colt sniffed his hand and nibbled at his outstretched palm, which he held flat so the colt would not bite him.

"Hungry, Sport?"

Mitch reached inside his bag, retrieved an apple, and broke it in half. The horse took his offering eagerly and ate it with relish while tossing his head. Mitch fed him the other half and scratched his nose. The colt nuzzled him affectionately, then bolted and ran across the pasture again.

Mitch picked up his bag and continued down the road. The colt played and ran beside the fence while he walked. Finally, the colt reached the end of the pasture. Mitch walked on, surveying the country around him. He saw rolling foothills to the south, foothills and mountains to the north. Ahead, to the east, the highway lost itself over a rise. Behind him were friends.

At times he wanted to turn back to the peace he'd left there. At the same time, he knew he must press on and find what waited over each rise in the road.

The horse stood quiet and watched until Mitch was gone over the hill, then he trotted back to where the other horses grazed. He stopped once to gaze back over his shoulder after the man who had helped him into this world early one winter morning; the man who had bottle-fed him after his mother was killed by lightning; the man who had taught him to love humans, yet the man who hadn't recognized the prized stallion he had kept a secret from his wife until her birthday, last June.

♠ ♠ ♠

Forty minutes after Donna called the bus station, the telephone rang. Tom answered it and listened for a few seconds, then nodded his head and said thanks to someone on the other end. A tense silence permeated the cabin when Tom hung up.

"Well," Tom said, heaving a big sigh. "It could be good news, then again, maybe not. He didn't catch another bus to Texas.

"He caught a cab," he said.

"He went home!" Donna said and ran to the phone. She punched in a series of numbers and waited.

No answer.

She dialed again; still no answer. Stifling a rising panic, she called information. Without writing the number down, she hung up, punched the numbers quickly, and waited.

"Dispatch, please." Donna waited, trembling. Steven paced the floor. Tom packed his pipe and lit it.

"Yes, could you tell me if one of your drivers picked up a man at the bus station at about ten this morning?" A short pause ensued, then, "Yes, that would be him." They endured another painful moment of waiting. Tom puffed on his pipe and prayed silently. Steven stood with Barney at his side at the entrance to the living room and watched a spot on the floor. His mind was reeling, his thoughts spinning, his fear working overtime.

"He did?" she said. "Where? No! NO!

Donna slumped to the floor.

"NO! No, I-I cannot lose him again. I can't, I caaannn't," she screamed shrilly.

The phone dangled limply by her side.

"Mom?"

Steven ran to her.

"What happened to dad? What happened?"

Tom pushed him gently aside.

"On a shelf in the linen closet in the hallway there is a leather bag. Get it and take it into the living room."

Tom picked Donna up and carried her to the couch. Steven met him there with the medical bag as Tom laid her gently down.

"Son, go into the kitchen and get me a glass of water." Steven ran quickly to the kitchen as Tom opened his bag and took out a bottle of pills.

"Are you allergic to Valium?"

"No," Donna shook her head, "no pills. I'll be alright."

Steven returned with the water.

"Donna, I'm a doctor. In my opinion, you need it." Donna looked into his eyes.

"So am I."

"Well, then, I can't tell you what to do, but in good conscience—*listen to me, he thought*—I have to suggest that you shouldn't self-diagnose and treat yourself."

She saw that he meant what he said. In an instant, she trusted him and took the pills.

"Donna, after years of examining dozens of patients a day, I can tell in a heartbeat if someone is ill. What's wrong with you?"

"I've had a hysterectomy. I missed my shot two weeks ago, but I saw my doctor yesterday. I'll be fine as soon as the hormones kick in. And by the way, I'm a psychologist."

Tom acknowledged that with a smile and a knowing nod of his head but plunged straight on and asked about her recent medical history. Then, with her permission, he gave her a thorough examination. Satisfied, he put his things away and closed his bag.

"Would you like me to put that back for you?" Steven asked. Tom nodded.

"Thanks, Son," he said.

The activity had helped to settle Steven down—as Tom knew it would—and when he came back, he sat beside his mother and took her hand.

"What did they say, Mom?" Donna took a deep breath and then let it out slowly.

"They said the driver dropped him off at the city limits. Mitch told the driver he was going to walk to Texas."

"Damn!" Tom said, shaking his head at Mitch, across the distance.

"That hardheaded fool! Anything can happen now. Mitch is tough though, and he's smart; he'll make out. Nevertheless, I'm still going to call the Highway Patrol; see if they can find him."

"Donna, you should go to San Antonio. I told him that I used to live down there. We talked about it and he decided that was where he would go. I may have been wrong, but I told him there was something about him, a quality that convinced me he was from that part of the country. It's a long shot, but if the cops don't find him, you might run into him."

"The River Walk!" she said. "We used to live in San Antonio. The River Walk was a special place for us. He'll go there. He may not know why, but he'll be drawn there."

Donna was again filled with hope. She sat up straighter on the couch.

"You are right, Tom. I must go."

"I told him to call me as soon as he gets there," Tom said. "Steven should wait in Boise, and I'll wait here."

"He proposed to me on the River Walk, Tom."

"Now don't forget, Donna, Mitch is not himself. He remembers virtually nothing about his past, although yesterday he remembered getting a haircut when he was a kid. It might be coming back to him."

Tom twisted his mustache, thinking.

"When he calls, I'll tell him to stay put. Steven, if your father regains his memory, he will call home." He smiled. "Don't worry, we will find him. The Lord has kept him alive; we must believe that He will bring us back together."

"That's right," Donna said. She stood up and embraced him. "All of us."

A light came into Tom's eyes and he knew at that moment he would never be alone again.

"Do you have plenty of cash?" he asked suddenly.

"I'm Ok! Why?"

"I just want to be sure you have enough. It's going to cost you a bundle for a plane, motel, car rental, and all the extras."

"Tom, you needn't worry about that," Donna said. She laughed as she sat back down. "We've more than we know what to do with."

"OK. Well, then how about lunch?"

"We haven't had a bite since yesterday evening," Donna said. "We've been too anxious to eat. I don't know about Steven, but I am famished."

"I could eat a horse," Steven said.

"Come back to the kitchen with me. We can talk while I whip up some sandwiches; I'm curious to know how you knew where to look for him."

Donna and Steven sat down in the dining room. Barney had taken an immediate liking to Steven and stayed close to his side.

"Barney's a heck of a dog," he said.

"That he is, Son, and he sure likes you. Barney was the same with your father." Tom opened the refrigerator and removed the makings for turkey sandwiches. Donna insisted on helping, so Tom let her slice the lettuce and tomatoes.

"When did you say Mitch left Boise?" Tom asked as Donna's earlier comment finally sank in.

"He left Tuesday, the 8th of April."

Tom shook his head slowly as he spread mayonnaise on wheat bread.

"What's the matter, Tom?"

Tom dipped his knife into the jar and said, "We found him the following Sunday. I'm just wondering what kind of hell he went through after the crash."

"How bad was he hurt?" she finally found the courage to ask.

Tom sighed heavily. He knew she would ask eventually. He had hoped for later.

"When we found him," Tom said, closing the jar, "his hands and knees were torn and raw. He had several cracked ribs and a punctured lung. He also had a broken leg. He was in pretty bad shape." Tom hesitated, not wanting to tell her the rest, knowing how it must hurt her.

"Go on, Tom, I know there is more. I have to know."

"Mitch had a small laceration over his right ear, and," Tom drew a shuddering breath, "his skull was fractured, but not seriously. It wasn't an impact wound; it looked more like he'd received a glancing blow. Had it been blunt impact trauma I might have done differently," Tom said defensively

Donna drew a sharp breath at his mention of a head injury, but then she visibly relaxed after his second statement.

"Hon', I didn't expect him to live. I should have taken him to a hospital, but I-I, I kept him here."

Tom sniffed back tears of shame over his actions, and of fear of what could have happened to Mitch under his care.

"It's alright," she said, putting her arms around him. "You did what you thought was right and he made it. And if I know my husband, he probably refused to go."

"He did, but I...."

"But nothing, it's alright. Forget it." Donna hugged him. "It's in the past. Just let it go. He's alive and that's what matters."

They finished the sandwiches and took the lunch into the dining room.

"I couldn't keep him down," Tom said. "I've never seen such strength and courage in a man."

Donna winked at her son.

"Tom that man used to be the number one bronc rider in the state of Texas, and a darned good bull rider, too. You ought to see him handle a rope. If it's got hooves or horns, you can bet he knows how to handle it, and they don't make men any tougher."

"Well, I'll be danged. I knew there was something

about him," Tom said with a huge grin. "I just knew it. You should have seen how he handled the twins."

"He loves horses. We're building a ranch outside of Boise. We have thirty head of registered Quarter Horses, five Appaloosas, two paint stallions, and about a hundred head of cattle. It's a mixed herd, mostly Black Angus, but we're introducing Brahma and the Japanese shorthorn breed of Wagyu into the blood. We also have a small herd of Longhorn cattle."

"Wagyu?"

"Yeah, sounds funny, but tastes great. Their meat is said to be low in bad cholesterol and high in the good stuff. Mitch is confident we'll be competing with Japanese markets in just a few years."

Tom brightened.

"Would you two spend the night? It would sure make an old man happy."

"Well, shouldn't we be on the road pretty soon?"

"No reason to rush it. Mitch can't possibly get to San Antonio before the day after tomorrow, and that's *if* he can find a ride. I assume that's his plan. He'll hoof it, but not all the way. He needs time to think, but he won't waste a lot of time getting there.

"You could leave tomorrow morning and fly down tomorrow night. He has my number, and if he wakes up, he'll have yours. I'll call the highway patrol and let God do the rest."

"Sounds like a plan," Donna agreed. "We'll stay the night. We still have a lot to talk about."

"And I want to see the twins," Steven said.

"We'll walk down after lunch," Tom said with the biggest smile on his face.

CHAPTER THIRTY

Mitch had walked twelve miles in three hours. He was getting tired. An eighteen-wheeler was parked on the shoulder a few yards ahead. Mitch left the road, crossed the ditch, and continued walking. As he passed the semi-trailer, Mitch saw the driver standing between it and the tractor, cooling the tires. Embarrassed, he averted his eyes and looked to the right as he passed. A few minutes later he heard the big diesel engine roar to life.

Mitch's feet were getting sore. He was wearing good hiking boots and thick socks, but he needed a rest. He called himself a fool and hoped the driver would offer him a ride.

The truck's shadow overtook him and then the shiny new rig stopped beside him. He heard the rush of escaping air as the brakes were applied. The engine was silenced and the passenger window slid down.

"Climb on up," the driver yelled. His voice was thick with a south of the border accent. Mitch stepped up on the running board.

"Where are you going?" The driver was about thirty. He was tall, dark, and wiry. He wore a weathered ball cap and a tank top t-shirt. He was clean-cut, freshly shaved and spoke good English.

"San Antonio."

"That's a long way to walk, Mister?"

"Well," Mitch said with a grin, "I imagine it has been done before. But no, I was gonna take it one day at a time."

"I am not in the habit of picking up riders. But you look OK, for a gringo." He said and grinned, showing perfect white teeth. "Climb on in and I will take you as far as we can get along."

Mitch opened the door and climbed up and in.

"Thanks. Name's Mitch," he said extending his hand.

"Gilbert Rodriguez," the driver said. "Some people call me Gil. My handle is J.B. That's because when I'm not in the cab I'm always wearing a John B. Stetson cowboy hat. Pleased to meet you. You're lucky my bladder was about to burst. I'm on my way to Dallas. You're welcome to ride. If we get along and you're still with me when we get there, I'll see you get a ride to the Alamo."

Mitch grinned lopsidedly and said, "Nice rig."

He sat his bag on the floor between the seats.

"Thanks," Gil said. "The seat is air operated. Look behind your left calf. See that silver knob? Pull it out to let the seat down, push it in to raise it up."

Mitch pulled the knob and, to his surprise, the seat sank to the floor. Gil chuckled. When Mitch pushed the knob in, his feet left the floor and his head bumped the ceiling.

"Uh, I forgot to mention how touchy it is," Gil said and laughed. "Truth is truckers lack for entertainment."

"I just bet you do," Mitch said, rubbing the top of his head. He cautiously lowered the seat and made himself comfortable.

"Better strap in," Gil suggested. "It is the law, you know."

Mitch buckled up as the friendly driver checked his mirrors and slowly eased his way through the gears and out onto the pavement. Then he plugged a tape into the cassette player and set the cruise control at 70 mph.

"Who's that?" Mitch asked as the speakers issued an upbeat western tune.

"That's Chris Ledoux."

Chris' mellow baritone bellowed out of the speakers as he sang a steppin' tune about him and his girl at the county fair.

"I like the sound of that," Mitch said.

J.B. smiled, pleased, and said, "He passed on recently but he sang about ranching and rodeo for over thirty years. He was a real family man. I guess that's why I like his music so much."

Gil Rodriguez reined in his tongue and said nothing for several miles. Neither did Mitch as the silence thickened. Mitch thought how much Tom would like this guy. He felt like he should say something but Gil's sudden silence had him stifled.

Suddenly J.B. spoke. "Do you have family?"

"I don't know," Mitch said.

He rubbed the scar above his right ear and then spent the next two hours telling his story while Chris and his band entertained them.

CHAPTER THIRTY-ONE

Eighteen wheels hummed on hot pavement between white-line borders and sagebrush-covered hills. Mitch dozed in the sleeper while the cool wind blew through a vent across his sore feet. Gil hummed along with the radio or CD player as he worked his way up and down the gears, up and down the hills on I-84, a hundred miles north of Salt Lake City, Utah.

Mitch had told his story while Gil drove in silence. Gil nodded his head in fascination as Mitch talked. When he was finished, he asked him to tell the part about the bear again. Mitch retold the tale and made Tom out to be the hero.

The miles rolled by.

They had stopped three hours earlier at Twin Falls, Idaho, for a quick cup of coffee and then moved on, with Mitch taking rest in the sleeper at J.B.'s insistence. He explained that he would need the sleeper later during the night and that Mitch would have to make do up front.

Gil played his music low, left the CB radio off, and tried to miss all the bumps in the road. He knew what it was like trying to sleep in a big truck while it was moving. On a rough road, it could be compared to trying to sleep on a trampoline with someone jumping on it.

At about ten that night the lights of "Salty" came into view and Mitch crawled bleary-eyed from the sleeper.

"Hey, Mountain Climber." Gil said. "Get any sleep?"

"Only a wink, maybe two. How in the heck do you guys sleep when you run double?"

"After a couple of days of hard driving, one is so tired that he falls asleep before the other driver gets going down the road, but sometimes doesn't get any sleep at all. Some of these roads are so bad that it's better to ride upfront and doze off and on.

"You won't find too many hands these days that are willing to run team. Not enough money in it anymore. One truck just won't support two families."

"You sound like an educated man. Why do you do drive a truck?"

"Yes, I have two degrees. Been there, done that. I had a good job in Chicago and was making good money, but I just, I, well, suffice it to say I wanted a change of pace. I stayed on the road because most of the time I like it. It got in my blood. I've tried to go back to working a regular job. I just can't stay away. Even after nearly two million miles I can't stay home for more than a few days before I get antsy and have to hit the road again. I can't sit still."

It was Mitch's turn. "Do you have family?"

Gil got a lost and lonely look in his eyes and said nothing for a long time. Once again, Mitch felt that choking silence. When Gil finally did speak, his voice was riddled with pain and sorrow.

"That's the main reason I hit the road," he admitted. "I went home one day and found a new pickup in the driveway, and a new man in my bed. I packed my things and left. I haven't been back. She knew I was born to live out here. She knew it before we were married. Her father drove a rig. But I loved her and I wanted what was best for us all. So I stayed home and went back to school. I had a lot of success. I was a lawyer. But the road always called to me. Once we had it made and we were living comfortably, I bought this truck. At first I just drove it one weekend out of the month and I hired it out the remainder of the month. When I found her in bed with that man.... I had two thoughts, kill them, or just get gone. So we divorced and split everything. Now this is my only home and I've been gone ever since."

Mitch did not mention family again.

After they had fueled and eaten in Salt Lake City, Gil felt like driving some more, so he encouraged Mitch to crawl back in the sleeper again and try to get what sleep he could.

Many hours later and five hundred miles farther down the road Gil weaved his way through the myriad rows of trucks at the Giant Travel Center, seventeen miles east of Gallup, New Mexico. He found a parking space close to the main entrance and backed the rig into place, then he reached back and shook Mitch awake.

"C'mon, hand. Rise and shine."

Mitch rolled out of bed and squinted his eyes at the bright morning sunlight.

"Where are we?" he asked as he pulled his boots on.

"Giant Truck Stop, east of Gallup."

"New Mexico? I thought you were going to pull over and get some sleep."

"I did. You were sleeping so soundly that I, well, I slept fine up here. Get yourself together and we'll go inside and clean up. I fueled already and we've got showers coming. We'll freshen up and get on down the road."

CHAPTER THIRTY-TWO

Showered and fed, Mitch and Gil were back on the road within two hours.

Mitch was enjoying the trip immensely and his eyes were constantly scanning the landscape. He was intrigued and enchanted by the high desert. The Earth was at once dying and being reborn before his eyes.

Buttes and mesas lined the highway by the hundreds, their bases littered with gigantic boulders and alluvial fans. Cedars, cacti, mesquite, and desert grasses grew sparsely among the rocks, creating shade and fodder for desert sheep, mule deer, rodents, and the occasional herd of pronghorn.

The morning sun bounced off the cliffs, illuminating an arch here, a cave there, and weather-worn holes in the sandstone. The object of many an artist's greatest works, the countryside blossomed in a rainbow of pastel colors.

Mitch and Gil talked the miles away and before they

knew it, they had crossed the Texas line and were fast approaching Dallas.

Gil got on the radio when they hit town and, true to his word, by the time they reached the other side, he'd found Mitch a ride. Gil was on a tight schedule and couldn't stick around, so they parted with a hand-shake, but promised to keep in touch. Mitch watched with a sense of loneliness as Gilbert Rodriguez's truck roared off toward Houma, Louisiana. Mitch ate a quick lunch with his new ride before they headed south.

His new chauffeur was older than Gil and would not give his real name but insisted on being called "Ram-rod." The driver's hat appeared to be older than he was, and the cigar he chewed was bigger around than his thumbs. The old man was a talker though, and when he was not jabbering with his buddies on the radio, he was telling jokes and stories.

The miles flew by, but the closer they got to the "Alamo," as they call it on the road, the less he really heard, Ramrod. Mitch was not ignoring him; he just found it hard to follow along. He was deep in thought and had a feeling the journey through his inner dark-ness was about to end. At the same time, he feared what lay behind the veil. He told himself it was alright to be afraid but that he should at all times be in control of his fear so that, if pressed, he could use it to his ad-vantage. He had a feeling these were not his own words, that he had heard them somewhere before, yet in a different way.

As that thought ran through his mind he found him-self staring at, Ramrod, only it was not a grizzled old trucker he was looking at. For a brief moment Mitch was not in the truck, and it was not I-35 south they were traveling. The muffled roar of an airplane engine had replaced the steady hum of big tires on hot pavement. A stinking, ripe, and rotting corpse sat behind the wheel. It spoke to him with a hoarse, raspy wheeze.

It was the voice of death.

"You forget, Mitch, whether it's under power or not, an aircraft will usually remain stable at the minimum speed at which it was designed to fly."

Mitch went berserk.

CHAPTER THIRTY-THREE

Tom woke Steven and then knocked on Donna's door. He received no answer, so he tried again.

"Breakfast is ready."

Steven stepped out of his room down the hall. "That's funny," he said. "Mom is usually the first one up."

The words had barely left his lips when the front door flew open and his mother breezed in.

"Well, it's about time ya'all got up," she hollered as she threw back her wind-blown hair. "Tom? Did you know Dallas is with foal?"

"What?"

"She's at least four months along. I have a minor in animal husbandry; she's pregnant!"

"I'll be dipped. Guess I'll have me a talk with Brad. One of his stallions must have jumped the fence. Well, come eat, it's on the table. Dallas is with foal? We're gonna have a baby. Yee Haw!"

♠ ♠ ♠

By nine, all arrangements had been made, and they were saying their goodbyes.

"Don't worry, Donna, Mitch will be fine; he's a survivor."

"I know, Tom. Thanks for everything."

She gave him a warm hug and then climbed into the Jeep. She rolled down the window.

"I'll call you when I get there."

"I'll be waiting. Good luck!"

He slapped Steven on the back.

"Chin up, Pard', this will work out."

"Thanks, Tom. We appreciate what you did for my father, and for us. So long, we'll see ya."

Tom moped around the cabin for most of the morning, doing chores recently neglected, such as scrubbing bathrooms and dusting. After lunch, he checked on the twins where they relaxed in the corral, swishing their tails at the flies. He could not see any difference in Dallas, but he trusted Donna's opinion. He supposed it was more a mother's intuition. He started to climb up on the fence to sit and scratch them behind the ears but he didn't make it past the second rail.

A few minutes later he woke to find himself lying beside the fence, unable to move. His mind reeled. He tried to yell but only managed a whisper. God, I've had a stroke. Barney was immediately by his side. Tom struggled and managed to raise his right arm and touch his dog on the face. He tried to speak out, to tell the dog he needed help but the words that came were garbled with paralysis. With a groan Tom dropped his arm and went limp.

Barney turned and ran a few feet but didn't understand what to do. He returned to Tom's side and crawled up on his chest. He whined and nuzzled at Tom encouraging him to try to get up. Tom gasped and cried out in fear, and managed a slurred, "Go." Barney whined and barked at Tom, trembling with conflicting urges to both run and stay. Then suddenly making up his mind he jumped up and ran as fast he could up the hill, past the cabin, and down the driveway to the county road.

The twins stood by the fence, calmly watching but not comprehending. Dallas nudged Tom's side with her nose. It was Tom's turn to fight for his life, and his chances were not near as good as Mitch's had been. He shook with fear until he felt his wife's soft fingers touch his cheek, and smiled with the right side of his face and went to sleep.

In Riggins, Clara was cleaning at the front of the café.

"Yeah, Baxter was in this morning, Joe. He and his wife were on the way to Boise to do some shopping. I imagine they'll be in tomorrow and I'll tell them you said...Tom."

"Tom?"

"Braden, Dr. Braden."

"What's wrong, Clara," Joe said when she abruptly backed away from the table, looking off toward the county road leading to Tom's place.

"He just came to mind out of the blue, and I got me a bad feeling. Something's wrong.

"We're closed," she suddenly shouted over her shoulder as she ran back to turn off all the equipment. She grabbed her keys, quickly sorted through her meal tickets, passed them out to her half a dozen customers and told them to shut the door behind them when they left. She rushed out the front door, climbed in her Ford pick-up and sped around the corner to the county road. She met Barney half way.

CHAPTER THIRTY-FOUR

Donna was a nervous wreck by the time the plane landed. She enjoyed flying, but the flight had been rough, and she was anxious and expectant, afraid of the stranger she might find in her husband. She worried she'd lose him again.

Her rental car was waiting; she drove immediately to their hotel by the river. The first thing she did was undress and step into a hot shower. The water rained down on her as it had that morning she last saw her husband. Every shower she'd taken since had reminded her of him, though he was never far from her mind. This shower was no different.

After her shower, she read from her Bible, finding peace, renewing her strength, and bolstering her faith. She prayed.

Through her prayer, she realized she was Mitch's beacon, his light in the storm. Then she remembered Tom. When she called, he did not answer. She figured he was with the horses. She would try again later.

She called home and touched base with Steven. Molly was there. Donna spoke with her for a few minutes, then hung up and tried Tom again, with no answer.

She tried again a few minutes later, to no avail. She told herself he was still with the horses but did not believe it. Something was wrong.

Tom said he would wait by the phone. He would have fed the horses early so as not to miss her. She decided to call him again in a few minutes, but she plopped down on the bed to relax and fell asleep.

Donna slept soundly, awakening at six in the morning when the front desk called. She remembered Tom and tried to call him again. The phone rang off the wall. She tried again after she showered, and when he did not answer, she called Steven and told him to try and to keep trying. Then she put on her face and her prettiest, sexiest dress, and went down to have breakfast on the terrace by the river.

After Huevos Rancheros, she sipped coffee and watched the people and the boats glide back and forth beneath the overhanging branches of the cypress and palms that bordered the river. She waited.

CHAPTER THIRTY-FIVE

H ey, Buddy! Whoa! Hey! Come out of it." The old trucker reached over and slapped him. Mitch almost hit him back, but as his fist flew up, he stopped himself. He came to his senses and calmed down. He had been yelling at the top of his lungs.

"What the hell is wrong with you?" The driver shouted. "Are you one of those crazy vets?"

"I'm sorry, Mister. I-I don't know what happened. I haven't been myself lately." He stared at the floor, cussing himself, and then stared out the window to his right. It was fifty miles to San Antonio, and for fifty miles he watched the hills pass by and spoke not a word. The bitter, angry old driver kept a wary eye on him and when they reached the city limits, he pulled over and stopped.

"I only carried you this far 'cause I told that other driver I would. This is the end of the line. Get out!"

Mitch grabbed his bag.

"Can I pay you for your trouble?"

"Get the hell out of my rig. NOW!"

Humiliated and ashamed, Mitch bailed out and started walking again. Eight weary miles later he found a convenience store, bought a soda and a candy bar, and called a cab. He drank the soda in a matter of seconds and bought another one. He tried to eat the candy bar, but his stomach revolted. He trashed it, leaned against the brick wall in front of the store by the phones, and waited for the cab.

He scuffed his boots against the sidewalk and wondered what would happen next. He'd read the city limit sign; the population of San Antonio was just over 1.2 million.

"Where do I start?" he asked a cricket that was scuttling along a crack in the cement. "Where would you look?" The cricket stopped, rubbed his hind legs together, jumped three feet away from Mitch, jumped again, and flew off.

"Yeah, that's what I thought, the phone book. But you didn't have to run away. I wasn't going to eat you." Mitch heard something and looked up to see a young preppy couple staring at him with obvious dislike. He tried to explain that he didn't always talk to himself. But they backed away, got in their car, and sped off to use the phone elsewhere.

"I ain't a crazy vet!" Mitch yelled.

"Well, why not? Everyone thinks I'm crazy. Might as well act like it."

He looked at his reflection in the window.

"Don't look crazy. Are you crazy? No, don't think so. Are you sure?"

He saw the haunted look in his eyes and did not blame the world for turning away from him.

"Mister, you're in a heap o' trouble," he said to himself as a young woman hustled a little boy out of the store and into a little red pickup.

"Manager's gonna call the cops on you. Shouldn't tell you this, but you better get, or get throwed in jail."

"Piss off, Lady," he hissed. Immediately he felt sorry and walked forward to apologize.

"I-I didn't mean that, Ma'am, I'm sorry."

"Kenny, lock the door and roll up the window. NOW!" she screamed. "Hurry!"

Mitch stood beside the car with his hands held out in front, palms up, gesturing helplessness and regret. Frantically, the woman put the truck in reverse and threw dirt at his feet as she raced backward. She slammed into a metal post by the pumps. She didn't seem to care; she just burned rubber and raced away, barely missing the cab as it pulled into the parking lot.

Mitch grabbed his bag he had left by the telephones.

"Impeccable timing," he said to the driver. "Take me to the nearest motel and don't waste your time."

"You runnin' from the law? If you are, I can't help you."

"I'm running from my ex-wife," Mitch said. "That was my girlfriend you just missed. She found out I'd been with my ex a few times this last month. My wife and I have always had great sex and didn't let the divorce get in the way of that. My ex-girlfriend has other ideas. She's on the way to see my ex-wife. I gotta find a place to hide. They both own guns."

"Are all your ex's in Texas?" the driver asked. "Don't worry, there's a motel just a few miles down the road."

Fifteen minutes later, Mitch was staring into a cracked bathroom mirror at a haggard and frightened stranger. The sickening smell of fear tainted his cloth-ing.

He shaved, then showered and put clean clothes on, but it didn't help. His stomach threatened to turn itself inside out in rebellion. A cockroach ran up the wall. A siren wailed somewhere down the road.

Mitch thought of the cabin. He remembered the mountains and the clean air. A drunk stumbled past his door, mumbling obscenities. A couple in the next room fought and screamed at each other. He turned the television on to drown them out.

"Have to get my mind on something else," he said.

Snow drifted across the screen in front of a vivid porno scene. He quickly flipped through the channels and found nothing but game shows and an old western. He watched the movie until interrupted by a fast food commercial. His stomach heaved and he lurched off the bed. He stumbled to the bathroom with one hand cupping his mouth and the other groping for the doorknob.

Vomit sprayed through his fingers as he fell to the floor in front of the commode. He threw up until he was too weak to kneel and then he just leaned against the toilet and dry heaved until he passed out.

When he came to he was lying on the floor between the toilet and the tub. A cockroach skittered toward him along the rotten baseboard behind the toilet. He staggered dizzily to his feet and leaned against the rusty sink. After a minute to clear the cobwebs, he turned on the cold water. He washed his hands and face, cleaned up his shirt as best he could, dried off with a threadbare towel, and then staggered to bed.

Lying on his back on the thin, hard mattress, he tried to squeeze the image of the cadaverous trucker from his mind. Try as he might, the image persisted.

It spoke to him again.

"Hope you make it, Buddy." Then, "this is going to be hard on the women." The last word echoed in his skull like a jackhammer until he couldn't stand it anymore. He jumped up off the bed, jerked open the door and ran out into the night. He ran without care for direction. He ran until his breath came in ragged gasps and then he sank to his knees in a dimly lit parking lot, two miles from the motel. He leaned forward until his head touched the pavement, clasped his hands over his head, and rocked back and forth on his elbows, wondering if he had lost his mind.

When his breath came easier, he sat up and found himself groveling in a shadowed corner of a lot next to a flashing neon sign. He listened and faintly heard a jukebox spinning out a country tune. He listened for a minute and then rose unsteadily to his feet. He leaned against the brick wall for support.

He found himself thinking of the river and the cliff. The lost and helpless feeling came back. He felt the fear and desperation. He could hear the roar of the river; feel the spray.

He felt the pain in his side and in his head.

The roar of the river became louder. It raged inside his head like a bulldozer out of control, until suddenly he found himself inside the cockpit of the Cherokee, diving into the forest.

When he came to, his head was throbbing and he had vomited again. He pushed himself to his feet and wiped his face, then stumbled into the bar. It was nearly deserted. Only two people sat at the bar and the tables were empty. Mitch wondered why the place bothered to stay open. He went to the restroom and cleaned up as best he could and then found himself a dark corner table. He ordered a beer.

A dark, skinny, and not-so-pretty waitress, in tight cutoffs and a red tank top, brought his beer and a coaster to set it on. She smiled, made it obvious she was available for a price, and swiveled her hips at him as she walked back to the bar. He didn't even notice her. Such was the condition of his mind and emotions. The girl frowned and virtually ignored him thereafter.

Mitch sipped his beer as the jukebox belted out the country blues. It was only after another girl brought his third beer that he started to relax. During his fourth beer, two rowdies, one big and tall, the other short and ugly, swaggered inside and set up at the bar next to a nice-looking blond in a short skirt and black leather jacket who had been talking with one of the bar maids since before Mitch arrived. The two men came onto her. She politely refused their advances, but they persisted. The woman finally had to raise her voice, which raised Mitch's head.

He looked over at the bar as the big man grabbed her by the arm.

"Let her go."

The big man turned slowly and glared at Mitch. Mitch glared back at him.

"Who the hell invited you?" Big and Tall said.

"Nobody, but I'm telling you to let her go."

"Screw you, asshole," Short and Ugly yelled. Mitch ignored him; Big and Tall had the girl.

"Stay out of it, Frank," Mr. Big said. "This asshole is mine."

Mitch noticed with foreboding that the bar had grown seriously quiet. The not-so-pretty waitress unplugged the jukebox. The blond winced in pain and Mitch stood up. He strode deliberately up to Big and Tall, stood toe to toe with him, and though the other man was half a head taller, poked him in the chest with his left finger and said, "Let her go, Jack!"

"Fu..."

Mitch cut him off with a swift right to the Adam's apple and followed with a wicked uppercut with his left. He threw a roundhouse with his right, splitting Big's ear and showering them both with blood. Mitch hit the big man twice more, then slapped him in the face and kneed him in the groin. Big and Tall hit the ground so hard it jiggled the bottles on the shelves behind the bar.

Mitch looked for Short and Ugly, but he was a split-second too late. He felt a thud on the back of his head and went to his knees. Short and Ugly kicked him in the ribs, and the lights went out as Mitch gasped in pain. As he fell the blond hit the door running and disappeared. Short and Ugly grinned and stared proudly at the beer bottle he held in his right hand. Within minutes, Mitch was carried outside and shoved into the backseat of a police cruiser.

"He started it," the big man said. "He insulted a lady, and when I tried to stop him, he went crazy on me. Shit! My ear hurts like a Mutha!"

"Shee-it, man," Short and Ugly said. "He hit Jesse and came after me, but I decked him with this." He held up the beer bottle like a trophy.

Mitch was hauled off to jail, to be charged with assault and battery, disturbing the peace, resisting arrest, striking an officer, and public drunkenness.

CHAPTER THIRTY-SIX

itch opened his eyes and found himself in a filthy, graffiti-decorated cell. He lurched to his feet, enraged, only to be struck by a wave of nausea and slump back on the foul-smelling bunk.

He once again held his throbbing head in his hands and fought a dizzying headache. He rocked back and forth on the dingy mattress, trying to quell the rising gorge in his throat.

"What the hell did I do to get in here?" Then he remembered.

In a rush, it all came back to him. He remembered everything. The bar, the fight, the truckers, Tom, the bear, the river, the crash."

"Greg?

Mitch turned pale.

"Oh no! God, no!" Mitch moaned as he hunched forward on his knees and cried into his hands. Tears flowed like the river that had taken his friend, the river that had almost taken him, the river he had beaten. He cried openly, unashamed. Soon heads were appearing from around corners, hurried footsteps resounded down the hall, and a big black cop stood tall and wide in front of his cell.

"Hey, shut it up!"

Mitch looked up and sniffed. "I remember."

"Remember what?"

"All of it. Everything!"

"You're talking crazy," the cop said. "You're still drugged up, psycho, just like last night when they brought you in. They said you were mumbling all sorts of weird stuff. Cussing and screaming about cadavers and such."

"I was drunk."

Mitch suddenly laughed for joy, in spite of his grief for his friend.

"You were definitely that," the cop said. "And I wonder what else?"

"I'm not on dugs. I assure you, it isn't that." The cop raised his eyebrows and took an appraising look at him.

Mitch had been transformed in a moment. He was no longer Mitch Cooper, the rough-and tumble-cowboy. He was once again Mitchell Anthony Cooper, city councilman, rancher, and businessman from Boise, Idaho.

"Why am I being incarcerated?"

The cop caught a smile and said, "You'll get your chance to talk in a little while."

"I've just got a few questions. It won't take a minute. First I want to know why I've been placed so disgracefully in this nasty, suffocating jail cell."

"Drunk and disorderly and disturbing the peace, for starters. Then you assaulted a man, busted his face and nearly tore his ear off. You spit on an officer, resisted arrest, kicked the window out of a cruiser, you broke...."

"I get the picture," Mitch said and waved the big cop silent. He thought a minute and felt of his head. He found a tender spot on the back of his head. He looked around the cell. He saw the filth, smelled the stench, and for the first time noticed he had a few cellmates. None of them looked particularly friendly. He turned back to the jailer.

"Can I make a phone call?

"I'll check on it."

The cop turned and walked down the hall. He returned a few minutes later to find Mitch staring out the small, barred window in the back of the cell. He was looking north and west with a worried look on his face.

"Mister, you can have your telephone call. You had better call your lawyer. For your sake I hope he's good. You're going to have to pay some damages."

The cop led Mitch to a phone at the end of the hall, still behind bars.

"Make it fast. I've got other things to do."

Mitch hesitated by the phone and then reached for the receiver. Quickly he punched in a series of numbers, and then waited. His heart raced. The phone began to ring. It rang twice, and then he heard his son's voice.

"Cooper residence," Steven said.

Mitch tried to say hello, but the words would not come.

"Hello?" Steven said a little louder.

"Son?" Mitch forced around the lump in his throat. "It's your father."

Silence held the line.

Then Steven spoke, "I missed you, Dad. Glad to have you back."

"Yeah, I'm back. I'm in San Antonio. Sorry I missed your birthday."

"Well, it was like a major catastrophe, you know, but I got over it."

"Son, I had an accident. I-I, it's a long story, but here's the gist of it. I lost my memory two months ago when we crashed into the mountain. It only came back to me a few minutes ago. Up until two days ago...."

"We know."

"I was living up in the mountains with an old man and his dog. The dog found me after the crash. He's a great dog...."

"Dad! We know all about it."

"I was dying, but they saved me. I stayed with them until...what did you say?"

"We know all about it. Tom told us."

"What? How? I-I don't understand."

"We saw you the other night across the fire. We saw you and Tom and Barney."

"Son, but I, still don't understand."

Mitch was dumbstruck.

"How do you know their names?"

"Dad, we, I mean Mom, she figured out where you were. It would take too much time to explain over the phone, but she knew you were alive. She felt it when you went down but she knew you weren't dead. When we saw you and Tom across the fire, well, she knew where you were because we saw Tom and Barney down by the river when we were searching for you."

"Well, I'll be dipped." Mitch said. "Let me talk to her."

"She's not here, Dad. She's there. She's in San Antonio."

"Huh? This is too much. Hold on a minute." He turned to the cop.

"How much time do I have?"

"Don't worry about it."

"Thanks."

"So, your mother is down here? You found Tom, and he told you I'd be down here, and she's here to find me?"

"That's right, Dad."

"How about that! She knew."

"Are you two alright?"

"We are now. It was rough for a while. But mom never gave up on you. She nearly gave up on herself but never gave up on you.

"She knew all along that you were alive," he spoke through his tears. "Sorry, Dad, I don't mean to cry."

"Don't ever be ashamed to show your feelings, Steven. If I have learned anything these last two months, it's that life is very precious and that you have to be strong for those you love and not be afraid to show it. Many people have lost that. They need tough men like you to show them the way. The good in this world is shadowed by much evil. It is individuals like us who hold back the darkness with the fires of the heart. Stay good and stay strong, Son, and show it. Do not be afraid of your emotions.

"Now, listen, uh, I'm in some trouble. I'm in jail. I do not want to go into the reasons why at this time but I need you to call my attorney. You know the number. Stay by the phone in case your mother calls. I'll have the officer here give you all the information you need."

He gave the cop a questioning glance. The cop nodded back in agreement.

"If your mother calls, um, when she calls tell her that I'll meet her at our hotel by the River Walk."

"Dad, she's waiting there for you now."

Mitch grinned.

"Ok, Son, if she calls before I'm released, tell her to call here." He thought a minute. "No, don't. I'll just meet her there. Just tell her to wait. I won't be long."

The cop handed him a slip of paper. Mitch relayed the information and then said goodbye. Immediately he turned to the cop and asked for another cell.

"Don't push your luck," the cop said and locked him back up.

An hour later, his reputation and his position in the City of Boise afforded him a quick release. His attorney got all charges dropped on the condition that Mitch make full restitution to the city and pay Jesse Alvarado's medical bills, plus $10,000 for pain and suffering. Within two hours of talking to his son, Mitch was back at his motel room. He showered, changed into his last clean set of clothes (jeans and a western shirt), and then caught a cab to the River Walk.

His insides tumbled and rolled. His hands shook with excitement as he paid the driver. The cabby drove away, leaving him at the curb in front of the restaurant where he and Donna had dined away many a romantic evening. He knew she would be either in the lobby in the adjacent hotel, up in a room, on the terrace, or walking along the river.

He gathered himself together and checked at the desk. She was checked in. He had the clerk ring the room. She was not in, so he made his way to the restaurant in the back.

CHAPTER THIRTY-SEVEN

Donna paused at the bottom of the steps a moment. She looked up and down the walk, searching the faces, but her husband was not in the crowd. After waiting in the restaurant for two very long hours, she had called Steven who just hung up from talking to Mitch. Relieved beyond measure, her heart racing at the thought of seeing him again, she began to walk back and forth along the river's edge, waiting for him to find her.

She looked up and down the walk, searching faces, but her husband was not among the crowd that milled along the cool, shadowy recesses along the river. Tour boats traveled the water between the towering trees and hotels that lined the meandering course through downtown, within a few yards of the Alamo.

She walked in a daze of expectancy until she found herself standing in the center of a crossover. It was where he had asked her to marry him. She felt a light touch on her shoulder and her heart leapt. She turned slowly, expecting to see him at last, but it was only a young girl.

"Would you take a picture of me and my boyfriend?"

Donna could not speak. She trembled visibly and leaned against the railing for support.

"Are you alright?" the girl asked.

"Sorry, Kids, you just startled me. I thought you were someone I was waiting for."

♠ ♠ ♠

Mitch was jelly inside as he walked down the back steps of the restaurant, onto the tri-level terrace between the river and the building. Donna had not been inside and she was not at any of the tables on the terrace, but a waiter told him he had served a woman earlier that fit her description.

"A real looker," he had said. He told him she had come back, then left again only a few moments ago, and he pointed to the river.

Mitch could not hear the chatter of the diners on the terrace, nor the birds in the treetops overhead. He could hear nothing over the thunder in his chest as he walked along the river to the spot where he knew she would be waiting.

The air was thick and hot. Perspiration coursed down his brow and trickled down his sides, but he didn't feel it. His stomach was growling; he hadn't eaten in nearly twenty-four hours, but he didn't feel that either. He was oblivious to any sensation other than the one in his heart, and as he rounded a curve and saw the crosswalk it swelled until he was breathless with longing. He stopped on top of the crosswalk to rest and to try to slow his rampaging emotions.

He saw her.

She sensed his gaze and raised her head. Their eyes met, their hearts reached toward each other, and of their own volition their feet began to move.

Time seemed to stand still and the distance between them vanished. She was just suddenly in his arms, kissing the wetness away. She smelled so good. She felt so warm, so alive, so Donna.

Her lips found his.

His head swam, his heart ached; he had been missing her for so long. His ears rang with the sound of her voice as she called his name repeatedly.

He held his wife tightly to his chest. Even behind the veil, he had missed her.

"I've missed you so much," he heard himself say.

"I missed you," she cried. They held each other for a long time, unable to speak, unable to let go. It seemed like hours had passed before Mitch finally raised his head from her shoulder and looked into her eyes. He kissed her passionately, tenderly, softly, then pushed her gently away and drank her in with his eyes.

"I love you more than life," he whispered and then pulled her to his chest again, held her close, kissing the tears away as they rocked back and forth. It was many minutes before they were able to find words again. Then the words began to flow, and they talked as they walked, arm in arm, side by side, inseparable, back to the restaurant, where they dined together once again. They sat close, never more than inches apart, always touching, kissing, and meeting each other over and over again, until suddenly Donna remembered Tom.

CHAPTER THIRTY-EIGHT

Tom was awake when Mitch, Donna, and Steven walked into his hospital room. He looked bad, but Mitch could see a fire in his eyes. Tom was lucky that Clara had followed her instincts and had gone to check on him. When she'd found Barney on the county road she stopped and picked him up, and then sped to the cabin. When she skidded to a stop at the end of the driveway, Barney immediately jumped out of the back of the truck and ran to where Tom lay prostrate under the bottom rail of the fence. With surprising speed Clara jumped out and followed. She panicked when she saw him, thinking he was dead, but when he turned his head in her direction she let out sigh of relief and knelt by his side. He was barely coherent but able to tell her he'd had a stroke. She tried her cell phone but couldn't get a signal. Telling him to rest easy now, she turned got up quickly and ran to the cabin.

She called emergency medical services in Riggins and in less than twenty minutes they had him loaded up and back in Riggins where they met a chopper. They flew him to Syringa General Hospital in Grangeville, where he was treated with tissue plasminogen activator to dissolve the blood clot in time to arrest the damage to his brain.

Although in critical condition, physically and mentally damaged, Tom was coherent. Mitch went quickly to his side and reached for Tom's outstretched hand. He could feel the weakness in Tom's grasp but he dare not let it show.

"We're here, Tom."

"How's your head?" Tom whispered.

"I'm fine. I remember everything. It's going to be OK now, and so are you."

Mitch had prepared himself for the worst, had known he would have to be strong, but he didn't know if he was strong enough to watch Tom die.

"Don't be so sure, Son. I'm old," Tom said. "And she's waiting."

Tom released Mitch's hand and pointed to a man in a business suit, standing off to one side.

Tom motioned him over.

"My lawyer," Tom mumbled, "Phillip...McIntyre."

Mitch greeted the attorney.

"Pleased to meet you, Sir. What's going on?"

"I believe he wants to tell you. I am here as a witness, to make it official."

Puzzled, Mitch returned to Tom's side. Donna and Steven moved closer. Tears welled up in Tom's eyes as he began to speak. With great difficulty, he raised his hand and pointed to Mitch.

"Son," he spoke with admiration.

"Yes?" Mitch replied, unable to hide the trembling inside him.

"What I owned is yours now. I'm giving you the land, cabin, money, and the twins. Barney is already yours.

He made that decision weeks ago."

He reached for Mitch's hands.

"Mitch," Tom's voice broke and he shuddered and became still as his hand relaxed and fell to the bed. Mitch leaned forward quickly as a hush fell over the room. His heart raced. It was breaking.

"No, Tom. Don't leave us. Fight! You can't leave us now. It's not right."

Tom's eyes flickered open. He looked up at Mitch.

"Come here, all of you," he said in a feeble voice, distorted by paralysis on the right side of his face. Donna walked around to the other side of the bed and took one of Tom's hands. Steven held his mother by the shoulders.

"Mitch, Donna, Steven, thank you for coming into my life. You've made me a very happy and proud man. I love you all, especially you, you big buzzard turd. Come closer, Mitch."

Mitch leaned forward and with sudden and surprising strength, Tom reached up, grabbed him by the shoulder, and pulled him close.

He whispered in Mitch's ear.

"It wasn't fool's gold! Be careful."

Tom released his grip and Mitch eased back. His expression was blank, unrevealing.

"Follow your dreams, Son." A single tear ran down each side of Tom's face, but his eyes revealed only joy. He grabbed Mitch's hand again and squeezed hard.

"I love you like my own."

"Likewise," Mitch said and prepared to let him go.

"Thanks for saving my life."

Tom did not reply, he just glanced up at the ceiling as if to say, "Him, not me." And Tom closed his eyes.

CHAPTER THIRTY-NINE

EIGHTEEN MONTHS LATER

Tom's mountain ranch glistened beneath two feet of new snow. Smoke curled lazily from the chimney and swirled over the cabin and through the pines. The yellow skeleton of a new building stood resolute between the barn and the cabin. It waited for spring, and for Mitch's skilled labor to resume. Lumber and boxes of nails were neatly stacked to one side. Mitch had painstakingly covered the building supplies in canvas tarps to protect them from the winter's snow and ice.

In the barn, with its mother, a ten-month-old sorrel filly dozed peacefully; waiting for 6:30 A.M. and the gentle touch of the man who had imprinted himself as her other mother. Mitch had spent several hours each day with her, from the very moment of her birth. In this fashion her life had begun and would continue through her gentle breaking and training. She would be a people-oriented horse for the rest of her life.

As the sun sank toward the western horizon, on approach to tomorrow, light from its farewell burning danced off the top of the double headstone by the river. A healthy rose bush, dormant for the winter but holding a promise of beauty to unfold in the spring, stood guard in front of it. One side of the marker was yet to be engraved. The other side bore the name of Natalie Braden, beloved wife, always loving, ever loved. Born 1923, died 2006.

Up at the cabin, Christmas lights adorned the windows and flashed a bright red, yellow, blue, and green on the blanket of snow. It was cold on Tom's mountain, but the cabin was warm and cozy. Mitch and Donna sat on the couch with the quilt on their laps. Barney slept at their feet on a rather large and unusual bear rug. The fire crackled and popped as they watched the flames dance and shimmer, waiting for Steven to call from Pocatello University. He called them every Friday evening at 7:30.

Donna shifted her feet under the quilt and turned a page in her book. Barney stood up and stretched, then jumped up beside Mitch and lay with his head in his lap. Donna yawned sleepily and put down her book. Mitch looked at her and smiled as she picked up a corner of the quilt. She held the corner that told the end of the story as it stood so far. The last block was light blue, like the sky, with a single red arrow pointing to one outside edge, and three words: "To Be Continued."

Mitch kissed her cheek.

"I love you," he whispered in her ear.

"I love you more," she whispered back. "I wonder why they haven't called. He's fifteen minutes late."

"I wouldn't know," Mitch said, shaking his head and fingering his mustache.

"You are tired, aren't you?" Donna said.

"A little, but I'm just about finished. Until spring, that is. I'll straighten things up down there in the morning, and then we'll rest for the winter while I draw up plans for the mess hall. If all goes well, we can have the entire complex finished by next fall and open by the following summer.

"Sounds great!" Donna said, then again, "I wish he'd call." She rested her head on the back of the couch. "I'm anxious to know when they'll be up for Christmas."

"He's probably lost in his studies," Mitch replied. "He'll be in touch."

At that very moment, Steven and Molly were turning into the driveway and they stopped to view the new entrance to the property.

Overhead, supported by two thirty-foot totem poles, hung an eight-by-forty foot sign, sandblasted from redwood planks.

WELCOME TO THE BRADEN/COOPER RANCH
'WILD' WESTERN RETREAT

"Wow!" Molly said, "Your father did a great job on that."

"He designed it himself," Steven said, "but he had help building it. He hired a friend of his to help run this place. He was the driver who gave dad a ride all the way to Dallas. He goes by the name of Gil Rodriguez."

"I can't wait to meet him," she said. "And I can't wait to see the look on your mother's face when we surprise her."

"Donna, do we have any ice cream?" Mitch asked. "I've got a sweet tooth."

"Yeah, I think we have a gallon. Should I get you a bowl?"

"No, not yet. I was just thinking how good it would taste with a big slice of that cake cooling in the kitchen."

"That cake is for day after tomorrow and you know it."

"Well, I'll settle for the ice cream then."

"I know you will," she said as she leaned over and gave him a kiss on the cheek.

She turned to the kitchen. Barney jumped off the couch to follow her but suddenly stopped in his tracks. He cocked his head back and forth, listening. Then he ran to the front door and started barking.

Steven quietly shut Molly's door. They didn't want to alert anyone until they knocked. The snow had effectively masked their approach so far. All they had to do now was make it to the front door.

"What is it, dawg?" Mitch drawled. "Bet it's that buck. Probably smelled your cake. He's looking for another treat."

He got up and went to the front door.

Donna followed him.

"I hear someone talking outside," she said. "Are we expecting anyone?"

"I don't know, but I'm fixin' to find out."

He reached for the doorknob.

"You ready?" Steven asked, standing before the heavy door that Mitch had brought from their home in Boise.

"Yeah, and hurry, I'm freezing," Molly said.

Steven reached up to knock, but Mitch opened it before his hand touched wood.

The surprise was mutual.

"Merry Christmas!" The kids shouted.

"Merry Christmas, ya'll! You're early. I didn't expect you till eight."

"Mitch?" Donna shrieked. "You knew?"

"For two weeks. I'm surprised you didn't read my mind."

"You ornery turd!"

Mitch laughed. Everyone was laughing.

"Well don't just stand there freezing," Donna said. "Get in here."

Mitch shut the door behind them. Steven handed his mom the packages he was carrying and greeted Barney with enthusiasm.

"Where's Grandpa?" Steven asked, as he played with Barney. "Did he go to bed early?"

"I hope not," Molly said, "I've got an early present for him."

"No, I'm still up and around," Tom said as he walked slowly into the living room, aided only by a cane.

"What do you have for me, Darlin'?"

"A Great Big Hug!" She ran and threw her arms around him.

"I love you, Tom."

"I love you, girl, and I've missed you."

"We missed you a bunch. How are you getting along?"

"Hon', it's been a long, hard recovery, but I'm gettin' better everyday. I've decided I'll stick around for a while and see what kind mischief I can get into in my old age."

Mitch just beamed his lopsided western grin and heaved a big sigh. Can it get any better than this? His mind wandered out back behind the cabin. He thought about the day he woke up on Sampson's ledge and all the events since, and he knew it could never get any better.

Once Tom had gotten well enough to go home, they all got together one night and talked about what to do with their combined assets. Tom didn't hesitate to say he liked the company and wanted more of it. That was when Donna got the idea of a bed and breakfast. Mitch suggested building an outdoor arena and putting on rodeos and other horse related events in the summer. Steven wanted to open four-wheeler trails, but Tom ruled that out immediately, and they decided on hiking and riding trails instead. They all agreed with a Born-Again Mitch, that no matter what, they would let God handle the details. They'd already framed most of the twelve-room inn out in back. Gil was on the road for the winter but was going to retire come spring and work full-time with his new partners. He'd saved enough money to buy into the business and was also dating a young woman who lived in town.

Tom had initially lost the use of his left side but had made a remarkable recovery. He was walking with a cane now and was able to get along fairly well. His speech was still slightly slurred, but that was also improving. His only serious deficit was that he wasn't completely aware of sound and sight to his left. His hearing and eyesight had not been injured by the stroke, yet the brain damage had caused a lack of awareness of what he did hear and see on that side. But his spirits were high and his eyes gleamed with happiness. He might have lost a wife and son, and some physical abilities, however he'd gained an entire new family and he wasn't complaining.

He walked over to the window to the left of the fireplace and looked out upon his snow-covered yard. A mule deer doe stood at the edge of the woods. He puffed on his pipe, sighed contentedly, turned to the tree in the corner, and said, "I don't know about the rest of you, but life is short and my patience has worn thin.

I'm dying to know what's in that big box with my name on it."

"Let's open presents," Molly shouted. Donna looked at Mitch. He grinned and looked at Barney.

"What do you think?" Barney barked twice and raised his right paw in the air at Mitch.

"Aw, what the heck, let's do it," he said and beat the whole bunch to the tree.

The End

Jim lives with his wife and critters on a small farm in central Arkansas. He is finishing undergraduate studies in psychology, and he and his wife, Carol, are in the process of founding an Equine Rescue and Rehabilitation Center.

Printed in the United States
213864BV00001B/2/P

9 780980 172584